Shock
and Paw

St. Martin's Paperbacks Titles
by Cate Conte

Shock
and Paw

CATE CONTE

St. Martin's Paperbacks

This is a work of fiction. All of the characters, organizations, and events portrayed in this novel are either products of the author's imagination or are used fictitiously.

First published in the United States by St. Martin's Paperbacks, an imprint of St. Martin's Publishing Group.

SHOCK AND PAW

For information, address St. Martin's Publishing Group, 120 Broadway, New York, NY 10271.

www.stmartins.com

ISBN: 978-1-250-88397-1

Our books may be purchased in bulk for promotional, educational, or business use. Please contact your local bookseller or the Macmillan Corporate and Premium Sales Department at 1-800-221-7945, ext. 5442, or by email at MacmillanSpecialMarkets@macmillan.com.

Printed in the United States of America

St. Martin's Paperbacks edition / September 2024

10 9 8 7 6 5 4 3 2 1

For the Five-Leaf Clovers.

Acknowledgments

I can't believe this is book number eight in this series. Time really flies when you're spending it on a beautiful island surrounded by cats and murder! As always, a huge thank-you to the St. Martin's team—my editor, Claire Cheek; my amazing cover designer, Danielle Christopher, who never fails to create the best representation of JJ and the town; and all the editors and production team, and agent, John Talbot, for helping bring this book to the shelves. I'm so lucky to be published with this house.

Special shout-out to Meg Jackson, my longtime friend and fellow writer who came up with the title for this book. It's absolutely fabulous, and I never would've thought of something so good myself.

Electrocuting someone isn't as easy as it sounds, especially when you have to make it look like an accident. Thank you to Jack Hibbard, my old friend and master electrician, for sharing his expertise and putting up with my relentless, perfectionist questions. It's been a long time since we've worked together, and I was so grateful to be able to do it again.

This book has a lot of newspaper-related content in it,

and I have to acknowledge all the hard work that newspaper reporters are doing out there. It's even harder today than it was back in the day when I was doing the job. Thinking of my friends still in the biz—thank you for your dedication to a sometimes thankless, but always necessary, career.

And to all the rescuers out there who are fighting every day for the lives of animals stuck in shelters and in danger of losing their lives, thank you. It's heartbreaking sometimes to do rescue work, but these poor deserving babies need us. This book is definitely a plug for "adopt, don't shop."

Jason Allen-Forrest, my first reader—thank you so much for your feedback and for always having the best eye for what the book needs. You are awesome.

My Wicked sisters—Sherry Harris, Jessica Ellicott, Julie Hennrikus, Barb Ross, Edith Maxwell/Maddie Day—thank you all for still being there as my support system. Love you all, always.

And thank you to all the readers. Seriously. Without you there would be no books, and I am grateful every day for you choosing mine to add to your shelves. Keep reading.

Chapter 1

"I swear to God if I find the person who's putting these flyers up, I'll murder them."

Every head in my cat cafe, JJ's House of Purrs, turned in Katrina Denning's direction at those words. I flinched, seeing my unexpected Christmas season boost in patrons dwindling as people decided they didn't want to be party to a murder.

"Can you keep it down," I hissed, clamping my hand on her arm and dragging her to the front desk area while subsequently smiling through my gritted teeth at the concerned cat lovers who were watching us a bit warily.

She shook me off, still annoyed enough to not care who she was freaking out. "Sorry, Maddie, but for real? Who puts flyers advertising designer cats for sale in front of a rescue? And I bet whoever it was had something to do with *this*!" She held up the cat carrier she'd brought in with more force than necessary, jostling its poor occupant. I reached for it to get the innocent cat huddled inside out of the line of fire.

She had a point, of course. Katrina was the Daybreak Harbor town animal control officer and a fierce animal advocate. Her job wasn't just a job to her—it was a chance to make our little island better for animals. And she really, really hated breeders. She loathed when animals were used for purely moneymaking purposes. She'd never even watched the National Dog Show on Thanksgiving Day because she hated the Kennel Club. She'd grudgingly acknowledged when they'd put a rescue dog category in the show, but she was still not a fan.

Adele Barrows, my shelter manager and fellow cat aficionado, glanced up from where she was restocking the new JJ-branded Christmas mugs in the corner of the cafe where we sold merch. My cat, JJ—short for Junkyard Johnny—had been an instant hit with not only the island dwellers and visitors, but people who'd read about his story in some of the extensive coverage on the mainland that we'd gotten over the past year. His stray-to-star story had hit home for so many people. It helped that he was the cutest orange kitty alive—at least in my opinion. The cat cafe was created in his honor, and as such, he'd taken on the role of the face of stray cats on Daybreak Island and beyond. And people were on board—he'd become the island's biggest star. His adorable face and rags-to-riches story attracted people from far and wide to the cafe, and inspired lots of adoptions, which was a perk. Plus, everyone wanted to take some JJ home, so I'd jumped on that. And that was where we'd actually been making money. Our admission price to the cafe was cheap—ten dollars per visit—so food and souvenirs were the real moneymakers that allowed us to help more cats.

"What's going on?" Adele asked sharply. "Who's selling designer cats? And who's that?" She nodded toward the carrier.

Katrina's voice rose to dangerous levels again. "I have no idea who's selling them. But like I said, when I find out—"

"Give me the flyer," I interrupted before she could start yelling about murder again. I handed the carrier to Adele. "Apparently it's our new resident."

Katrina shoved a half-crumpled piece of paper into my hand. "He can't be adopted yet. He's on a three-day stray hold," she said to Adele, nodding toward the cat.

I took it, scanning the text. "'Designer cats for sale,'" I read, noting the photos of the fluffy kittens. "'Unique, pedigreed, adorable. We also have hypoallergenic cats. The *best* Christmas gift for the cat lover in your life. Multiple price points and breeds available. Our cats are *one of a kind*! Ask us!'" I looked up at her. "Multiple price points? One of a kind? Where did you find this?"

"They're posted all around town! Including near the animal care facility, and one on the pole right outside your place." Katrina jabbed a finger toward the street. "I just noticed it when I came in. Can you believe it?"

"Well, who's the breeder?" I scanned the flyer again, noting the number. "Can we look it up?"

"I tried. Nothing's coming up. It's probably a burner phone. And Mick won't check for me. I asked him yesterday when I pulled down the flyer from outside my place." She looked disgusted. "What's the point of having a boyfriend who's a lieutenant in the police department if he won't do you a favor once in a while?"

In an interesting twist, Katrina had been seeing Lt. Mick Ellory of the Daybreak Harbor Police Department. Mick and I went way back. Well, way back to when I'd first moved home. I'd been a suspect in a murder case then, and we hadn't gotten off to the best start. But our relationship had improved over time, and was actually good now. Part of that was his relationship with Katrina, which had greatly improved his mood. Part of it was we'd kind of gotten used to each other, and he had even started to value what I'd brought to some investigations in which I'd ended up involved.

"He can't use police resources to check up on people who aren't actually doing anything illegal," I said automatically. That had been drilled into my head by Grandpa Leo since I was a kid. Although I suspect it hadn't stopped him from looking up my and my sisters' past boyfriends, though he would never admit such a thing. There were perks to being the police chief, and in the name of keeping his family safe, he would've used them without hesitation. "Did you call the number?" I asked.

"No. I don't trust myself to not flip out. But we're going to get someone to call and pretend to want a cat. Then I'm going to bust whoever it is."

I tried to hide my smile. Not that I thought the breeding of designer cats was okay in any way, but because Katrina's reaction was so, well, Katrina. And I could say that, because I'd known her since we were kids. Actually, she had been my babysitter once upon a time. Back in the day, a four-year age difference was enough to get her the job. My favorite memory of her was when I was in fourth grade and she was in eighth. Her class was "chaperoning" ours on a field trip to the beach, and one of her classmates threw a rock at a seagull. She'd picked up her own rock and hurled it at his head—and hadn't missed. I remember her asking him how he'd liked it even as she'd been suspended from school on the spot. I had mad respect for her after that.

In later years, we'd become friends. And now that I had moved home and we were both in the rescue business, she was back to being a big part of my life. Not only as my friend, but as my cat supplier.

"I don't think you can bust them," I said. "First of all, you don't have a badge. Second of all, unfortunately this crap is not illegal." I did hate thinking about all the cats sitting in shelters while greedy people tried to make money off breeds they thought people would pay for. And I had to admit, advertising right outside my cat cafe where rescue cats were waiting for new homes was pretty ballsy.

"I don't care if it's a legit breeder. They all stink, in my opinion. And they should not be advertising outside the rescues. And certainly not trying to get people to buy these cats as Christmas presents!"

"This is a fancy cat," Adele announced, cutting into Katrina's rant. She opened the carrier door and pulled the kitty out by his scruff. He looked like he wanted to flee into a corner.

But she was right. A fancy cat for sure, though I couldn't place what breed—oversized ears, short hair, and a few leopard-looking spots. Kind of an orangey-brown color, a bit like a Savannah but not quite. Still, Leopard Man, our quirky island character who dressed in leopard garb, would be all about this guy, I was certain.

"I told you," Katrina muttered.

"What kind of cat is that?" I asked.

"I have no idea. One that was clearly dumped."

I tuned her out as I knelt down to get a closer look at the cat. The poor thing looked sad. I immediately wanted to hug him—or her—but I resisted. If Katrina saw me being too soft she'd just start bringing cats over every day until we all had to move out to make room for them. "Boy or girl?"

"Boy. Super shy. Some lady who works at the laundromat downtown found him yesterday hiding behind a dumpster. He's clearly never been outside before. I had him at the kennel and he was terrified. So here we are."

"Maybe he's someone's cat. He doesn't look like any random stray. No chip?"

She gave me a look that suggested it was a stupid question. "No chip. I wanted him to be somewhere more comfortable while we wait out the hold."

"Did he get tested yet?" All the cats had to be tested for FIV—feline immunodeficiency virus—and feline leukemia before we added them to the general population.

"Yeah. He's clear. He's scared of dogs, FYI."

Well, that wasn't helpful since we had two. "Just dogs?" I asked.

"No. He's pretty much scared of everything," she said.

"Poor thing. Hi, buddy. You like other kitties?" I asked.

He didn't respond.

"He does. I tested him out with a couple of the cats over at the shelter," Katrina confirmed. "He's nervous, but he does like them."

"Okay. Maybe I'll put him upstairs for now. It's going to be a little crazy in here this weekend," I said, taking the carrier. "JJ can keep him company." JJ loved when new cats arrived in the cafe. He was like a one-cat welcoming committee. And when we had kittens, he was the best babysitter. "What's his name?"

"I didn't name him yet. You can do the honors." She glanced at her watch. "Crap. I have to go. But we need to figure this out."

"Frederick," I decided. "He looks like a Frederick."

Neither of them was listening to me.

"I'll call," Adele said, putting Frederick back in his carrier.

"No!" Katrina and I both said in unison.

Adele huffed out a breath. "Why on earth not?"

"Because the only person I trust less than myself to not freak out is you," Katrina said. "Plus anyone who knows you would recognize your voice."

"She's right," I said. Adele's throaty, two-pack-a-day voice was legendary. You met her once and never forgot it. But voice aside, her personality was ninety percent sass and ten percent cat-masquerading-as-human. Adele had volunteered for me before I made her my official, full-time shelter manager, so I'd gotten to know her well. Under the rough exterior, she had one of the most generous hearts I'd ever known. And even though that heart loved cats more than most people, the people she did love felt it fiercely. Sometimes through a tongue lashing, sure, but still.

But the cats were her top priority. And breeder beware, because if Adele got involved in this on top of Katrina it would end really, really badly for them.

Adele still didn't look happy, but she humphed at us and went back to her work. I could tell she was still listening, though.

"So who, then?" Katrina demanded.

"We'll think of something. Anything else?" I asked.

Katrina frowned at me. "Yeah. How many cats do you have right now?"

"You can't bring any more over! I'm full." I glanced behind me at the cafe full of cats and the delighted patrons playing with them. When I'd opened the cafe a year and a half ago with my business partner, Ethan Birdsong, and my Grandpa Leo, we'd been firm that we'd only have ten cats at a time. But over time, that number had gotten a bit more gray. Now I probably had twenty in here. And the fact that I didn't actually know how many was kind of a problem.

"Yeah, but a bunch will get adopted today," Katrina said confidently.

As if she'd staged it, a woman came up to the counter carrying one of our black kittens. "Excuse me. Can I fill out an application for this baby?" she asked.

Katrina grinned and plucked one from the stack Adele kept on the desk. "Here you go. Kittens really should go in pairs," she told the woman.

"Oh! Really?"

"Yes," Adele confirmed. "Let me show you which one he's bonded with." She led the woman over to the kitten cage.

"Case in point," Katrina said.

"Yeah, yeah."

"In all seriousness, I may need to bring a couple more over. I'll let you know." She took the flyer back. "Think about who can pretend to want a cat," she said.

"I will."

"Thanks. I've gotta go relocate a raccoon now." With a wave, she headed out the door.

Shaking my head in amusement, I picked up our new charge and headed toward the back of the cafe and the French doors that led to the rest of the house. It was really nice to see so many new faces in here in the winter months, I thought as I passed through the guests. It meant our Christmas tourism campaign was working. Usually once Labor Day hit, the island went from a population of thirty thousand to about five thousand. But this year, with our big Halloween event and now our Christmas extravaganza that was kicking off this weekend, people were coming to visit way offseason.

Which was good for all the local businesses. And for the cats who needed good homes, because it meant new people coming to the cafe looking to adopt.

I emerged from the cluster of people oohing and aahing over the cats when I noticed my boyfriend, Lucas Davenport, had just walked in from the main house. And he looked concerned.

"Hey," I said, walking up to him. "I thought you'd left

already." Lucas owned a grooming salon downtown—Diva Dogs and Classy Cats. It was the only year-round one on the island. Which meant he was always busy. On Wednesdays he worked late, so his other groomer opened the shop and he went in for the afternoon and evening shifts. The salon was one of the reasons we had been thrown together when I first came back to the island. He'd offered to help groom the strays that wound up in the town animal control facility to help get them into adoptable shape. But we'd first met in a pet store when one of his charges had peed on my leg.

"I was just coming in to say goodbye," he said, but he wasn't really looking at me. He kept glancing at the windows in the room that faced the street.

"What's wrong?" I asked.

"Nothing, I . . ." He shook his head. "Nothing."

I raised an eyebrow. "You sure?"

"Yeah." He turned and focused fully on me. "Just grabbed some lunch and I'm heading out. I'll see you later on tonight?"

"You bet," I said, leaning in for a kiss—but suddenly he jerked away from me. Startled, I stepped back as he pointed at the window.

"There! Right there," he said triumphantly. "I knew I wasn't imagining things. There's a woman staring in the window."

Chapter 2

I whirled around to follow his finger, alarmed.

And then laughed when I saw the mass of blond hair and the bright red glasses pressed against the ground-floor window. "Oh, that's just Donna." I caught her eye and waved. Donna waved back. The spot in the window where her face pressed against the glass had a film of fog over it from her breath.

"Donna?" he repeated, his gaze sliding back to me.

"Yeah, Donna Carey. The newspaper publisher. Becky's big boss." Becky Walsh, my best friend, was the managing editor of the only Daybreak Island daily paper. It had been her dream job since we were kids. And Donna's family had owned and operated the paper for a couple hundred years or something crazy like that, making it one of the only remaining independent newspapers not just here in New England, but probably in the country. Donna herself had been leading it for the past twenty-five years, since her mid-twenties, and had seen it through some of its toughest times. Becky was a huge fan of Donna's—both her style and her approach to journalism—and loved working for her.

"Okay," Lucas said, clearly still not getting it. "So why is Becky's boss staring in our window?"

"She does it every week. It's her thing." I shrugged. "You've never noticed her before?"

Now he was looking at me like he was worried about me. "I can't say that I have." He squinted, trying to get a better look at her without being obvious. "So . . . why does she do that? And, uh, don't you find it creepy?"

"Nah." I mean, it was odd, but who cared? She loved the cafe, sent people here all the time, and offered us free advertising in the paper. Who was I to judge? Plus, pretty much everyone on this island was quirky in their own way. It was part of the charm. Most of the time. "She loves cats. But she's allergic to them," I said. "Did I not mention that?"

Lucas started to laugh. "Nope, you left that out."

I grinned. "Sorry. Yeah, this is how she gets her fix." I forgot that Lucas wasn't always able to spend a lot of time in the cafe since he was busy running his own business. Which meant he wasn't up on all the quirky things we dealt with that had become the norm. I didn't mind. It had been a little strange at first when Donna asked if she could come visit from the outside, but hey, strange is relative, right? And I felt sorry for her that she couldn't have cats. That sounded horrible. And overall, she was a cool lady. I wouldn't let her peek in my windows otherwise.

"Well, as long as there's a reasonable explanation," Lucas said, and leaned over to give me a kiss.

"Hey, lovebirds." Adele appeared behind me. "Are you gonna stop canoodling long enough to tell me how you want this place decorated? The volunteers are coming this afternoon and I need a plan. I also need to know where all the decorations are."

"Canoodling? Really?" I muttered to Lucas, biting back a laugh before turning to Adele. "The decorations are in storage in Grandpa's office downstairs. I trust you and the team to set it up how you think. You guys will do an awesome job. Just make it look fun and Christmasy."

Adele rolled her eyes. "Between you and that grandfather of yours," she muttered. "One of you is obsessed and the other can't focus. Good thing you have me."

"We're totally comfortable leaving the plan up to you," Lucas cut in smoothly. "You know better than any of us the nuances of decorating in a cat-friendly way."

"Where is Grandpa?" I asked. I realized I hadn't seen him in a while, and he was usually here in the middle of things in the cafe.

"Last I saw him, he was outside fussing with the lights," Adele said. "But that was hours ago when I came in."

"Outside? Still?" I glanced out the cafe windows again. The ladder was still propped against the house in the same place it had been when I got home, in front of the window two over from the one Donna had been peering through. They must have been chatting. Grandpa could talk anyone's ear off, and he had known Donna forever. The time could pass quickly that way.

Adele was right though—Grandpa Leo *was* obsessed with the Christmas decorations. Especially because our house was on the roster for the annual Best Christmas Lights contest, a town staple he had always embraced. Typically it had been its own thing, with about twenty homeowners participating each year. Judges were sent in a limo to rate each display and give out prizes to the top three. That was pretty much the extent of it.

But not this year. The new Chamber of Commerce

leadership team was breathing new life into our Christmas activities with a lot of enthusiasm. Not only was the contest bigger and better, with more neighborhoods and corporate sponsors, there was a huge cash prize—twenty grand—for the house that won. The second-place prize was also cash, a mere five grand, while the third-place winner got a year's worth of pizza from Nick's on the Beach, a local favorite. There were also honorary mentions in multiple categories, such as Most Innovative Display, Best Color Scheme, and Best Island-Themed Light Display, to name a few.

It was a *big deal,* especially to people who had been doing this for years. It rejuvenated the whole spirit of the thing.

And it was the official start of our festivities. The contest was Friday night. The tours started on Saturday and were held every night through New Year's. The holiday bazaar also kicked off Friday night, a market that was being held in our high school gym for the next two weekends before the holiday. And our town tree lighting with Santa was happening Sunday night. This was a big weekend for us, as the biggest town on the island and the main ferry port.

The entire downtown area in Daybreak Harbor had been decorated professionally so the whole town would look classy when people went to see the houses. There were also formal bus tours taking people to view all the lights, complete with a stop downtown for a little holiday shopping. For those who wanted to self-tour, the Chamber had printed maps. And included on the maps were the local businesses who had agreed to participate with special holiday hours during the season, complete with decorations and late hours on tour nights.

And not only was our house on the contest roster, but

our cat cafe was on the map. So naturally, Grandpa was taking this year very seriously. Especially since last year he'd been so off his game. Our house, where we all—Grandpa, me, Lucas, my sister Val, and her fiancé, Ethan Birdsong, who was also my business partner—lived and where the cafe was housed, had been part of the Daybreak Harbor Christmas celebration for years. My grandparents had always been contest regulars, with at least ten wins under their belt—they were known for going all out. Every year since I was a kid the display had gotten bigger and brighter.

But last Christmas had been the first without Grandma, and even though Grandpa had tried to keep the spirit alive, none of us really had our hearts in it. We were also extremely busy last year, remodeling Grandpa Leo's house to seamlessly fit the cat cafe into our home without just feeling like we'd moved a bunch of cats in. But we'd figured out the remodel, created a whole new, separate wing for the cats with its own entrance, and now we were officially a business. Our detached garage had become the food cafe where Ethan prepared all the yummy goodies and coffee that were just as much of an attraction as the cats. We also were able to create a small seating area in there too, which we expanded outside so people could enjoy our beautiful views of the ocean during the nice weather.

This year, Grandpa's competitive spirit was back, alive and kicking. It wasn't the money—he didn't care about that, and if he won he'd donate it—but the glory. He was proud of this house. It had been in his family for generations. And he loved when it stood out as an island landmark. And the fact that we'd gotten some snow already—a few inches last night—had gotten him even more jazzed. There was just enough to get everyone in the mood and make things look pretty without being overwhelming.

Grandpa's rejuvenated Christmas spirit meant he was constantly finding ways to enhance our display, instead of just piling more and more lights on. He didn't believe in more is better. Instead, he believed that the presentation of the lights—*Colored or white? Blinking or steady? How did they illuminate the other decorations?*—was more crucial to the competition. And his tactics worked, because our house was a town favorite, as well as a continuous contest winner. And with our expanded presence because of the cafe, he definitely wouldn't settle for anything less than perfect.

He'd been out there perfecting things himself the past couple of days, despite the fact that we'd gotten someone to help. The town, on recommendation from the Chamber, had hired a local contractor to be the on-call handyman for the Christmas light contest, someone who could help with lights and other decorations as requested and also do any last-minute fixes for problems that came up. In her capacity on the event committee, my mother had just sent the guy over to handle our house. She hadn't wanted Grandpa trying to do it all himself, especially since ladders were involved and Grandpa tended to ignore his age. Grandpa had been less than on board with that plan, which likely explained why he was out there rearranging everything.

"I have a decorating plan, of course," Adele said. "I just want to make sure you didn't have a different one. When are you picking up the tree?"

"We're supposed to get it tomorrow," I said, moving closer to the window. "Do you have any idea where you want it?" I hadn't seen the ladder move at all. Unless there were a lot of lights specific to this side of the house he was rearranging. Which I really hoped he wasn't, because I thought everything looked pretty good already.

"You didn't see the big empty space in the entryway?"

I turned back as Adele's tone shot right back to annoyed, catching the tail end of an eye roll. "I'm sorry. Yes, I did see it. So no one has seen Grandpa come back in?"

Lucas and Adele both shook their heads.

"I'm just going to run outside and see if he needs help," I told Lucas. "Would you mind putting this guy in the guest room on the fourth floor before you leave?" I motioned toward the cat I was still holding.

"Of course." He took the carrier.

As I hurried to the side door leading outside to our driveway, I almost bumped into a frantic Donna Carey, poised with her hand already lifted to bang on the door, face drained of all color save for her bright red, cat-eye glasses.

"Maddie. You have to come right away."

Chapter 3

"I'm fine," Grandpa Leo insisted to the EMTs trying to load the gurney he was on into the ambulance. "Seriously. You need to let me off this thing. I would know if something was broken." He sounded like a petulant child who'd gotten on a ride he no longer wanted to experience at the amusement park.

Still trying to calm my pounding heart, I stepped up to his side. "Grandpa, stop. They're trying to help you. And if you hadn't been on the ladder in the first place—"

"Mads." Lucas took my hand and pulled me back a step, cutting off my rant. "Not the time," he murmured. He stepped up to Grandpa's side. "They just want to make sure you're all good, Leo. You could've hit your head and we need to get it checked. You'll be back home in no time. We'll be right behind you, okay?"

Grandpa sniffed, but stopped arguing. The female EMT who had been fighting with the blood pressure monitor shot Lucas a grateful look, then they hoisted him into the ambulance and got in the front. A minute later, the vehicle pulled away, silent but with lights flashing.

Adele squeezed my hand and went back inside. Ethan,

who'd come out of the garage where he ran the food portion of our operation to see what all the chaos was about, had stepped away to call my sister Val and let her know what was going on. Donna, who had seen Grandpa fall off the ladder and come running to get me, remained on the sidelines, watching. She'd been almost more upset than the rest of us. Now, she stayed far enough back so as not to get in the way, but didn't seem to want to leave.

Suddenly, the crowd and chaos around me had dispersed, and I felt the adrenaline whoosh out of me.

And now that Grandpa was out of my sight, I felt all the bravado drain away. I hadn't really wanted to yell at him about being on a ladder. I just wanted him to be okay.

"Stupid snow. The ground was probably slippery," I said. "He shouldn't have been up there." I felt the tears form in my eyes, inadvertently stiffening as Lucas turned back toward me. I hadn't yet had a lot of reasons to cry in front of him, and I wasn't sure I was comfortable with it. I mean, I was Maddie James. Strong. Always in control. I'd seen a lot of bad things and always managed to hold it together and figure out a plan. I didn't know if I wanted Lucas to see me falling apart.

But right now, I realized I had no control over any of this. Seeing Grandpa on the ground next to the ladder had nearly given me a heart attack. I'd immediately thought the worst, and the stabbing fear that resulted had been something I hadn't experienced in a long time. Not since the moment when I was probably seven or eight and I'd gotten separated from my parents in an airport. We'd been on a trip to Disney, and we were coming home. My parents, trying to manage all three of us kids, were focused on my youngest sister, Sam, still a pretty young toddler and having a meltdown about something. Wanting to get away from the chaos, I'd lagged behind and then paused in front of one of the airport stores to look at a stuffed animal. When I refocused on my surroundings, I realized I was all alone in a sea of people I didn't recognize. That moment was seared into my brain—the feeling of my heart plummeting so low it felt almost removed from my body, the sick feeling rising in its place. It felt like I'd lost the very thing I needed to survive.

That was how I felt when I'd come outside and seen Grandpa like that.

"I know," Lucas said, putting his arms around me and hugging me tight. "But he's going to be fine."

I buried my face against him as some insistent tears leaked onto his coat. I knew he was right. Grandpa had been conscious the whole time, and by the time he got in the ambulance he'd been sniping at people, which was encouraging. But those first moments were terrifying.

Lucas had immediately sprung into action, calling 9-1-1 and trying to keep a semblance of calm over the situation, keeping curious onlookers away with Adele's and Ethan's help while Donna and I had stayed with Grandpa.

Thankfully, it had looked worse than it was. Once he'd had a few sips of water someone brought, he told us that he'd been working his way down the ladder, tweaking the way the lights hung, when one of the strings over the first floor window went out. When he tried to find an errant bulb that was causing the outage, he'd gotten a little zap—which had knocked him off balance and he'd fallen. Luckily it hadn't happened when he was higher up. He'd only been a few steps up at the time, which could still have been horrible. But despite some pain in his right leg and ankle, he seemed lucid and able to move.

Now we just had to wait and see what the doctor said after a thorough exam.

"I thought . . ." I managed through my tears.

"I know." Lucas squeezed me tighter.

"I should have stopped him," I insisted. Despite the fact that Grandpa was super active for his age and in great shape, I still worried. I'd half-heartedly lectured him about the ladder business this morning, telling him he should leave it to someone else. That got me about as far as I thought it would, which was a big fat nowhere. It had also earned me a lecture about being *ageist,* a term he'd likely heard on one of his NPR programs and had decided would be his new counterpoint if anyone tried to rein him in from doing something.

At this, Lucas chuckled. "Have you met your grandfather? Do you really think you could have?"

I sighed. "No. Of course not."

"Right. So stop blaming yourself. We should get over there, yes?"

"Yeah." I pulled away and wiped my face with my hand. "I need to call my dad and make sure he gets him right in." At times like this, it felt like my dad's job was the best one anyone could have. If he had to pull the best doctor out of brain surgery, he would.

"I'm coming with," Ethan said as he hurried back over to us. "Val is meeting us there. You okay?" he asked me, the concern evident on his face.

"Yeah. Thanks. I'm glad you're here. For Val *and* me."

He squeezed my hand.

As we piled into Lucas's Subaru Forester, I called my dad's cell. He didn't pick up, so I disconnected and immediately called back, our family signal that if it was at all possible, we needed to answer the phone.

He did. "Maddie. Everything okay?" he asked immediately.

"Not really." I filled him in on what had happened. "The ambulance should be there any minute. Can you make sure someone sees him right away?"

"Of course. How did he seem? Did you call your mother?"

"You know Grandpa. He was resisting the idea of the hospital. Which I guess is good, right? I haven't called Mom yet. I'll call her now."

"I'll take care of everything. See you soon, hon. And don't worry. Leo's a tough old bird. He'll be fine."

"Thanks, Dad." I hung up and tried to breathe myself into a state of calm before I called my mother. She would certainly freak out. She and my grandpa were super close, and having lost Grandma last year, I knew she already felt even more protective of him.

She, however, didn't answer the phone, even after three subsequent calls. I hated to do it but I had to leave her a message that she shouldn't worry, but we had to take Grandpa to the hospital and she should meet us there once she got the message. I dropped my phone into my lap and stared out the window, feeling Lucas reach over and squeeze my hand as he drove. I squeezed back, grateful he was there. Then I remembered he'd said he had appointments.

"You need to get to the salon," I said, sitting up straight. "I'm sorry, I totally didn't think of that—"

"Maddie. I'm not going anywhere except with you," he assured me. "I already texted Caroline. She's taking care of the appointments and rescheduling what she can't fit in. Don't worry about it." Caroline was his other groomer.

I opened my mouth to protest but he shook his head. "Don't argue with me."

I debated, then gave in and nodded. "Thank you." I wasn't sure how to respond. I hadn't had someone like him looking out for me in, well, ever. I mean, I had my family of course, but I was usually the one holding things together or at least feeling like I had to try. It felt nice to not have to shoulder something alone, to have someone to lean on.

As we drove and my head started to clear, I replayed what Grandpa had told us about his fall. That he hadn't just lost his balance, but been zapped by the lights. The lights that the town contractor had helped put up. I needed to call that guy and chew him out—then make sure he got over here to fix whatever was wrong.

Grandpa would be murderous if something went wrong and ruined his chances at winning the contest.

Chapter 4

As I hurried into the hospital, I met my sister Val at the desk. She turned as we came up behind her and threw her arms around me, then Ethan.

"What happened?" she asked finally, her voice wobbly. "Is he okay?"

I told her what happened and what Grandpa had told us. "He seemed okay, but I have no idea if he hit his head. Has he gotten here yet?"

She nodded. "They just brought him in to a doctor. Dad apparently called down and let everyone know that he was top priority."

I felt kind of bad about that when I looked around and saw all the people waiting to be seen.

"It's okay," she said, reading my mind. "They would've taken him first anyway. Possible head injury, and given his age . . ." she trailed off. "You said he got a zap from the lights? Is that true? Was he messing around with them?"

"He definitely was messing around with them, but I don't know what happened for sure." But I needed to find out. "You got here fast," I said, changing the subject.

"Yeah, I was prepping for the party," she said. "The

hosts don't live far from here and I needed to bring over some decorations." Val had been tapped to handle the big party for the Christmas light judges on Friday night. The judging was an event unto itself. The judges had a cocktail party at someone's fancy house prior to the limo ride around town to view the lights, and the evening wrapped with a dinner party for them back at that same house while they tallied up scores. The town had hired Val's company to handle that on behalf of the people who had opened their home to the judges.

My sister had started an events planning firm last summer when she left her first husband and went on a quest to remake her life. She'd clearly found her calling—barely a year in and she was already hiring staff and having to turn work away. She'd gotten Ethan involved, too, as a caterer. He did love to cook.

Now she hesitated. "You know the host is Selena Boyle, right? Her husband is Todd Banks." At my blank stare, she sighed. "The handyman and electrician the town contracted for the lights and stuff."

"No way." I stared at her. I hadn't known that. "The guy who may have messed up our lights? Have you met him?"

She shook her head. "His wife is the one kind of running this thing. I haven't seen him at all."

"Come on, let's sit," Ethan said, taking her hand and motioning to a section of seats in the corner. Lucas joined us a minute later, and the four of us sat in silence as we waited for word. I had just started to wonder where my mother was—she hadn't responded to my voicemail yet—when a nurse came over to us.

"Maddie James?"

I nodded, rising from my chair.

"Can you follow me?" she asked with a smile. "All of you can."

We all followed her behind the double doors where a red sign warned us they were for Authorized Personnel only.

"Your father asked me to get you," she said, leading us to a corner room and pushing open the door.

I stepped in first. My dad was in there, along with a doctor. Grandpa Leo sat up in bed, one leg swung over the side as if he were trying to make a run for it.

My dad turned when we entered. "There you are," he said.

Val and I immediately stepped over to the bed. "Is he okay?" Val asked the doctor, then without waiting for his reply, turned to Grandpa. "Are you okay?"

"I'm fine," he assured her. "Aren't I?" He frowned at the doctor.

"He's fine," the doctor said, turning to us. "Nothing broken. A sprained ankle that he needs to stay off for a bit, though. I'm Dr. Cameron, by the way. We do want to keep him overnight just as a precaution. To make sure there was no sneaky head trauma that hasn't presented yet. But everything we've looked at looks good."

"Then I should be able to go home," Grandpa said. "Right, Brian?"

My father held up his hands and stepped back. "I'm not in charge here."

"You run the hospital!" Grandpa roared. I was relieved to hear the loud bluster in his voice.

"Not this part I don't. Besides, Sophie would kill me if I made the wrong call." He looked around. "Where is your mother?"

"I couldn't get her. I left a message," I said.

My dad frowned. "That's odd."

I thought so too, even though I was trying to not think about that. I didn't need two emergencies in one day.

"I'll have you transferred to a private room, Leo,"

Dr. Cameron said. "We'll get that done quickly so you can get some rest."

"I don't need rest. I need to go home and finish my decorating." Grandpa turned to me. "The contest—"

"Don't worry about the contest. We've got it under control," I said. "I can just get the electrician back to do whatever still needs to be done with the lights."

"Don't bother," he said, his voice full of disgust. "He messed something up with our electrical. That's what I was trying to figure out when I got zapped."

Dr. Cameron glanced at my dad, then back to Grandpa. "Zapped?"

"I got a shock," Grandpa said. "That's why I fell."

"Hmm." The doctor thought about that. "In that case, I'm going to run a couple more tests. I'll be back in a moment." He slipped out the door.

I watched him go, worried, then turned back to Grandpa. "We'll figure out what happened," I said. "Let's not jump the gun."

"He's a hack," Grandpa retorted. "That's what happened. And I should've just kept my mouth shut."

"The doctor is not a hack," I said.

"Not the doctor!" Grandpa frowned at me.

"Who's a hack? And what is going on?"

We all spun around as my mother barreled into the room, eyes wide in panic as she looked at each of us, her eyes finally resting on Grandpa. My sister Sam was behind her. She looked like she'd been crying.

"Dad! Are you alright?"

"He's fine, Soph," my dad said, going over to give her a hug.

"Damn right I am," Grandpa muttered.

My mother came over and took Grandpa's free hand. Sam hovered over her shoulder. "What happened?" my mother asked again.

"He fell off a ladder," I supplied.

"You what?" Sam's face fell as she turned back to Grandpa. "Why were you on a ladder?"

"First of all, why wouldn't I be? I had to do some work on the house. And second, I didn't just fall off the ladder like some frail old man," he snapped.

Sam looked like she was about to cry again. Grandpa never got mad at us. Well, at least since we were adults. I remember once or twice as kids when he'd had to discipline us. He'd seemed to hate it more than we did.

But he didn't seem to notice her distress. Turning to my mother, he said, "I got zapped. That electrician you insisted on sending screwed up something with my electrical. I got a little zap and it made me lose my balance. And now they want to run more tests. I shoulda kept my mouth shut," he grumbled.

My mother's hand flew to her mouth. "Oh no. Dad, I'm sorry. Let me get someone over to take care of it."

He scoffed at that. "No thanks."

I saw the hurt in my mother's eyes and jumped in. "Grandpa, I'll handle it. We'll get to the bottom of what happened. The house will be perfect by Friday. Everything will go off without a hitch. I promise."

Chapter 5

We all cleared out of the room while they got Grandpa ready to go. My mother, usually so bubbly and positive, looked like she was about to cry.

"It's not your fault, Mom," Val said. "He really shouldn't be up on ladders at his age." She immediately clapped her hand over her mouth and glanced at the door to the hospital room, clearly hoping Grandpa hadn't heard her.

"Well, we all agree on that," I said. "But I wonder if there was some kind of electrical issue. There was a section that kept going out. I thought it was just a bad string, but maybe not." I glanced at my mother, hesitating to ask because it seemed like a stupid question for someone who had been running these big events for years like she had. But I had to. "Did this guy have references?"

She sighed. "He runs a landscaping and handyman company. Electricity is apparently on his list of jack-of-all-trade services. But you're right. I should've done better due diligence. We hired him because, well, we only had two RFPs and his was frankly less expensive. And Eva wanted to spread the love this year. Give someone new a chance." Eva Flores was the new

Chamber president. "She was pretty firm that we were going to use him. She's trying really hard to do things differently, make things more equitable, and I have to support that."

The event committee—which my mom was on—and the Chamber staff had been working with the town on obtaining requests for proposals from anyone who wanted to bid on this year's contracts. What Eva and her new team probably didn't realize going in was how small of a pool of candidates there would be. Most businesses that worked out here weren't based here and got the heck out of Dodge for the winter.

"We've been using Bernie forever," my mom went on. Bernie Elliott, owner of Elliott Electric, had been on the island his whole life. "Which I also wanted to honor, but you can't argue with the idea that we have to open up the channels for new people to become part of the community. Todd and his wife are new to the island and we all thought it would help them get their name out. Plus he's the only nonseasonal landscaper and general handy person who can also do electrical work. Bernie is just electrical and charges a lot more. We needed to have someone on call for this event, especially with so many people wanting help with their lights and other decorations. It seemed perfect, but I think the demand might've been too much in retrospect. And of course, I'm hearing about it left and right from people on and off the committee. Camille Billings will not let up on me about it. She actually threatened to step down from the event if we don't end this contract, and I can't afford that because she's in charge of the bazaar and the tree lighting." She rubbed the back of her neck. "Honestly, the whole thing is giving me a headache. And now I'm worried about the tree lighting, too. What if *that* goes wrong?"

"Who's Camille Billings?" I asked, trying to follow the conversation. My mother was never this frazzled over events—she could basically do all this stuff in her sleep. But it sounded like there was way too much cat herding going on.

"I'm sure you know her. She works in the office at the United Methodist Church. She was in the garden club with your grandmother. She was all over us to get professional help for the contest entrants, and now she's not happy with it."

I still couldn't place her, but it didn't matter. "So are you getting rid of this guy, then?" I asked.

"I'm working on what to do."

"Well, he better get it together if he thinks he's going to get any kind of work after this," I said. Although it was harder to find options for any kind of service in the winter months—something he was probably banking on. Still, I figured he'd learn pretty quickly that he couldn't phone it in around here. Daybreak Islanders—the year-rounders—were tough. Living in a place where they had to depend on themselves during most of the year to get by meant that when they trusted you with something, you'd better deliver. Otherwise you were basically done around here.

But right now my mom looked so sad I couldn't take it. I gave her a hug. "Grandpa's fine, Mom. I'll get the electrician back to check out the house and get everything up and running. Just send me his number. And if he can't do it, we'll find someone who can. By the way, where were you when I called earlier?"

"I was in a committee meeting about the bazaar. I had to shut my phone off because I was getting so many messages about things going wrong. And there are some problems with the contract for the high school. Some concerns that we were going to have to find a new space before Friday. And I also had to pick up the maps."

The holiday bazaar was scheduled to be held in the high school gym. And since it was two days before the market opened, I figured it would be decorated and ready for vendors to move in. I couldn't believe how unorganized this event sounded. But I managed to keep my mouth shut. After all, I wasn't involved in this one, by my own choice.

The James family was a big part of the community, which meant I was voluntold for a lot of local happenings. My dad was the CEO of the Daybreak Island Hospital, and he and my mom were an island power couple, involved in a lot of events and organizations. Like this event, where he'd been tapped as one of the "celebrity" judges. And my Grandpa Leo was the former chief of police in Daybreak Harbor. As a result, my two sisters and I always ended up involved in some activity or event. I just finished running a huge Halloween event, the first of its kind on the island, which hadn't gone exactly as planned and had been super stressful. I needed a break. I wanted to focus on the cat cafe, and actually being there to run it for a change. Besides, something always went wrong with these things and the stress could kill you. My mom was a good example of that right now, as part of the Chamber's advisory committee. She looked exhausted. I didn't envy her.

No, having this time off from community stuff was good. It meant I could focus on my own business. Be the face of the tours here, talk to people who came through about our mission and our cats, refill the cookie platter with Ethan's special holiday cookies. And we'd hopefully have lots of new visitors. Especially since we were highlighted on the map. Which I hadn't seen yet, and now I was excited.

"The maps! Yay. Do you have them with you?" I asked.

"I do." My mom opened her giant tote bag and pulled out a cardboard box. I removed the cover and eagerly pulled one out.

And tried to hide my reaction. The cover design was rudimentary at best—one step above clip art. The printing was subpar too, with the ink already smeared in a few places. I managed to keep my face neutral as I opened it to the map, searching out our part of the town and the cafe.

But when I found it, I frowned and looked at my mother, who was waiting for my response.

"They spelled the name of the cafe wrong."

"Oh no. You're kidding." That almost-teary look was back on her face. I was a little worried about her—my mother was always calm and cool under pressure. This seemed very out of character. Then again, she'd just had the life scared out of her because of Grandpa. Added on to the stress she appeared to be under, her reaction was understandable.

"I'm not, sadly." I jabbed at the tiny type where *Purrs* was spelled with only one *r*. To me, it was glaring. And just bad form. Had these people never heard of spellcheck? Did no one proof the product before it went to the printer, or even after when they'd printed a sample? This never would have happened if I had been on the committee. The marketing materials and promotional stuff were my forte.

As if she'd read my mind, my mother eyed me. "Want to help? There's still time," she said, sounding hopeful.

I didn't answer. My initial reaction was to agree and jump right in, just because I was kind of Type A and I knew this was a big deal, but on the other hand, I had my own stuff to do. I was enjoying having an event off.

But would I still be able to enjoy it if things were obviously going wrong?

"I'm kidding," my mother said, seeing the look on my face, although I knew she wasn't. "I'll get it fixed. Anyway, we're figuring it out, but there are a lot of things falling through the cracks. Clearly." She took the map back and shoved it in her bag. "I'm trying not to overstep since I'm advisory this time. But there are too many cooks in the kitchen and not enough experienced people."

I sympathized. I could also feel Lucas's and Val's eyes on me.

Resist, Maddie, I heard a little voice in my head saying.

But you want the event to succeed, a different voice in my head argued.

Before I could say anything, they wheeled Grandpa out of the room on his way upstairs. The attention turned from me—thankfully—and my mother hurried over to see Grandpa before they took him to the elevator.

I noticed Lucas grinning out of the corner of my eye and turned. "What?" I demanded.

"Nothing," he said innocently. "Just wondering how long it's going to take for you to come to the rescue."

"I'm not coming to any rescue," I said. "I just can't believe they spelled the cat cafe name wrong. How hard is *JJ's House of Purrs* to spell?"

"Right," Lucas agreed. "They probably need someone to show them how to do this stuff." His eyes were twinkling.

I crossed my arms protectively over my chest. "I haven't even recovered from the Halloween debacle yet. And I have so much with the cafe and now the decorating since Grandpa is laid up . . ." I trailed off

"I know Halloween was tough. But this stuff is in your

blood, Maddie. You need to be involved in these things. No, you need to *run* these things," Lucas amended. "That's when you're happiest. When you're stressed out and spending too much time on town events." He kissed me, daring me to disagree with him.

I started to protest, then kissed him back even though he was wrong. I was *delighted* not to be involved.

When he pulled back, he grinned at me. "So are you going to do it?"

I frowned. "Absolutely not." I brushed past him to go give Grandpa a kiss before they took him to his new room, trying to ignore the louder voice—which of course was the one telling me I should help out.

Chapter 6

When we got home from the hospital it felt like midnight. I was surprised to realize it was only six p.m. It felt like we'd been there for days.

I hated hospitals. Even though I'd spent a lot of time in one given my dad's job, being on the actual floors where people were sick or hurt felt very different than being in his office on the top floor. It freaked me out.

And now that I was home, I was restless. The house felt weird without Grandpa in it. Which I knew on some level was silly—he was out all the time on normal days. He had a more active social life than any of the rest of us. But I guess it was just the knowing of where he actually was that made it strange. And it meant I didn't really want to be in the house. Our dogs, Ollie and Walter, could sense that something was off—they both glommed onto me as soon as I walked in and didn't stray very far. Ollie, an older pit bull mix, was Lucas's dog that he'd re-rescued last year and brought to live with us. Walter the schnoodle puppy was the newest addition to our growing family. He was a rescue that Katrina had coerced Lucas into fostering. She knew what she was doing—she'd pretty much bet on us keeping him. Of course, she'd been right. She was a good saleswoman. And we all knew I couldn't turn away an animal in need. It was the reason why I now had double the amount of cats I'd planned to have in the cafe at any time. Honestly, I'd lost count.

Adele and Harry, one of our other volunteers and Adele's now boyfriend, were still in the cafe even though we were closed for the day. They had brought JJ in to play with the other cats while they waited on word about Grandpa. Once I assured them Grandpa was fine, they headed out. They had a standing Thursday night dinner and live music date at the yacht club, which was hilarious for those of us who knew Adele. Before Harry, she had basically only interacted with cats and worked her multiple jobs to make ends meet, spending her evenings with some wine and her own cats. She also held a grudge against the kind of people who hung out at a yacht club—which was probably still true on some level. But Harry had broadened her horizons, and with his extensive friend base had started to get Adele out and experiencing some new things. I was happy about it. She deserved an easier life than she'd had.

After they left, I went into the kitchen, followed by JJ and the two dogs, not really sure what to do next. Lucas poked his head in.

"I'm going to go clean up outside. Then we should get some dinner," he told me.

"Clean up? You mean hide the ladder before Grandpa comes home?" I asked.

He smiled a little. "Maybe. You want me to take a look at the lights while I'm out there?"

"No. Please. I don't need anyone else winding up in the hospital today," I said. "What I do need is for that guy to get back here and fix whatever he messed up. I should call him."

"Ethan and I are heading to his house now." Val walked into the room just as I said it. "We can talk to him."

"That would be great." I didn't really trust myself to call him right now. Val wouldn't risk losing the job by punching the guy in the face.

"Not at all. I'll let you know when he's coming."

"Thanks." I looked at Lucas. "You sure you don't have to get to the salon?"

"Nope. We already moved things around. I'm all yours." He kissed me, then walked outside.

I watched him go. If I was in a cartoon, little heart bubbles would be appearing over my head. I was smitten. I still couldn't believe I'd found my perfect person in my hometown, of all places. When I'd moved back a little more than a year and a half ago, I'd had low expectations about my love life, given (1) my typically poor choices in men and (2) the fact that the population on my island during the majority of the year was about five thousand, and I'd known about four thousand ninety-five of those people since I was a toddler.

But somehow, the Universe had delivered Lucas to my door.

Dopey smile in place, I fed JJ and the dogs and took the dogs out to go potty. When Lucas came back in, I finally had a sense of purpose.

"Want to run an errand with me and then we can get some dinner?" I asked him.

"Sure. What are we doing?"

"I want to say thanks to Donna. If she hadn't been outside looking in the window, who knows how long he would've been out there without us knowing he'd fallen." I didn't really want to think about it. This whole thing could've ended so much worse.

"That's nice," Lucas agreed. "Want to get her flowers or something?"

"Flowers. Yes. That's a good idea."

We got in the car and headed to town. It was dark, and everything was lit up—the first time I'd seen it all done. I'd been to town over the past week, but mostly either during the day or in the early dusk. I was surprised at how beautiful it looked. Whoever had done all the decorating this year had done a fabulous job. Not only were all the buildings perfectly lit like a scene out of a Christmas photograph, but the lights were all consistent—multicolored, which I loved so much more than plain white lights—and all the streetlights were wrapped in color as well. They'd also strung up lit stars along the street so it looked like they were hovering over the town. It looked magical.

The flower shop was still open, a perk of the holiday festivities. Shops that normally closed early—or didn't open at all during the sluggish winter months—were open regular hours for the season. We had one really nice flower shop in Daybreak Harbor—The Lotus Petal. The woman who ran it, Annie Daniels, was a close friend of my mom's. I'd heard they were doing centerpieces for the judging party, so they were probably working on those since it was two days away.

When we got there, they were getting ready to close, but as soon as Annie saw me she opened the door and grabbed me in a big bear hug. "Maddie! My goodness, I just heard about your grandfather," she said, her voice muffled in my hair. "I'm sending all good vibes his way!"

I loved Annie. She exuded warmth and good juju. You always felt like you were with a particularly loving mother figure when she was around. She was also cool—today, her long hair had turquoise ends, including her bangs, and she wore a shimmery silver dress that would've been perfect for a New Year's Eve party.

I couldn't really speak, she had me smushed against her chest so hard. Once she realized that, she let up a little. I took a breath. "Thanks, Annie. He's going to be fine."

"Well, of course he is," she scoffed. "He's Leo, isn't he?"

I laughed. "That's for sure. Have you met Lucas?"

"I have." She turned an appraising eye on him. It was a silly question, I knew. Everyone on Daybreak knew everyone on Daybreak. It was a perk—and also maybe a downfall—of living in such a small town on a small island. Even if she hadn't met him in the capacity of my boyfriend, she certainly knew who he was, even though she didn't have a dog or cat to get groomed. And probably everyone was on standby to judge him if things between us went awry—which probably wasn't cool, but if he realized it he didn't seem to mind.

"Good to see you again," Lucas told her.

"You too, sweetie. Now what can I do for you?" Annie asked.

"I need some flowers." I explained how Donna had alerted us to Grandpa's predicament.

"Ah. Well, that calls for a big bouquet," she declared. "You wait right here and I'll whip something up."

Once we had the bouquet—an enormous, brightly colored mix of daisies, lilies, and roses, we got back in the car. I was googling Donna's address when Val called.

"The electrician isn't home," she said when I answered. "His wife says he's out on a job. She did look worried when I asked about him, which may not be a good sign. I didn't tell her anything, just asked her to have him get in touch with us."

"Thanks for letting me know." He was probably out fixing something else he'd done wrong.

I disconnected and turned back to Google Maps. Donna lived just outside of the downtown area of Daybreak Harbor, right on the water. Her family was old Daybreak money, so it made sense they would have a spot like that. Of the five towns on the island, Daybreak Harbor was not the bougiest of them all—it had its fancy areas and its less fancy ones—but the area she lived in was pretty expensive, full of large homes on the water. The neighborhood was a mix of older, statelier homes and new construction—what some of the more judgmental, old-money residents thought of as too flashy, the "new rich" trying to show off their money.

Donna's house was one of the older homes, in her family for generations like ours, although our two homes couldn't have been more different. Grandpa's house was four floors, and each generation had renovated and added on. The result was a pretty new old house that had its own unique style. The Carey home was a traditional Cape-style house through and through, though much larger than the average. But the weather and long winters had taken a toll, and it didn't look as though there had been much done in the way of upgrades over the years. Still, she was part of the Christmas light contest, as was her whole neighborhood, from the looks of it. Every single house had lights, and as we drove to the end of the street where she lived, I saw people still outside in a lot of yards, tweaking and adjusting.

Donna's house, when we pulled up to it, was spectacular. She had really gone all out this year. The people down the street were probably trying to catch up to her. Every square inch of the house that could have lights, had lights. But it wasn't overkill—they looked like they had been strategically and systematically placed to give maximum impact without looking like Christmas had thrown up all over everything. They were a mix of white and very light blue lights, which together gave a shimmery, silvery look and feel, almost ethereal. On the front lawn, a recreation of Santa's toy workshop was lit up, with elves working inside and reindeer waiting patiently out in front with a sleigh.

"Wow," Lucas said, slowing as we approached.

"Yeah," I said. This was a serious contest this year. And from the looks of things, Donna was going to be a serious contender. Although Grandpa's was, in my humble opinion, better.

We pulled up behind a white van in the driveway. "I'll just run to the door if you want to wait here," I told Lucas.

"Sure. I'll find us someplace to eat while you do that." He pulled out his phone.

I bypassed ladders and some errant extension cords on the lawn mixed with cigarette butts that told me things were still in process as I headed to the front door and rang the bell. No answer, but all the lights in the house seemed to be on. And I thought I heard voices. I leaned against the door to listen, then realized they were coming from somewhere outside. I went back down the stairs and around the side of the house to the back, stopping short when I saw Donna standing just outside her back door, her voice raised in what was clearly a chastising tone. Donna looked like she'd been having a cozy night at home: hair piled on top of her head, the colorful skirt and boots she'd worn earlier—which seemed like days ago—swapped for a pair of leggings and a sweatshirt. She still wore her fun glasses, though. The guy getting the tongue lashing wore a long leather duster coat that didn't seem warm enough for the weather and a leather driving cap pulled low over his eyes. An unlit cigarette hung off his lip. Another woman stood slightly behind Donna, arms crossed over her chest, an uncomfortable look on her face.

"You've got one job, and you've completely screwed it up!" Donna jabbed a finger in the guy's face.

Chapter 7

I watched the man shrink back a little from Donna's long, glittery fingernail jabbing at his face. Becky had always told me Donna was a formidable opponent. She could morph from the fun-loving, easygoing I'm-your-friend persona into the made-of-steel, badass businesswoman in the blink of an eye. "It's a whole strategy," she'd said admiringly. "She gets people to let their guard down, then cuts them off at the knees the next instant."

Just hearing a bit of this made me never want to get on her bad side. I wondered what this person had done to draw her ire.

The woman watching the fight noticed me first. She reached forward to touch Donna's arm and murmur something, nodding in my direction.

I took that as my chance and cleared my throat. "Excuse me, so sorry to interrupt."

Donna and the guy both turned to stare at me. I thought I saw relief in the guy's face. "I told you I'll take care of it. I'll call you tomorrow," he muttered around the cigarette, then stalked away around the side of the house. I heard his engine start a minute later.

Donna met her companion's eyes, lips pursed, then

turned back to me and motioned me over. "Hi, Maddie. Sorry about that. Did you ring the bell?"

"I did. Sorry to show up unannounced," I started to say, but the other woman cut in.

"Maddie? Are you Maddie James?" She stepped forward eagerly, holding out her hand.

I realized who she was just as she said it. "Eva Flores."

"The new Chamber president," I said, finally placing her. "Good to see you."

"Your mom has told me so much about you." Eva clasped her hands together and beamed at me. "She said we might be able to get you to help us out a bit in our last-minute scramble to put this event on." Her eyes twinkled at me.

Eva was a pretty woman, tall with long, thick black hair and perfect skin. Her eyes were deep brown and friendly and she looked like she wanted to wrap me in a hug.

Leave it to my mother. She'd clearly been manipulating me earlier to get me on board when she'd already decided I needed to help. Maybe her whole spiel at the hospital had been dramatized just to get me sympathetic to the cause before she turned the pressure up. "She did, did she," I said noncommittally, but couldn't help but smile back at Eva. She had a good vibe.

"Well, I won't pressure you, but we'd love to have you. Donna, I'm gonna go. I'll call you tomorrow," she said, giving Donna a hug and a quick kiss on the cheek. With a wave at me, she hurried off around the side of the house.

I turned back to Donna. "Again, sorry to interrupt but I wanted to bring you these. As a thank-you for being there for Grandpa today." I held the bouquet out.

"Not at all. It's lovely to see you." She leaned in and air-kissed my cheek before accepting the flowers. "Beautiful, and completely unnecessary. You know how I feel about Leo. That was so scary. We were talking, then all of a sudden, he just lost his balance and fell." She shuddered a little. "It could've been so much worse. How is he?"

"He's fine. And I think it's because you were there. So really, thank you."

"Ah. So peeking in your windows is a good thing," she said with a wink. "Come on inside. It's freezing out here." She held the door open. I realized she wasn't even wearing a coat and followed her inside.

"I can only stay a minute. Lucas is in the car. Sorry again to interrupt." I stopped short of asking who the guy was.

Donna waved me off. "It was a useless conversation anyway. Do you know him?"

I shook my head.

"That was Todd Banks. Our illustrious town electrician, at least for this holiday season."

"Wait. That's Todd?" Crap. I'd let him walk right by me.

"It is." She appraised me, eyes big behind the red glasses. "Why?"

"He needs to come back to my house. He needs to . . . make some adjustments to our lights." I didn't mention the zap Grandpa said he'd experienced. I didn't want to scare her.

A light thud distracted me and I turned, catching a blur out of the corner of my eye as some creature ran into the room. It took me a second to realize it was one of those hairless cats, but this one looked a little different than any I had ever seen before.

"Oh my gosh, who's that?" I asked, crouching down and holding out my hand to the cat.

"That's Simon," she said.

I glanced up at her. "I didn't realize you had a cat! I

thought you couldn't have any? Is it a Sphynx? He looks a little different than how I remember them."

"I have two, actually. Simon and his sister Sheila. I just got them recently. And yes, they are Sphynxes. So they don't bother my allergies. Isn't he gorgeous?" She gazed at Simon lovingly. "They are unique. All cats look a little different, yes? I do still like to look at the furry cats, which is why I come to your place so often."

"Well, you're always welcome of course," I said. The cats were cute in that weird, hairless cat kind of way. Clearly cats that had been purchased from a breeder. I tried not to judge, although Katrina's angry face while shaking the flyer loomed large in my mind. Simon regarded me with an aloof curiosity, which probably had more to do with the smell of cats on me than anything about me specifically, then turned and left the room. Donna watched him go with a smile. "He's not very sociable until he knows you," she said apologetically.

"It's fine. That's how cats are." I stood. "Where did you get them?" I asked, trying to keep my voice nonjudgmental. I disliked the whole breeder thing, but didn't want her to get defensive. "I didn't know we even had cats like that around here."

"My friend helped me find them," she said. "She knows a respectable breeder on the mainland. Trust me, I know the issues with breeders. I don't love it as an option, but in my case, it was the only one."

I didn't want to make her feel bad. And if she'd gotten them off-island, they probably had nothing to do with Katrina's current nemesis. "Well, he's very cute. Anyway, I should go. Lucas is in the car. Thank you again, Donna."

"Oh, honey." She waved me off. "Nothing to thank me for. Anyone would've done it."

"Good luck with the Christmas light contest," I said.

"Although I do hope Grandpa wins." I winked at her. "I think it will cheer him up."

She laughed again. "I kind of do too. The other houses don't hold a candle to either of ours. And yes, I already scoped them all out."

I had to smile. Grandpa always did the same. Though this year he wouldn't be able to, since he couldn't drive. Which I'm sure frustrated him to no end.

"There are a lot more this year, with the changes. But Leo deserves it. I'll do my best to throw the contest in his favor. Although if my lights keep going out, I might not have to." Donna's lips pursed in annoyance at that thought, then she seemed to shake it off and led me to the door.

Impulsively, I gave her a hug before I turned to go. "Thank you," I said again.

"Oh, honey." She squeezed me back. "Of course."

She waved as I got in the car.

"All set?" Lucas asked.

I nodded. As he drove away toward downtown, I glanced in the rearview mirror. Her house looked great. I couldn't see any lights out, at least from my vantage point. I wondered what Todd hadn't done right that she'd been so upset about.

Chapter 8

Val stuck her head in my room the next morning, jolting me awake. "You better get up. Grandpa will lose it if we're late picking him up," she said.

I flung the pillow off my head and used one eye to look at the clock. Almost nine. How had I slept this late? I threw off the covers, startling JJ awake. My chunky orange sidekick had been sound asleep on Lucas's pillow, which Lucas had vacated already. "Is everyone up?" I asked.

Val nodded. "Ethan's got coffee going. Lucas took the dogs out. He wanted to let you sleep."

I'd been exhausted. I guess Grandpa's accident had stressed me out more than I'd let on, because I'd come home after dinner and crashed pretty early. I hadn't even woken up once last night. "I'll be right down."

"We're picking him up at eleven and going to get the trees," Val reminded me. "It was the first thing he said when he got on the phone."

"He still wants to get the trees?" Before the accident, we'd planned to go get the Christmas trees for our house and the cafe this morning, so they'd be up and decorated before the festivities kicked off on Saturday. But I'd figured we'd be pushing that timeline back some.

But Val was nodding. "Yep. He insisted. And he's already in a mood because he'll be in a wheelchair with his ankle."

"That'll be a sore spot," I agreed. "No pun intended." Which meant he'd be in rare form, barking orders at us from his throne. I hoped Ethan had made the coffee extra strong. Something told me today might be tough to get through. "Are they definitely releasing him, or is he just releasing himself?" I asked.

"Mom talked to the doctor this morning. She's the one who called. No signs of head injury, thank goodness. And no issues to his heart or anything from the zap. They said it must have been very small."

I breathed a sigh of relief too. "It really was lucky he was so close to the ground when he fell." Which reminded me that I had to follow up with the electrician. I'd called him last night after he'd slipped by me at Donna's and gotten his voicemail. I'd left a curt, urgent message that we needed him back ASAP. I didn't mention Grandpa's injury—I didn't want him to think we were going to sue him or something and not come back. I checked my phone. No messages.

"Mom also said that we needed to take our time with the trees because she's planning a little welcome home party for him. She wants to get people over here while we're out to surprise him. She promised to take care of everything," she said when she saw my face. "I had the same reaction, but she swore we wouldn't have to worry about anything. Anyway, hurry up." Val left, closing the door behind her.

I looked at JJ. "Guess we're having a party."

He squeaked—his signature sound. It had taken me

by surprise the first time I'd heard it, out in the cemetery near my grandmother's grave where I'd found him watching me from afar. The high-pitched squeak completely contrasted his strong, stocky looks. But he was very self-conscious about it and hated when anyone pointed it out. Usually, they got the tail—the cat's middle finger. I headed to the bathroom to take a quick shower. When I finished, JJ was waiting at the door.

"Breakfast time," I told him. "And you can come with us to get the tree."

He squeaked again, then trotted downstairs behind me.

Everyone was gathered in the kitchen when I went downstairs—Lucas, Ethan, Val, and the dogs. I was hyperaware of Grandpa's absence. His usual chair was loudly empty. And while we were all relieved that he was fine, I felt like it was a reality check of sorts. He was in his late seventies. He had to be more careful now. And even if he was, he wasn't going to live forever.

The thought made tears spring to my eyes, and I hurried to the counter, pretending to take my time choosing a mug and pouring my coffee so no one would notice. Focusing out the window, I noticed it had snowed again. Another two or three inches on the beach, which actually looked cool.

"How many trees are we actually getting?" Ethan asked, drawing my attention back into the room. "I think we need one for the outside cafe too."

"Definitely," I said. "And one for the cat cafe and then the big one for the house." I looked at Lucas. "How come you aren't at work?"

"I'm helping with the trees," he said simply. "You're down a pair of hands, yes?"

If he kept this up, I might cry. We agreed to take two cars—Lucas's and Grandpa's truck. "You want us to go get Grandpa and we can meet you at the tree farm?"

I asked Val. "Maybe you guys can start scoping out some trees in advance. You know Grandpa might be a little . . . testy because he can't do a lot of this himself this time."

"Good call," Val said. "We'll give you a head start then. We've got to make some menu adjustments for the party tomorrow anyway. Apparently they forgot to tell me one of the judges is vegan." She sighed. "At least Ethan has been testing out new vegan recipes."

I grinned. "He's a Californian. Of course he's good at vegan recipes."

"And they taste good, too," Lucas said. "Which I never thought I'd say about vegan food."

Ethan smiled modestly. "I think we'll attract more people to the cafe if we have a robust vegan and gluten-free menu."

"I agree," I said.

Ethan headed out to the cafe. Val started to follow, then turned to me. "Hey, did you ever hear from the electrician?"

I realized I hadn't. "No. I'll call him."

"You sure?"

"Yeah. Thanks for trying." While I finished my coffee, I called Todd Banks. No answer. I left a message, then with a sound of frustration, I dropped the phone.

"The electrician?" Lucas asked, glancing at me.

"Yeah. And I think I need to find someone else. If this isn't fixed today, Grandpa's going to be back out there trying to climb the ladder. But I'll worry about that after the trees. One thing at a time." I finished my coffee and poured more into a travel mug. "Ready?"

"I'll go warm up the car."

While he did that, I got JJ into his harness. He loved to go out. He was like a celebrity around town—people were always happy to see him, and most of them had treats they carried around especially for him. It was kind of a given that he would show up in some town establishment at least once during any given day, and people wanted to be ready. He knew it too. He swaggered around town with the full, confident knowledge that he was completely and utterly adored, and expected to be treated that way at all times. It was kind of hilarious given his humble beginnings living outside in the local cemetery.

We drove to the hospital with him standing on my leg, looking out the window like a dog, nose pressed against the glass. People in cars next to us beeped and waved. It lifted my spirits as much as it lifted theirs. I loved that I had a cat who brightened people's days.

When we arrived at the hospital, the royal treatment began. The nurses at the station sprang to attention when they saw us. One of them came around with a handful of the Temptations treats they kept especially for him. I handed Lucas the leash so he could let JJ visit his friends while I went to see about Grandpa.

I found him in his room, waiting for the final discharge papers, my mother and a hospital-issued wheelchair that my dad had gotten him by his side. He had a splint on his right foot, which my dad had told us they were giving him to keep the sprain from being aggravated. For someone being sprung, Grandpa didn't look happy. I understood. I would hate to feel like any part of my independence was taken away. And for someone who walked as much as he did and was just generally active, this would be a blow.

"Hi!" I said, leaning down to hug him. "You look good!" I glanced at my mother over his head. She nodded and smiled, signaling that all was well.

Grandpa gave me that look that said, *Stop fussing,* but

he hugged me back hard. "We're going to get the trees, right?"

I nodded. "Val is meeting us there."

"Good. Now if they would just sign me out!" He raised his voice loud enough that the nurse passing by could hear him.

"Dad!" my mother admonished.

The nurse paused, sticking her head into the room. "The doctor will be right in to see you, Leo."

"Humph," he grunted. But they didn't make him wait long. Dr. Cameron arrived a few minutes later and went over the discharge instructions, which basically involved Grandpa using the wheelchair until his follow-up visit in two weeks when they would reassess. He didn't love it, but he wanted to get out of here, so he agreed.

"I stayed overnight," my mother told me when Grandpa was busy with the nurses who came in to finalize everything and help him into the wheelchair. "I just felt so bad."

"Aww, Mom. It's not your fault." Come to think of it, she looked worse than Grandpa. Her curly hair was pulled back in a severe bun with a headband covering most of her head, and she wore a pair of sweats and a sweatshirt that she'd clearly slept in.

"What's the story with the electrician?" she asked, ignoring my comment.

"I haven't gotten a hold of him yet. I actually saw him at Donna Carey's last night, but didn't realize it was him until he'd left already. I don't know if he's just busy or avoiding my calls. She was pretty mad at him too."

My mother frowned at that. "She was?"

I nodded. "Seems to be a theme."

"Are you sure you don't want me to deal with him?"

"No. Between Val and me, we'll nail him down. I

mean, unless you're firing him from the town contract. If I can't get him next time I try, I'm going to get someone else."

"We'll get Bernie. Just let me know."

Lucas returned to the room and handed me JJ's leash. "I'll get the car and meet you downstairs," he told us.

"Thank you," I said.

My mother checked her watch. "People are going to start showing up at the house soon for Grandpa's welcome home. I need to head over there."

My phone chimed with a text message. I pulled it out and saw that it was Ellen, the town librarian. I tapped on the message.

Hi Maddie! I have a problem—the library schedule isn't showing on the Christmas event website. We really want people to find our programs. I haven't been able to reach anyone at the Chamber. Can you help?

Ellen was super dedicated to the library and made sure they were involved in any festivities the island was hosting. I hated to think she—or anyone, for that matter—was having a bad experience. These events, especially the offseason ones, were the lifeblood of our island tourism. The more we upped our game, the better it was for our year-round residents.

But I wasn't sure why she was texting *me*. I held the message up to my mother. "Why does Ellen think I'm in charge of the event website?"

My mother read the message. "Probably because you're usually in charge of that kind of thing when we have events. I'm not sure."

I thought of Eva's comment yesterday about my mom mentioning my possible assistance. "Well, who *is* in charge?"

"The Chamber has a marketing person that's supposed to be doing it."

"Is she doing the maps also? Did you tell them that they were wrong?" I asked.

"No, Madalyn," she snapped. "I've been a little busy."

Whoa. I inadvertently took a step back. I hadn't heard my mom sound that stressed in a long time. She thrived on being part of everything going on on the island. And she hardly ever snapped at us.

"Is everything okay?" I asked after a minute. "Is this about Grandpa, or is it something else?"

She paused for a long moment, then sighed. "I'm sorry. I'm just having a hard time with the way they're running this event, and I can't just step in and take it over since it's a whole new group. I'm trying to be a team player, but it's frustrating. And now your grandfather . . ." She trailed off, then squared her shoulders and looked at me. "I know you wanted to stay out of the planning for this one, but I could really use your help."

She was looking at me so earnestly.

I had to hand it to her. She never asked us for much, so when she did, we felt incredibly guilty saying no. I could feel my resolve caving.

I sighed. "What kind of help?"

Her eyes brightened, but she was still treading carefully. "Well, the marketing for one. And there are some loose ends with the bazaar, which starts tomorrow night. That's giving me agita. The contract is still under debate, people want to get in there to set up, it's chaos." She shook her head. "I need someone to basically direct them on what to do. You're good at that."

I was. But I'd always been a little bossy.

"I guess I can help get things off the ground," I said, resigned.

"Really?" She clapped her hands then threw her arms around me. "Thanks, hon. I promise, it won't be so bad."

"I've heard that before," I muttered.

She stepped back, grinning. She looked much better than when I'd first arrived. "I promise. I'll send you some emails to get you started. Now. Make sure you keep your grandfather out for at least two hours," she said, dropping her voice. "I've got a party to set up."

Chapter 9

The Cranberry Bog Tree Farm was hopping when we arrived. Most of the island was trying to get Christmas-ready, especially the people who were in the contest. All the participating homeowners wanted to make sure their trees were also visible in a window to add to the effects of the outside lights. It was part of the whole package. And the homes that were part of the contest were usually big, which meant they had big windows and, therefore, big trees that enhanced the ambiance.

We didn't have that one big window on a high floor, but we had the perfect spot in the living room. Our windows were oversized anyway, so there would be a good shot of the tree. And Grandpa had a knack for picking out the perfect one.

Grandpa made a move to get out of the car when we arrived, but I shook my head. "No way. You've gotta wait for the wheelchair. You heard the doctor."

"And just how do you plan to roll that thing around the forest?" he asked, glowering at me.

"The same way they push carriages and other things on wheels," Lucas assured him. "Don't worry, Leo. I got you."

I stood back with JJ and let Lucas take the lead helping Grandpa out of the car and getting him into the wheelchair. He looked sullen, probably wondering what everyone would think and what he would tell them. But also I knew he didn't want to miss the adventure, so he would suck it up.

JJ was excited. His little nose was already going a mile a minute, sniffing around the ground at our feet, straining at his harness to try to reach some of the trees. I could imagine how much there was for him to smell. The dogs would be in heaven too if they could've come, but they weren't allowed at the farm. No one wanted to buy a tree that had been peed on, I guess.

But it was beautiful just being here. The grounds were still covered in a thin coating of snow, and the trees looked like they were from a New England postcard, tipped with icy whiteness. There was something magical about snow near the ocean too. Despite the cold, it made me happy. I took my first peaceful breath since Grandpa's accident.

I texted Val to find out where she was, then slipped my hand into Lucas's and surveyed the rows of trees in front of us to figure out where to start.

"Go that way," Grandpa directed from his chair, pointing to where the tallest trees on the farm stood. "I want a really nice one for the house."

I suppressed a smile. He'd never not had a "really nice one." Grandpa took the Christmas tree selection process as seriously as he took the light contest, and he expected us to as well.

I did relish this annual trip to get the trees. It had been one that my sisters and I looked forward to as kids. It was one of the things I'd missed most when I lived out West.

But I was here now, and I was going to enjoy it. Also it helped that JJ was having fun. He looked like a bloodhound, nose glued to the ground, straining against the leash as he tried to get me to move faster.

I was so intent on the maze of trees that I didn't notice my sister and Ethan until Val stepped out in front of me.

"You made it," she said, leaning down to kiss Grandpa. Her gaze traveled to his splinted ankle. "How are you feeling?"

"I'm fine," he said, waving her question off. "Why wouldn't I be?"

She smiled. "Gee, I don't know. I guess that was a silly question."

"How about this one?" Ethan called from the grove next to where we stood. Waving, he held onto a tree that was at least nine feet tall. For him, it probably didn't look that big—Ethan was six two—but to the rest of us it was a monster.

"For the house, maybe. Not for the cafe," I laughed. "Can you imagine that thing crashing down when the cats start climbing on it? It would probably go through a window."

"You might want to get a fake tree with cheap ornaments for the cafe," Val, ever the pragmatist, offered. "With the cats and all."

The rest of us turned and stared at her as if she'd just suggested we skip the Christmas tree this year altogether.

"We must not have raised you right," Grandpa said sadly. "A fake tree? That's disappointing, Valerie."

I tried to stifle a laugh with a fake cough as Val opened her mouth to defend herself. "I think we'll just get a smaller one," I said, putting an arm around Val's shoulders. "But maybe that one for the main house, if you think it'll fit."

Grandpa motioned to Lucas to push him closer to the tree. I watched him taking measurements in his head.

"This one might be too big," he said finally. "I want people to be able to see the top. We have that star your grandmother loved," he reminded us.

"Okay. Onward," Ethan said, heading deeper into the rows of green.

Lucas watched the whole process with some trepidation, clearly not sure if he dared to suggest a specific tree for fear of making a choice that might have unforeseen repercussions.

I was about to follow him when I heard someone shouting. A man's voice. "I already put a marker on that one!"

"I don't see a marker!" A woman's, just as loud and insistent. "I want this tree, and I'm taking it!"

I turned to see who was shouting, surprised to find Angelo Longo, the owner of our local grocery co-op, having a face-off with a woman who stood at least a whole head shorter than him. And Angelo wasn't tall. Both of them had a possessive hand on another giant tree that rivaled the one Ethan had been eyeing. The woman had reddish-blond hair cut in a stylish, long-in-front, short-in-back style and wore a fuzzy coat that made her look like a bear. I didn't recognize her, at least not from back here.

Angelo was one of Grandpa's buddies. He came to many of Grandpa's card games. I'd always known him as a soft-spoken man with a slight Italian accent. His wife had died years ago, back when I was in high school, and it had been just him and his daughter, Molly, ever since. Molly was a year younger than me, so she'd been a teenager when she'd lost her mom. As a result, she and her dad had become even closer. Molly worked with him at the co-op to this day, and though she was all grown up and married, they actually lived on the same street.

"Camille. It's right here," Angelo insisted, pointing at the base of the tree. Then he stopped and stared. "Did you take it off? You took my marker off!"

Another man stepped up next to the woman. "Why are you yelling at my wife?" he asked. His voice was much lower, but a lot more menacing.

Angelo wasn't fazed. "She took my tag off. This is my tree."

Beside me, Lucas made a sound of disbelief. "Are these grown adults really fighting about a tree?"

"I told you, they take Christmas seriously around here," I said, eyes glued to the action.

The new guy, who I also didn't recognize, stepped forward, chest puffed out. "If my wife wants this tree, she's getting this tree."

Angelo stepped in front of him, trying to match the bravado. "I said, it's mine."

The other guy went toe-to-toe with him, then used his shoulder to shove him aside. As he made a move to heft the tree, Angelo shoved him back, causing him to lose his balance and fall, taking the tree with him. The guy went down in a shower of pine needles, landing in last night's fresh snow. The woman screamed and jumped out of the way.

I sensed nothing good was going to come from what happened next. Already a hush had fallen over the farm as the gathered crowd watched with bated breath as the guy got up, slowly, and advanced on Angelo.

Next to me, Lucas swore. "Should I go try to help?"

Before he could start toward the ruckus, an ear-splitting whistle shattered the moment. I pressed my hands to my ears, then realized it was Grandpa who had made the sound. He'd always done that when we were fighting as kids to get us to stop.

His whistle slowed down the confrontation long

enough that a couple of the workers could run over and intervene. One of them righted the tree while the other got in between the two men, who were about to start throwing punches.

I glanced at Grandpa. "Well done."

He shrugged. "That always works. Takes people right out of their insanity."

"What the heck is going on with my father?"

I looked up at the voice behind me and did a double take when I recognized the face partially obscured by a knitted hat pulled low over her forehead. "Molly?"

Molly Longo—actually I had no idea if she still used that last name—glanced at me, then brightened when she recognized me. "Maddie!" she exclaimed. "How funny. I was talking to myself, by the way. Good to see you. It's been forever." She gave me a hug.

It had been. Probably I hadn't seen her except in passing since I'd graduated. We definitely hadn't run in the same circles. She had been a big-time swimmer, competing nationally and everything. It had all stopped when her mom died, and after I left I lost track of her except to see her at the co-op every now and then when I was home. She'd seemed to embrace her life here with her dad and the family business from the jump, whereas it took me a decade to have any desire to come home.

"How's that cat cafe of yours? I've been meaning to get over there," she said. "What a cool idea."

"It's awesome," I said. "You really should come by sometime. Are you in the market for a cat?"

"I have been for a while." She shrugged. "I'm being picky, though. But I'd definitely love to see the place."

"Well, once you're done here, come on over. My mom is throwing Grandpa Leo a welcome home party. I'm sure he'd love to see your dad, and that way you can check out the cafe."

Molly looked interested now. "Cool. Let me make sure we have enough coverage at the store. Anyway, what happened?"

"They were arguing over the tree," I said.

Molly cringed. "I really hope my dad didn't start it."

I refrained from answering that one.

"I better go help him. Good to see you." She rushed over to her dad, who was off the ground, still facing off with his nemesis. The other guy's wife fawned over him, but he was glaring at Angelo over her head.

Grandpa shook his head. "Shame on them."

"Who was that Angelo was fighting with?" I asked.

"Camille Billings. And her second husband, Ray." Grandpa made a face. "He's kind of a piece of work. Works over at the yacht club."

"Camille Billings, like the one in Grandma's garden club?" I asked.

Grandpa nodded. "You remember her? Your grandmother never really liked her."

I didn't, but I remembered the name because my mom had just mentioned her as being involved in the event and giving her a hard time. Which meant she'd likely end up giving *me* a hard time once I was involved.

Terrific.

"I haven't seen Molly in years," I said to Grandpa, changing the subject.

He nodded. "Still working at the co-op. Angelo says she's doing well. Aside from that lawyer she's married to." Grandpa made another face. "Angelo isn't thrilled about him. But it could be that no one is good enough for her in Angelo's mind."

I got his point. Molly and Angelo were super close, perhaps dysfunctionally so—but in this case I suspected Angelo was right. Molly was married to a guy named Brandon who worked at the same firm Val's

ex-husband's family owned. He'd been a huge jerk in
school. With guys like that, it usually only got worse.

Grandpa motioned to Lucas. "Come on, let's go back
to the tree search."

Chapter 10

As we rounded the corner into an aisle of trees, I saw Becky and her new boyfriend, Damian Shaw, heading toward us. Becky's blond curls peeked out of a hot pink slouchy hat that asked "Got news?" Ever the newsperson, that one. She and Damian held hands, which I just loved. I hadn't seen my best friend this happy in years.

"What was that kerfuffle about?" she exclaimed, rushing over then doing a double take when she saw Grandpa in a wheelchair. "And what's *that* about?"

"I'll explain later but he's fine," I said. "And those two were arguing about a tree, seems like. Hey, Damian."

"Hey, Maddie." He grinned at me. "You're always present for the mayhem, aren't you?"

I rolled my eyes. "Don't remind me."

Becky looked like she didn't know what to focus on first—her eyes kept roving to Grandpa, but the look on my face must've discouraged her. "Must be contest related. People are getting nutty this year with this stupid cash prize," she said, rolling her eyes. "We just reported on someone sabotaging someone else's house because they thought the lights were better. They've been disqualified, but still! They may have criminal misdemeanor charges filed against them. Can you even imagine?"

"Wow," I said. "I hadn't realized it had gotten that out of control."

"Yeah, well. People are nuts. So what happened?" She dropped her voice and indicated Grandpa.

"I saw the ambulance yesterday at your place," Damian said in a low voice. "I was worried. I didn't want to intrude, though."

"Thank you. He's okay," I said.

Damian nodded and stepped forward to shake Grandpa's hand and greet Lucas, making small talk about the weather, the trees, the upcoming holiday festivities, easing everyone effortlessly into the conversation. Damian was a transplant to the island from the Midwest. He owned and operated the Lobstah Shack, a popular restaurant right down the street from us next to the ferry dock. He'd bought it from a local family who'd run it their whole lives, and many natives had scoffed at the idea of a Midwesterner moving to our island and successfully running a seafood shack. They figured there was no way a guy who had barely seen the ocean was going to make a go of cooking seafood on a quirky island like ours where the majority of the year was freezing and desolate.

Yet he'd proven them all wrong. In just two years he had expanded it so it was way more than just the roadside shack for which it had been named. Now it was both a place where you could pick food up at the counter and eat out at picnic tables, staying true to its roots, but it also had a sit-down dining room and a fish counter inside so he could stay open year-round. He'd made friends with some local fishermen and, using his Midwestern charms, had managed to move himself to the top of the list for fresh fish to sell.

Basically, he was rocking it, and rumor had it that he'd already managed to start turning a profit despite being so new to the venture.

And in a recent development, he was now seeing Becky. He'd managed to win her over too, which was probably harder than winning over the whole island. He was good for her—Damian had a calm, easygoing way about him that seemed to instantly rub off on my high-strung, breaking-news-minded best friend.

Becky pulled me out of earshot. "So?" she demanded.

"The short version is he sprained his ankle falling off a ladder. I'll tell you the whole story later. Are you getting a tree for your place?" I forced the subject change. I was a little surprised to see her there. She usually didn't bother decorating her small condo—she spent Christmas at our house anyway, and the rest of the time she was at work.

"The newspaper office," she said. At my raised eyebrows, she added, "We're opening the newsroom for anyone who wants to tour this year."

I was surprised to hear that. I'd figured the businesses that were going to be open were the stores, maybe some historical town buildings. The newsroom wasn't really an open-to-the-public type of place. And I hadn't noticed it on the map I'd been scrutinizing like a hawk. "Really? How come?" I asked.

She shrugged. "Donna's idea. The paper is the platinum sponsor of the event, so she wants to be super visible. We're taking people through who are interested, giving them an idea of how it all works. She figures people should get engaged in how local news is really made. Which I agree with, of course. I think the more people know about how we work the better off we are. So I volunteered to help."

"Wow. That's cool," I said.

"It kind of is, right? I'm glad you said that, actually. I could use your help decorating later. I couldn't get a lot of volunteers from the staff, so Damian and I are doing most of it. And Alice." Alice Dempsey also worked at the paper, a former columnist who had recently taken on a new role working directly for Donna as a chief of staff.

I hesitated. We had to finish decorating our house, and now I had an event to manage . . .

"I'll take us all to dinner after," she said, to sweeten the deal.

I laughed. I hadn't seen much of Becky lately, so this might be fun. Also watching her deck the halls would be an experience. "Sure, why not? As long as I can slip away. Grandpa's kind of on a tear." I glanced behind me, watching him barking orders at Ethan and Lucas. Apparently we'd found at least one tree.

"I'll text before I pick you up," Becky said. "Bring your holiday cheer."

Chapter 11

Despite the crazy in the air around us, the tree selections went more smoothly than I expected, for which I was grateful. We finished the whole process, including getting the three trees netted and tied down onto the cars, in just under three hours—which was perfect for my mom to get the party set up at home. I hoped Grandpa would be happy about it. I wondered how many people I'd find in our house when we got back. I hoped she'd warned Adele. If as many people as I suspected were on the invite came, it might throw a wrench into cafe parking, and she might get cranky about it. Well, there was no *might* about it. She would be cranky, period.

When we got back to the house, cars lined both sides of the street for as far as we could see. Guess that answered that question. I tried to ignore it, but Grandpa leaned forward from the back seat once he caught sight of the vehicles.

"What is that about?" he demanded.

"What?" I asked.

He gave me a look. "The cars, Madalyn."

"I don't know! I guess we're having a run on the cafe. I hope Ethan had enough people working today." I smiled

sweetly as Lucas parked and I jumped out, tucking JJ
under my arm. Val and Ethan pulled into the driveway
behind us. Lucas and Ethan had to help Grandpa up the
steps since we had no wheelchair ramp—something
we'd never given a second thought to needing. Val and I
brought the chair. Once Grandpa was situated in it again,
we opened the door and pushed him through.

And were greeted by a loud cheer.

"Welcome home, Leo!"

I stepped inside, my eyes widening. Our living room
was crammed with people. They even spilled into the
kitchen. I had been expecting a lot of people, but this was
above and beyond. My mom had done a good job in a
short period of time. Also between our visits to the hospital and the tree farm, word must have spread fast that
the beloved Leo Mancini had been involved in some
sort of accident and people were immediately springing
into action.

So here they all were, in our living room, which was
now not only decorated for Christmas but also with a
huge Welcome Home banner and covered with flowers,
gift baskets, food, and other goodies. Everyone on the
island knew that Grandpa had a sweet tooth, and the
amount of candy and cake-type stuff I could see on my
first scan of the room was staggering.

Tons of people from around town were talking all
at once, trying to get to Grandpa. Leopard Man, our
resident quirky character, and his girlfriend, Ellen, the
librarian—who I realized was still waiting for me to respond to her text—had balloons. They were an adorable
couple. They'd fallen in love over Shakespeare and now
they were inseparable. Grandpa's card-playing friends
were here. I caught sight of Donna Carey's bright red
glasses as she huddled with Annie from the flower shop.
Adele and Harry had stepped away from the cat cafe to

join us. Adele had also had the foresight to make sure the main house was closed off from the cats, which was good given Donna's allergies.

I also spotted Angelo Longo and Molly. I wondered if they'd come because of my invite to Molly, or if Angelo had already been planning to come. Either way, I'd have to make sure to take her through the cafe. Damian was here solo. Becky was probably back at the office. My friend Cass Hendricks, who sent Grandpa tea every week. Katrina. Craig Tomlin, my ex-boyfriend and a local detective. And I even caught a glimpse of Lt. Mick Ellory. He and Grandpa also worked together— unofficially—a lot when the opportunity arose. Grandpa had started his own PI firm after he retired as the chief of the Daybreak Harbor Police Department. He just couldn't stay away from law enforcement. Also, he was nosy. He liked to know everything that was going on around town and the island, and his direct line to information had been severed. So after moping around for a few months, he put up a shingle and got in the new chief's hair as often as he could.

Grandpa, who was never at a loss for words, seemed overwhelmed by the outpouring. He wasn't even giving anyone a hard time for all the fuss, which he normally would be doing. In fact, he looked downright emotional, although he tried to hide it. I knew how he felt.

"Not getting enough attention lately, eh, Leo?" One of his poker buddies came over and clapped him on the back. "Had to get all drastic on us?"

"Well, you slackers haven't been around much," Grandpa returned.

"Didn't you hear? We're playing cards tonight," another chimed in. "My house. We'll pick you up. Game starts at seven! You better be ready."

I was relieved to hear that, since we were all going

to be mostly out and I didn't want Grandpa home alone.
Which I'm sure my mother had something to do with.

"Hey. Why didn't you tell me what happened?" Katrina demanded, coming up to me and giving me a fierce
hug. I hugged her back. Grandpa was like family to her.

"I just didn't have a chance yet," I said. "It's been a
little crazy."

Craig and Mick joined us. Mick slung an arm over
Katrina's shoulder. "I'm sorry that happened. But he
looks like he's good, save for the foot. You guys need
anything?" he asked.

"I don't think so, but thanks. I'm glad you came," I
said. It made my heart happy to know so many people
loved my grandfather.

"So weird to see him sitting in a wheelchair," Craig
said in a low voice, as if he could read my mind.

"Tell me about it. You should have been here yesterday when I found him on the ground." I had tried to
shake that image off multiple times, but it kept creeping
back into my brain, hovering at the edges of my vision,
waiting to spring into view as soon as I closed my eyes.

"Yikes. You doing okay?" Craig asked, his voice full
of sympathy.

"Yeah. It's all good. He's fine." I put on a brave smile.
Lucas came up and slid his hand into mine, nodding at
Craig. The two of them didn't love each other, but they
got along for my sake. I was grateful that Craig and I
could still be friends, especially after I'd turned him
down when I moved back and he'd attempted to rekindle
our relationship.

"How are you gonna keep him off that leg?" Mick
asked. "Between Christmas and his job, I'd say you have
your work cut out for you."

"I don't know if he has any jobs right now," I said.

Mick laughed. "He's always got a job."

My mother joined us, holding two cans of seltzer water. She handed me one. "There's food in the kitchen. Go get some. I'm sure you haven't eaten today. What's top of mind?"

Food. Yes. I was starving. I hadn't had anything but coffee yet today and wondered how I was still standing. "The lights and the contest. Which reminds me." I pulled my phone out and checked for voicemails from the electrician. Nothing yet.

"Oh my God. Don't tell me he didn't come," she said, immediately onto what I was doing.

"Shh. I haven't told Grandpa yet," I said. "But no. And I left two voicemails."

She looked like her head was about to explode. "I need to do something about this," she muttered, then marched away, grabbing her coat off the hook near the door and leaving before I could stop her.

"What was *that* about?" Katrina wanted to know.

"Long story. I'll tell you later."

Damian came over. "Sorry to interrupt, but Becky's coming to pick us up around six," he said. "She wasn't able to get away to come to the party but wants to run in and bring Leo something later. And I need to run back to the Shack. I left the garland there to decorate the newsroom."

"I'm leaving anyway," Mick said. "Gotta get back to work."

I hugged him, impulsively. "Thanks for coming."

He hugged me back awkwardly, then left, giving Katrina a quick kiss.

"We came separately," she explained. "I wanted to stick around. We need to talk about that phone call we need to make." She raised her eyebrows, clearly hoping to convey that I should know what she was talking about. I did. The breeder.

"Okay. Give me a minute. I'm starving." I started to head for the kitchen to grab some food, when a blur of fur bolted down the stairs, through the living room and onto the table, landing right in one of the casserole dishes someone had left on the table. I gasped in dismay as I realized it was my new charge: Frederick, our fancy cat.

Frederick looked as startled about his predicament as the guests. Using his back legs, he vaulted out of the dish, spraying mac and cheese everywhere—including Molly Longo's hair and Ellen's pretty pink skirt—and bolted toward the back of the house.

How had he gotten out of his room? Someone must've left the door open.

"I'll get him," Lucas said, touching my arm. He was so good.

"I'm so sorry," I said, handing napkins to Molly and Ellen.

Ellen laughed and dabbed at her clothes. "I never know what to expect at your house, Maddie."

I mumbled another apology, grabbed the ruined bowl of food, and hurried for the kitchen. But as I was about to push the door open, I heard Grandpa's voice. "I don't know for sure yet, but I'm still working on it," he was saying. "This damn leg threw off my schedule."

"Don't worry," a female voice said. "Just get better, please. I know you'll get to the bottom of it, but the sooner the better, of course."

Was that Donna? Deciding to be nosy, I pushed the door open. "Get to the bottom of what?" I asked.

It was indeed Donna Carey, having some kind of private conversation with my grandfather. She jumped up from the chair she sat in. "Maddie! Hello." She glanced at Grandpa, waiting for his response.

"Hi, Doll. None of your business," he said cheerfully. "Just chatting."

"Fine, be that way." I made a face at him and deposited the plate in the sink. "Don't ask. And don't eat it." I grabbed a tuna sandwich off a plate on the table then headed back out. I was curious about what they were talking about, but figured I'd probe more later.

I did wonder if it was business like PI business, or some other kind of business. It could be anything—he and Donna were old friends. If it was *business* business, I'd get him to tell me eventually. We always played this game with his work. He pretended he wasn't going to tell me anything. Sometimes he didn't. Most often, he did. Sometimes I even helped him out, which technically put me on staff, which meant he wasn't breaking any confidences by telling me things.

But I was preoccupied now. And probably I should go help Lucas with the cat. But the doorbell rang so I veered over to the front door, still stuffing my face.

And was really surprised to find Todd Banks, notorious electrician in question, standing on the porch. He wore the long leather coat he'd had on at Donna's last night. It reminded me of the full-length leather jackets that were cool when I was in high school and definitely not cool now. At least there was no cigarette hanging out of his mouth. I stepped onto the porch, closing the door partway behind me so no one else—like Grandpa—noticed him.

"Hey," he said. "I'm here to check on the lights. So where's the issue? I need to get to a few other jobs tonight."

Repairs, I figured, but refrained from asking that. I found myself getting even more annoyed with this guy. Bad enough that he was crappy at his job, but he didn't even seem to realize. Or care. "Follow me," I said, and led him over to the section that was out.

He pursed his lips and studied the house, then finally nodded. "Easy fix."

"Great. Can you text me when it's done?" I asked. "Don't go to the door or anything." I wanted to keep Grandpa out of this as much as possible.

"Sure. Won't take long." He walked away to his van, the leather coat billowing around his ankles.

I watched him go, fingers crossed that he actually knew what he was doing and could fix the problem without causing any more havoc.

Chapter 12

The celebration went on for a couple hours until people started drifting off, heading out to dinner or home to their families. Lucas had retrieved Frederick, and at Grandpa's suggestion, put him in the first-floor guest room Grandpa was staying in so he wouldn't be lonely. Now he and Ethan had moved on to the job of setting up the Christmas trees. Katrina was still waiting for me, and I had to address her plan to call this breeder before Becky came to get me. Grandpa lingered in the living room, surrounded by candy and the other goodies most of his admirers had brought, surreptitiously ignoring the healthy goodies like the fruit baskets and even some of the soups and casseroles well-meaning neighbors and friends had brought over.

"That's not what friends bring," he'd informed me at one point when I'd pointed them out. "Friends recognize this is a great time to eat bad food, and they help you out."

He was also pretending his ankle wasn't bothering him while giving directions, which the boys took in stride. The dogs raced around, even older gentleman Ollie, the excitement of all the activity—and having trees in the house—too much for them to handle. Walter, of course, tried to christen the tree, but luckily Lucas caught him and brought him right outside.

It was chaos, but at least Grandpa was home and things were feeling normal and almost festive again.

Katrina had been waiting patiently for me to pay attention to her. She was in the kitchen with Sam when I finally joined them.

"Sorry," I said. "Crazy day. I didn't know you were still here," I said to my sister.

She smiled. "Story of my life. Mom left without me, so I figured I'd hang out."

I had to laugh. Our mother was clearly a little overwhelmed these days. I took a seat, grabbing a cookie from a tray. Then I noticed the piece of paper on the table in front of Katrina. The fancy-cat flyer.

"It's a new one," she said, following my gaze. "For every one I take down, more pop up. It happened again outside my place too. I got this off the pole outside again."

"You're kidding. At your place too? Don't the police have cameras out there?" I asked.

She gave me a look that said, *Fat chance.* "The chief doesn't really think what I do is super important," she said.

That was kind of an understatement. The current chief didn't love Katrina's approach or her enthusiasm for her job. He definitely didn't like it when she made waves, and had almost fired her once. He preferred the ACO to respond to calls, do what needed to be done, and stay quiet.

It was definitely not Katrina's MO.

It also meant she had to tread carefully with this situation. But it was clear she was getting more fired up by the second.

"So is your new cat who crashed the party from this same person?" Sam pointed to the flyer.

"No idea. There are a lot of people doing stupid things with animals to make money," Katrina said. "There are definitely way more odd mixes of fancy breeds out there. I saw a whole thing about it in one of the animal groups I'm in on Facebook. But it could be the same person. I hope there aren't that many breeders out here on the island." She rolled her eyes at the thought.

"You know," I said thoughtfully, "I saw some cats last night. Sphynxes."

"Where?" Katrina asked.

"Donna Carey has them. Said she just got them from somewhere on the mainland." I shrugged. "She's allergic to cats with fur. That's why she comes here and watches them from outside."

"She does? That's weird," Katrina said.

"Sure it is. But that's not the point. The point is, maybe it's all the same breeder? I mean, clearly breeding different kinds, but who knows? Could they be sending cats over here to someone?"

"Could be," she said. "I'd love to get a handle on the breeder licenses on file and make sure anyone who's registered is doing things on the up-and-up."

"How do you do that?" I asked.

"Well, I could make sure they have the right licensing for their operation. Massachusetts has specific laws." She shrugged. "I could figure something out. But also, not everyone doing this is registered. They're just flying below the radar. Then I have no idea. So. You ready to call this number?" She jabbed a finger at the flyer.

"Me? No way," I said. "You don't think I could actually pretend to be interested, do you?"

She narrowed her eyes at me. "Of course you can. You're a good actress."

"Why do *I* have to do it?"

"I just need the address!"

"So you can go over there with guns blazing? Literally?" If she could get Mick to play along, she probably would.

"Well, someone has to call. I need to figure out what they're doing," she said. "Who can fake being interested without getting all mad like you or I would?"

We both fell silent for a minute, thinking. Then, we both turned in unison to look at Sam.

She frowned. "What?" she asked warily.

"Can you make a phone call for me?" Katrina asked sweetly. "I'll give you the script."

Sam hesitated.

"I just need someone nice to talk to this person for me. And we all know I'm not nice," Katrina said to Sam.

Sam took the flyer and studied the picture of the kittens. They looked sort of Russian Blue but clearly with something else mixed in. The ears were almost too small for their head, reminding me a bit of a Scottish Fold. "What kind of cat is that?"

"I don't know. It's clearly some weird hybrid that they figured out they could charge thousands of dollars for. I'm dying to know how much. So? You in?"

She shrugged. "Sure. What do I have to do?"

"Just tell them you're interested in a cat. Ask for the breed, and the price, and if there's paperwork. Then try to get an address from them. Say you want to go see them first."

Sam pulled out her phone, tapping the number in. She looked startled when someone answered. "Yes, hello, I'm calling about your cats," she said. "The ones on the poster?"

Katrina gestured for her to put it on speaker. Sam complied.

"What would you like to know?" The voice on the other end was male, pleasant-sounding.

"Uh . . . what breed of cat? I couldn't tell from the picture," Sam said.

"They are a mix of some truly stupendous breeds," the man said proudly. "A Russian Blue and Egyptian Mau."

What? I raised my eyebrows at Katrina. I'd never even heard of an Egyptian Mau.

"I see," Sam said, looking at Katrina for guidance.

Katrina grabbed a paper napkin and scribbled a dollar sign with a question mark.

"And how much are they?" Sam continued.

"Typically we would charge about twenty-five thousand," the man said, and I nearly fell over. Twenty-five thousand dollars for a cat? Were they high? "But we're offering steep holiday discounts because these cats are so special and we want them to have good homes for the holidays. So we're offering them for eighteen."

"Eighteen thousand?" Sam repeated, looking as stricken as I felt. I didn't dare look at Katrina. I could feel her head exploding even from where I sat.

"Correct."

"Okay. Can I, um, come see them first?"

"Certainly. I can arrange a meetup," he said. "Where do you live?"

"Turtle Point."

"How about we meet this afternoon? I can bring the litter." He paused. "What's your name?"

"Linda," Sam said after a split-second pause.

"Excellent. So does that work, Linda? I can come to you."

"Actually, today's not great," Sam said, eyes on Katrina who was vigorously shaking her head no. "Can we perhaps meet over the weekend sometime? I can call you back tomorrow to confirm."

"Absolutely. You have a pleasant day," the man said. "Thank you for calling." He disconnected.

I finally risked a glance at Katrina. Her face was bright red. "Easy," I said. "Don't have a stroke on me."

She opened her mouth, letting out a string of curse words.

"Is that typical for that kind of cat? That amount of money?" Sam asked.

"I've never even heard of an Egyptian Mau," I said.

"And I have never in my life heard of real people actually selling cats for that much," Katrina said. "I mean, not in real life. I've heard there are very fancy cats out there that can cost up to a hundred thousand, but I thought it was very specialized. That can't be happening here on the island." She shook her head in disgust. "I knew a guy selling Maine Coons for a grand and I thought that was wild. And clearly these people are trying to keep this on the down-low. Notice they didn't ask you to come to them. That's classic for a sketchy breeder. They're hoping people won't see that as a red flag and just think they're super accommodating."

Sam nodded. "So now what?"

Katrina thought about this. "You up for another mission?"

"Heck yeah," she said. "What do I need to do?"

Chapter 13

I had to leave Sam and Katrina to their plan. Becky was on her way to pick me up.

She pulled into the driveway as I was putting on my shoes. She hopped out of the car, leaving the door wide open, and ran up to the porch with a bunch of balloons in one hand and a giant box of candy in the other, letting herself in.

"Leo! I'm so sorry I couldn't get here earlier," she said, going over and giving him a fierce hug. "Brought you a little something."

He grinned, accepting the candy. Russell Stover, his favorite. Those candies had been a part of our holiday season since I was tiny. I was surprised they still made them, actually.

"Thanks, honey," he said.

Becky tied the balloons to the back of his wheelchair. "There. Now your ride is all spruced," she said, then turned to me. "Ready? Sorry to run, Leo, but I'll visit you this weekend," she called, dragging me to the door.

"Jeez. What's your rush?" I paused to grab my coat, and she almost ripped my arm out of its socket.

"I still have some work to do for tomorrow's paper," she explained. "And we have a lot to do to get the newsroom set up. I won't have much time to do anything tomorrow, and the tours start Saturday."

I followed her to her car. Todd's white van was still out front. I didn't see him anywhere. I wanted to go check up on him, but Becky waited impatiently for me.

I got into the passenger seat, glancing back at the house. JJ sat in the living room window, tail swishing, obviously displeased I'd left him behind. I waved at him. I swear he flipped me off with his tail.

"So Leo's okay?" Becky asked immediately when she'd gotten into the driver's seat.

"Yes, he's doing fine." I loved that she loved Grandpa Leo as much as I did. "Grumpy, as expected. He hates not being able to do anything."

"Well, he's pretty independent," Becky pointed out. "This has to be hard, even if it's not serious."

Becky had grown up at my house. Her mom had been working all the time, trying to make ends meet as a single mom. Her dad had died when she was super young. So my family had adopted her. She'd spent as much time at Grandpa Leo's as I had when we were kids—he was like her own grandfather. Seeing him vulnerable in any way had to be tough on her.

She pulled into the parking lot of Lobstah Shack to retrieve Damian. The Shack was right down the street from our house, next to the ferry dock. Damian had been waiting—he emerged before we'd even stopped the car and hopped into the back seat.

"Hey, ladies," he said, leaning forward to kiss Becky's cheek. "I brought the garland." He held up a shopping bag. "And some lobster decorations the prior owners left behind."

"You don't want them for your tree?" I asked.

He laughed. "I took what I wanted. Using them all would've been overkill."

"Did you bring enough garland?" Becky asked. "The newsroom is pretty big."

"Oh, we'll make it work. Don't you worry," Damian assured her. "Just leave it all to me."

"I would," I told Becky. "The Shack looks awesome." When I came home last night, I'd noticed how great Lobstah Shack looked, even though I hadn't been in much of a Christmas mood. Damian had lined the entire building with colored lights and decorated the fences on either side of the parking lot with the same color. Icicle lights and sparkly decorations hung off the tree near the picnic tables. The bigger tree outside was decorated in lobster motif, and he'd also put a tree in the big dining window area inside that he'd chosen to decorate all in white so it stood against the colors outside.

"Gotta get in the holiday spirit," he said with a grin. "Hey, doesn't Santa come in on a boat one of these nights?"

"Yeah, the night of the tree lighting," I said. "This weekend."

"Cool. We have to go to that, right, Beck?"

She glanced in the rearview at him. "Seriously?"

"Well, yeah." He looked at her like she had two heads. "Where's your holiday spirit?"

I saw Becky really think about that. "I never thought about it. I mean, I'm sending a reporter."

Damian laughed. "Doesn't count. I want to go. You're not going to deprive me of Christmas joy, are you?"

"We'll see how busy the paper is," Becky said, but I could see a faint smile playing on her lips. Damian was good for her. He was making sure she had fun, which was something my workaholic best friend could use way more of in her life.

She pulled up to the curb in front of the newspaper building, snagging a parking spot easily—which would never happen during peak season. She peered up at the brightly lit building critically. "I guess they did a good job with the town lights."

That was an understatement. The three-story brick building that housed the newspaper office looked almost magical, between the outside lights, the candles in the windows, and the rooftop Santa and reindeer—not the cheesy kind, either, but the classy, small-white-light kind. "It looks amazing," I said. "The crew they hired is no joke." It clearly hadn't been Todd Banks. They probably should have this crew come back to make sure the town tree was in good shape for Sunday. Given Todd's track record, it was an iffy proposition to leave him in charge of it.

We got out of the car and followed her to the newspaper's employee entrance. She swiped a badge at an electronic box outside the door and held it open for us. I led the way up the huge staircase to the top floor where the newsroom was. The first floor was advertising and sales offices. Second floor was executive offices. The newsroom took over both sides of the third floor, with all the activity happening on one side and the kitchen and a few extraneous offices and conference rooms on the other side. When they needed to interview serious political people, they used that side of the floor.

Becky led us into the newsroom, which was pretty quiet tonight. No breaking news, which was a good thing. We'd had our share of it lately on the island, and I think even Becky was grateful for a reprieve. The assistant who sat at the front had gone home for the day. There were a couple of copydesk and layout people in the back of the room, working on tomorrow's edition. The sports editor was at his desk near the door. He was so focused he didn't even glance up when we came in.

I paused and glanced around. The newsroom was barren of any festive objects, barring a leftover paper turkey hung on one of the office doors and the Christmas tree they had dropped off earlier sitting naked in its stand in the middle of the room. "Wow, we're really starting from scratch."

She turned to give me a look. "We're running a newspaper here, remember? That kind of takes priority."

"Sorry," I muttered.

"You think that's the best place for the tree?" Becky surveyed its location critically. "It's kind of in the way, no?"

"You want it to be obvious, not hidden," Damian reminded her.

"I think it's perfect right there." We all turned as Alice Dempsey emerged from the back, holding another box of decorations. "And I found these."

"Alice!" I rushed over and gave her a hug. I was happy to see her. She'd had a hard couple of months. But aside from looking a bit too skinny, she seemed like she was hanging in there.

"Hi, Maddie." Alice dropped the box and hugged me back. "It's good to see you too."

"How's Balfour Junior?" Her recently acquired black cat was almost as popular on the island as JJ. It was cute. They'd made a good Halloween pair.

"He's perfect," she said.

"Hey, Alice." Becky joined us. "You sure about the tree here?" She gestured to the location in question.

"Positive," Alice declared. "Let's get decorating."

"The rest of the stuff is in my office," Becky said, motioning for us to follow as she headed there.

"Hey Beck?" One of the copydesk people called, rising from her chair. "Rick called and left you a message. Said to make sure you get it when you come in tonight."

Rick was the executive editor, Becky's direct boss. He was the one layer between her and Donna.

Becky waved a hand in acknowledgment and pushed open the partially closed door to her office. It was in its usual state of chaos—stacks of papers tilting precariously off her desk and piled up on the floor, notepads strewn across whatever surface of the desk was available, books opened and marked haphazardly with Post-its. "This dude needs to text me like everyone else in the world," she said. "I mean, who leaves voicemails anymore?" She picked up her phone and jabbed at the buttons while Damian and I started to lay out the decorations to see what we had.

A minute later she hung up the phone, frowning. "I have to run downstairs for a minute."

"To get coffee?" I asked, brightening. I had forgotten to ask her to stop on the way over.

She rolled her eyes. "No, to deliver something to Donna's office. But we can use the fancy kitchen down there to get you coffee," she added. "Everyone should be gone by now. Rick forgot to send the editorial page stuff for the weekend down, so I have to do it. Want to come and pick what you want?"

"Totally," I said. "Damian, Alice, want anything?"

Alice declined, holding up her water bottle. "Trying to hydrate more," she said.

"And I'm wired enough on holiday spirit," Damian said with a grin, pulling what seemed like miles of garland out of his shopping bag. "I'll just be here decking the halls. Hey, can we put Christmas music on?"

"Yeah!" the copyeditor responded enthusiastically, peering over the top of his cube.

Damian took that as his cue and fired up his iPhone. Pretty soon "Jingle Bell Rock" was blaring through the newsroom.

I followed Becky to her boss's office—the one with the turkey on the door. She went in and grabbed a large envelope off his desk. While I waited, I took the turkey down. "Past his time," I told her when she came out. "Also, he looks like he's from 1957."

"He probably is," Becky said, tossing it on the desk where the reports had been sitting.

We went down to the second floor, which unlike the newsroom had a big fancy door right off the steps leading down a hallway with new, plush carpeting. Everything here felt more expensive. And much quieter.

"Kitchen is right there," Becky said, pointing to the door behind me. "I'll just drop this off on Donna's assistant's desk." She moved to the door across the hall and two doors down, with a gold plate on it that read Donna Carey, Publisher.

Then she paused. The door was already cracked. And it seemed like the office was occupied. A male voice was speaking, getting louder with each word.

"Time's about up, Donna. You can't drag this on forever."

Chapter 14

Becky and I looked at each other. "I thought this floor was empty," I stage-whispered. Donna had just been at our house chatting with Grandpa. But apparently she'd decided to come back to work.

"Yeah. Guess not," Becky muttered.

"Should we come back?" I whispered, already turning to go. I figured we didn't want to be caught intruding, but Becky hesitated.

"Well, it's not as easy as you seem to think it is." Donna's voice this time. Unlike the man's voice, which was full of angst, Donna sounded calmer, more reasonable. "I'm well aware of the time constraints, Brandon. But it's a big decision. This place has been in my family for centuries. They'll just have to wait until I'm ready."

"What else can I do to help you decide?" Brandon's tone was full of frustration. "Are you leaning in a certain direction?"

Donna chuckled, the sound tinkling and pleasant. "I'll tell you as long as it's nonbinding."

"You're not taking this seriously enough."

Now there was a pause, and when Donna spoke again, her voice held that unmistakable note of steel and authority—the same one I'd detected when she'd been speaking to Todd Banks last night.

"I'm quite serious. Please don't misunderstand," she said. "I'm just wondering why *you're* taking it so seriously."

"Because it's my job," Brandon said, his tone indignant. "I'm here to advise you. Just like you hired me to do."

I glanced at Becky, trying to discern what was going on in there. She stood frozen, eyes and ears glued to the door in front of us. I was starting to think we shouldn't be there, but before I could try to pull her away the office door snapped open and a man moved into the doorway, still facing inside the office. But I could see his silhouette and the familiar voice clicked into place.

Brandon Tyson. The creep lawyer married to Molly Longo. Brandon was also best friends with Cole Tanner, Val's ex-husband. They both worked together at Cole's father's firm. I hadn't seen Brandon except for in passing since Val left Cole a year and a half ago. I didn't know him that well, but we'd gone to school together. He was my age, so we'd been in a lot of the same classes. In addition to being besties with a cheating liar, I remembered Brandon from school as a bully who had always suffered from the privileged-white-boy syndrome that affected a lot of boys on this island, unfortunately, since we didn't have a hugely diverse population. I remembered that he and Craig had once gotten into a fight because Brandon had been bullying an exchange student from Korea and it had made Craig mad. Craig had won.

And now, from the sounds of it, Brandon was trying to bully Donna into . . . something. Something that sounded like it had to do with the newspaper, if the phrase "this place has been in my family for centuries" held any clue. He clearly didn't know who he was dealing with if he thought he could manipulate her. She hadn't been running this business with an iron fist for the past nearly three decades because she was a pushover. But he'd find that out soon enough, I supposed. Despite myself, I inched a bit closer to the door too. Curiosity was contagious, even if it did kill the cat.

"Let's get real about this. Newspapers are a dying breed." Brandon let out a frustrated sigh. "Look. If you want the amount they're offering, they said they need a decision by Monday. The latest. Otherwise they're going to start deducting money. And I'm sure you don't want that. If you're going to sell, you may as well take the top number." A pause. "Do you need me to show you the numbers again?"

"I think I was able to understand them the first time," Donna said, the sarcasm biting, and I had to clap my hand over my mouth to avoid laughing out loud at her response to his mansplaining. Men like him were something else. She'd been running a business almost longer than he'd been alive, and he was lecturing *her* about numbers? I turned to Becky, expecting to see the same reaction. Then realized she had gone white as a sheet.

"You have to be practical," Brandon said. "Take the money and get out while they're offering it. The price is just going to keep going down, you know. No one cares about local news anymore."

At this, Donna laughed, but the sound wasn't friendly. "I do beg to differ on that. This whole island cares about local news, because this is the only world that matters to most people here."

"Well, the advertisers aren't getting enough business to justify it," he said flatly. "The numbers speak for themselves, Donna."

I poked Becky, trying to get her attention. I wasn't quite sure what to do. I was afraid if we moved, they'd notice us. But it sounded like the conversation was almost over and if they came out, they would find us anyway. I was more afraid that Becky was about to bust in there and start debating what was clearly a conversation about the importance of this newspaper and how much it was worth.

But she ignored me, clutching her envelope to her chest. I hoped she wasn't about to pass out or anything. I didn't often see my best friend looking like a deer caught in the headlights, but she did at this moment.

"Like I said. I need some time to think," Donna said. "Now if you'll excuse me, I have dinner plans."

Brandon stepped into the hallway with a frustrated shake of his head, then stopped short when he noticed us standing there. He glanced back at Donna, who waited impatiently to leave her office.

"Oh. Hey," he said with a nod of recognition. Then, "Excuse me," as he pushed past us. I couldn't help making a face at his retreating back as he strode down the hallway to the elevator. Donna stepped out into the hallway, pulling her office door shut behind her. Her face registered surprise when she saw us.

"Becky! And Maddie. We're seeing an awful lot of each other lately," she said to me. Her smile seemed a bit strained at the edges, but she hid it well.

"Donna," Becky said, after what seemed like an interminable pause. "I . . . sorry to interrupt. Rick asked me to give this to you." She handed her the envelope.

"Oh yes. Thank you." Donna accepted the envelope and tucked it into her oversized shoulder bag, tossing her thick hair out of the way as she adjusted the strap. "So, what brings you both here tonight?"

"We're decorating the newsroom. Since we're opening it for tours, we wanted it to look nice." Becky gestured awkwardly at me. "Maddie offered to help. She wanted some coffee," she added inanely.

"Ah, yes! Well. That's lovely. Thank you, dear. And thank you for helping, Maddie. I'm heading out now. Enjoy your night." She patted Becky on the shoulder and started to walk past us.

"Thank you," I said, telepathically willing Becky not to say anything.

But she didn't get the message.

"Donna. Wait. I couldn't help but hear—are you thinking of selling the paper?"

Silence. Then Donna said, "Please don't worry, Becky. I can't discuss what our conversation was about, but I assure you that I am always thinking about what's best for the paper and our reputation."

Becky nodded slowly, but she couldn't let it go. "I know. And I apologize. I certainly didn't know you were in the middle of something when I came down here. But I do need to say that selling would be a terrible idea."

Another pause, then Donna nodded slowly. "I understand where you're coming from—"

"It's the only paper on the island." Becky's voice grew louder and more insistent as she got fired up. "People depend on us. And we actually still do the news right, which you can't say about a lot of outlets these days. We have an *obligation*."

Oh boy. I loved my best friend, but she sometimes didn't know when to shut her mouth. Arguing with the publisher was not going to get her what she wanted, and even if Donna didn't sell, there might not be a job to come back to if Becky kept at it. I desperately wanted to disappear into the floor.

We seemed to hang there in the balance of her words for a million years before Donna spoke again. Her tone was still pleasant, but that steel was back. "I certainly understand what we've been bringing to the community. Better than most, actually. If and when there's something to share, I certainly will. In the meantime, I would ask that this conversation stays between us." She glanced at me too, a silent reminder that she was speaking to both of us.

Thankfully, Becky didn't keep going. "Of course," she said finally.

I nodded, unsure what else to do.

"Thank you," Donna said. "Now if you'll excuse me." She waited for us to walk down the hall before she followed.

When we reached the main floor, Donna pressed the down elevator button, turning away from us to discourage any further conversation. Becky and I climbed the stairs back to the newsroom in silence, speaking only when we reached the top floor and were certain we were out of anyone's earshot.

I turned to her. "You okay?"

Becky shook her head, her face looked pale and stricken. "Not really, no. Did you hear—can you believe—" She threw up her hands, unable to even finish a sentence. "She's thinking of selling the paper." She swallowed hard. "If she does, that's it, Maddie. These big corporations will shut it right down. Or make it unsustainable to put out a good product. Or work here at all." She blinked, and I realized she was about to cry. "What am I gonna do if that happens?"

I had no idea. "Look, she's a smart lady," I said, trying to be reasonable. "She knows what's at stake. I'm sure she was just trying to get him out of her office so she could enjoy her weekend."

Becky didn't look convinced, but she didn't argue with me.

"Come on." I squeezed her arm and pulled her toward the newsroom door. "Let's go be festive. Plus you can't let on that anything's wrong in there."

"I know, I know." She took a breath, drawing herself up taller again. Even though she was five foot nothing, when she wanted to, Becky could appear larger than life. "I'll figure it out. There's no way she's gonna sell this place. I'll convince her." Nodding, she pushed the door open and marched into the newsroom.

I followed her doubtfully, wondering exactly how she planned to do that.

The rest of the night passed quietly. Becky begged off dinner after we'd finished decorating the newsroom, saying she needed to finish some work. Damian stayed with her. I felt bad for him because he had no idea what had happened downstairs, but was determined to cheer her up.

Because it was obvious that she wasn't cheery.

Lucas picked me up as promised and we went out to eat. I picked at my food, still troubled by what was going on. And when we finally got back to the car, I decided that not telling anyone didn't include him and poured the story out.

I'd just finished the story and come up for air.

All Lucas managed to get out was a surprised "Wow," before my cell rang. Grandpa.

Immediately worried, I answered. "Are you okay?"

"I'm fine, but there's a problem," he said. "You need to come home."

Chapter 15

Lucas sped home. My heart stayed in my throat the whole time. Grandpa had refused to say more and of course, I was imagining the worst-case scenario. He'd fallen out of his chair, or something had happened to Val, or someone else we loved.

Lucas had barely stopped the car before I jumped out and raced to the door, my angst heightened when I saw the unmarked car in our driveway. Grandpa was in the living room. So was Lt. Mick Ellory.

"What is going on?" I demanded. "Grandpa, what happened?"

Mick turned to me and wordlessly handed me a bag with a piece of paper in it. I took it and read the note: "Leave the flyers alone and mind your business. Or the next time someone will get hurt."

I read it twice, then looked back at Mick. "What is this?"

"Your grandfather found it on the bed in the guest room," Mick said, before Grandpa could speak.

"What?" My eyes went from Mick to Grandpa then back. I could feel my heart sitting in my throat, making it hard to swallow. "Someone was in the house?"

"There's more," Grandpa said grimly.

"More what?"

Lucas came up behind me. I handed him the note. I saw his eyes widen as he read it, then reread it.

"What is it? Just tell me!" I snapped.

"Frederick is gone."

I was sure I'd misheard. Frederick, our terrified, potentially breeder-dumped cat. I sank down on the couch. "What do you mean, gone? You must be mistaken," I insisted. Then I jumped to my feet, panic flaring. "JJ—"

"He's fine," Grandpa interrupted. "He was in your room. Valerie checked and he's still there. She was checking the rest of the house to make sure there was no place Frederick was hiding."

"And the cafe cats?" I was already heading toward the French doors, but Ethan shook his head. "Nothing in there was disturbed. The doors were still locked."

"Still, we should make sure everyone is accounted for," I said.

"Of course. You'd know that better than anyone," Mick said.

"Frederick's got to be hiding. He's super scared," I insisted. "Did you check—"

"We looked everywhere." We all looked up as Ethan came down the stairs, Val behind him holding JJ. I rushed over and grabbed him from her, hugging him tight. I should have brought him with me. "I'm sorry, Maddie. It looks like someone stole him."

Now I just felt sick. "But how? How did they get in the house?" I asked. Grandpa was religious about locking the doors. This was a safe island—mostly—but still, as the former police chief he was more aware than anyone about the importance of personal safety. He never left the doors unlocked. Or windows, for that matter.

He looked mad now. "Charlie."

"Charlie?" I was confused, then realized he was referring to one of his poker friends.

"He picked me up for the game. Had to help me get out because of this stupid thing." Grandpa gestured angrily at his wheelchair. "I think he didn't lock the door behind him and I didn't remind him. So it's my fault too."

"And we were out," Val chimed in. "I thought it was weird that the door was open when I got home because Grandpa wasn't here . . ." she trailed off.

"I got home after them and found the note. And Frederick had been locked in my room." Grandpa had suggested putting him in there after he crashed the party, so he wouldn't be lonely. "The door was still shut, but the note was on the bed," he finished. "I called Mick, then you."

The room went silent. I realized my hands holding JJ were shaking. Had Frederick been this mysterious breeder's cat? Had they somehow known Katrina had picked him up and brought him here? What had they done with him? I felt like I might cry.

I looked at Mick. "So what now?"

"I had a tech come and check for fingerprints, but there was nothing. They clearly wore gloves. And very brazenly walked in and out of here like they belonged," he said grimly. "I'll be checking with the neighbors to see if anyone saw anything unusual, or if anyone has cameras that may have captured anything."

"Thank you," Lucas said when none of us said anything. "Do you need anything from us?"

"Just keep the doors locked," Mick said. "Maddie, let's go check on the other cats."

I handed JJ to Lucas and led Mick into the cafe. All the cats were sleepy-eyed, even the kittens, and blinked at me when I turned the lights on. I grabbed Adele's

list—thank goodness she was meticulous about her records—and started checking to make sure everyone was
there. When the number of cats matched the number on
the list, I breathed a sigh of relief.

"All good?" Mick confirmed.

"Yeah. Mick, what the actual . . ."

"I know," he said grimly. "It's pretty ballsy to break
into a former police chief's house."

"You need to work with Katrina on this breeder thing,"
I said. "Clearly it's connected."

He nodded. "I know that too."

"Does she know yet?"

"No. But she'll be hard to keep in check once she
finds out."

Chapter 16

I woke up at the crack of dawn the next morning, my brain kicking into gear before my eyes even opened. A million thoughts flooded into my consciousness—the heaviness of what had happened last night, the realization that I'd be thrown into a bunch of event stuff today that I was now not in the mood for, whether the lights on our house were fixed and ready to be judged into first place, making sure Grandpa was okay, and also worrying about Becky after the whole bombshell with Donna last night.

Most of all, I was scared to death of what had become of poor Frederick, and worried that we'd never find him.

It was a heck of a way to kick off the Christmas season. In spite of all that, I knew I had to push through. With this weekend, Christmas would be in full swing, and there would be no escaping the good cheer. The tours would start tomorrow night, once the winner of the lights contest had been announced.

Thank goodness Adele was way on top of running the cat cafe, making sure we were staffed and everything was running smoothly. I did need to tell her to be extra vigilant with the cats. I wasn't sure what that threat had meant in the note, but I couldn't help but feel like the cafe was a target. It was definitely the one thing, aside from Lucas and my family, that would get my attention.

I'd also completely forgotten to check on the electrician's fix last night. The lights had been shut off when we got home. Grandpa had a hard and fast rule that on "normal" nights, the lights went off on a timer. On the tour nights he'd leave them on later, but he still was very cautious about his electric bill, which could go off the rails this time of year.

Todd had texted me that all was well when we were at the newsroom, but I had been really focused on Becky and the unfolding drama so I'd just said thanks and hadn't questioned it.

I was a little sorry I had signed up to help with the event. Right off the bat I needed to get the website fixed with the right events and times. But honestly, it needed a whole do-over, as did the maps. The design was horrendous, and we needed the errors corrected. My first task of the day—once it was daytime out West—was to call Bones, my web guy out in California, and get him working on the website. I had to ask our marketing volunteer, Clarissa, to redesign the maps. Then I had to go see Eva Flores at the Chamber and figure out where I could best jump in, since the Chamber was managing the entire event and the subcommittees. And my heart wasn't in any of it. I wanted to go pound the pavement looking for Frederick. But Mick had specifically warned me last night not to.

"You have no idea what this person is capable of, and if they find out you're looking, it could cause more trouble," he'd said, pulling me aside before he left. "Let us handle this. I promise we will."

So I had to trust him. Katrina would make sure he was

on it as soon as she knew—I had no doubt. And people were depending on me for this event, so I'd better get my head on straight.

All those thoughts were careening around before I'd even opened my eyes, which I tried to avoid until at least seven. When I did, I realized that despite the still-early hour, I was missing a few of my normal snuggle buddies. JJ was still curled up at the foot of the bed, but Lucas's side was empty and the dogs were also missing. I threw my covers off and got up. JJ did not.

I checked my phone. As expected, a text from Katrina awaited me, complete with a lot of curses and angry-faced emojis. Mick had filled her in. I'd answer her later. I headed downstairs. I expected everyone else to be around, but the only signs of life were the coffeepot in the kitchen, gurgling the lovely sound of almost-brewed coffee, and a note from Lucas propped up against my favorite mug, one of the original cat cafe designs with JJ's picture on it, which he'd put out on the counter, that said he'd taken both dogs and gone in for some early grooming appointments.

I sighed. I hated missing him before he left, but it was understandable he'd be busy. The Daybreak Harbor dogs had to look good for Santa, who was coming to town next weekend. He'd be taking pictures with both kids and pets, and really anyone who wanted a photo with him. We had some really cute photos of town elders on Santa's lap.

In any event, it was sweet of Lucas to let me sleep. He probably figured I wouldn't be doing much of that from here on out.

I tapped the note against the counter, looking around at the empty room. My first thought was that Grandpa must be out for his walk until I remembered he wasn't walking right now. He might still be in bed resting. Which felt wrong on so many levels, but if he was, I just hoped that meant he was getting stronger.

It was too early also to go over to the Chamber, so I decided to make myself useful here. I took my phone out of my pocket and checked my cafe to-do list. I had to get the Christmas collars sorted—we'd bought them for all the kitties in the cafe, and they were all super excited about potential adopters coming through. At least, I was projecting that they were. I definitely was. The cats were probably more excited about playing with the Christmas tree, which a few of them had already mastered climbing if the pictures Adele had texted me last night were any indication. Luckily the climbers were the littlest kittens, so the tree hadn't actually fallen over. Yet. I hoped that luck had held overnight. I also had to check the schedule and make sure the wait list was being managed, check on the social posts for the day, send out a newsletter, and I wanted to get a head start on the cleaning to surprise Adele. I needed to do something before I broke the news to her about what had happened.

I poured my coffee and turned to leave the kitchen. As I did, my eyes fell on the morning newspaper someone had tossed on the table—probably Lucas, grabbing it on his way out. My heart sank as I picked it up and glanced at the headlines, realizing just how accustomed to this ritual so many of us were. Even if we didn't realize it.

I couldn't believe Donna Carey might sell the paper. It was an institution here on the island—and the family-owned component was a big deal. So many of the most beloved places here on the island were family-owned. It was part of the charm of coming here—you weren't going to find a big box store in downtown Daybreak Harbor or any of the towns around the island. We were a close-knit population—even our newspaper, which could bring about a lot of strong feelings, was beloved. When it wasn't being hated, of course. I couldn't imagine anyone else owning it. And even though I wasn't embedded in the newspaper world, I knew enough to know that when indie papers were scooped up by bigger corporations, many of them didn't survive very long. I'd heard all about it from Becky, who monitored the goings-on in her industry like a hawk.

And truthfully, the thought of that happening here on Daybreak was heartbreaking. I sincerely hoped Donna was just entertaining the offer because she was a businesswoman and, well, that's what you did. Weigh every opportunity without the emotion first and see where you landed. Then you factored in the gut feeling of what was actually the right thing to do. At least that's how I ran my businesses. It hadn't failed me yet. But I wasn't running a newspaper.

Like all newspapers, ours had undergone massive transformation the past couple of decades, but thanks to Donna, it was doing much better than most. She had taken over the paper nearly twenty-five years ago, despite the naysayers who said someone in their twenties couldn't run a newspaper. But the business was in her blood.

Now in her fifties, she'd been the one to usher the paper into the new era of journalism with an eye to the opportunities rather than the perceived loss that came with a changing industry. The little island newspaper had seen some of its most successful years over the past two decades as other papers crumbled. Donna had led the charge in focusing on hyperlocal coverage, and they'd won a number of awards.

She was probably the last in the family line to run the paper at this point, though. She had no heirs apparent. I didn't know of other family members who could carry on the legacy when and if she finally decided she didn't want to steer the ship any longer, so maybe that's just what was happening here. Maybe she figured she'd taken it as far as she could, and it was time to redirect her attention to something else.

Who could blame her, really? It would just be a tough pill to swallow for her employees—and the residents.

I headed into the cafe. JJ must have heard the French doors opening from upstairs, and a minute later he appeared at my feet, his trademark squeak loud in the early morning quiet.

"You want to come with? Okay, let's go," I said, holding the door open. "I'll feed you with the other cats."

Delighted, JJ dashed into the cafe and made a beeline for the kitten crate. The babies were up and, as usual, they'd trashed their condo. Three of the four were hanging off the bars, mewling desperately like they were being tortured. They'd managed to spill their water and their food, and the cat litter they'd scattered had mixed with the water to form a gooey paste that would be fun to clean. But that aside, I had to stop and gape at how good the place looked.

Adele and team had done an amazing job. It looked like a winter wonderland in here, but it wasn't over the top or too cheesy. Each cubby space had a stocking hanging in front of it with the cat's name in glitter pen. Stars and twinkle lights dangled from the ceiling. The tree was still standing and still decorated—with all non-breakable items—and colorful lights. Rudolphs, Santas, Frostys, and Grinches decorated the walls, and in the spaces the kitties couldn't reach there were Christmas village pieces set up in fake snow. All our pillows and blankets had been swapped out for red, green, or Christmas-themed ones, and the counter up front was lined with garland.

I loved it.

I opened the crate to free the kittens and got to work. There was a peacefulness about being the only one here surrounded by purring cats, even if I was wrist-deep in a mess. Everyone was happy to see me and hungry for breakfast, but they waited patiently while I cleaned. Rory, our calm black-and-white kitty who'd been here for a while, came over and rubbed against my arm.

"Hey," I said. "I bet this wouldn't have happened if you were in charge."

Rory meowed her agreement.

When the crate was once again livable and I'd vacuumed up most of the litter scattered around the floor, I took out bowls and began dishing out Fancy Feast, most of our residents' favorite meal. It was a special day, after all.

I was so engrossed in the task that I didn't hear Adele come in until she came up behind me. "What are you doing?" she demanded, making me jump. A spoon full of food flew out of my hand and splattered on the floor.

"Jeez," I said, pressing my hand to my chest. "You scared me. I wanted to get a head start on the cleaning. You know, surprise you. By the way, the place looks amazing."

Adele didn't react to my compliment. She surveyed my work with pursed lips, no doubt looking for what I'd done wrong. She was a stickler for doing things her way. Sometimes I thought with some amusement that she had long forgotten it was my place. While I waited for my performance review, I bent down to clean up the food I'd dropped. JJ had beaten me to it. He'd already licked the spoon clean and wiped up what had hit the floor.

But she didn't lecture me. Instead, she said, "Thanks." A glint of a smile touched her lips. She didn't want to like the compliment, but she did.

I figured I wouldn't have a better moment as the morning went on, so I took a breath. "I have to tell you something. And I need you to stay calm."

"What?" Immediately she snapped to attention. "What happened?"

I gave her the abridged version of last night's events. "I just need you to be extra careful about keeping an eye on the cats," I said. "Is Harry working today? Maybe we can pay him to do some official security?"

Adele's eyes looked like they were going to pop out of her head. "What are we doing about this? We need to go find those people and get the cat back!" She looked like she was about to run out and stage a town-wide SWAT operation herself.

"Mick said to please let him handle it," I told her. "He said it could get dangerous if we don't. And I know you don't want to put any of the other cats in danger."

I had her there. She wouldn't do anything to jeopardize our charges.

She wasn't happy about it though. "He better be quick or I'll have no choice," she warned me, pulling out her phone. "I'll call Harry now. When are they coming to fix the lights?"

I frowned. "What do you mean? The guy came back last night. I thought it was all set." *But you haven't checked yet,* a little voice in my head chided.

"Well, if he did, he didn't do much." Adele waved her hand toward the window. "I just tested them. A bunch of them are out."

"What! Are you kidding me?" I so did not need this today.

"Go see for yourself," she said with a shrug.

"I'm gonna kill him," I muttered, pulling out my phone and jabbing angrily at the buttons. But of course, I got his voicemail. This time I didn't bother leaving a message. With a cry of frustration, I handed Adele the spoon and open can of Fancy Feast. "I have to go deal with this. Can you finish?"

She accepted the items and waved me off.

"Don't tell Grandpa if you see him," I warned.

Adele shrugged. "Figured telling you was enough to get something done about it. Good luck."

I didn't need luck. I needed someone competent. I wasn't messing around with this any more. I headed back into the kitchen. I needed more coffee if I was going to deal with this. On my way, I called my mother.

"The electrician came back last night to fix the lights and they're still out," I said when she answered, sounding frazzled. I hated to dump more on her, but she needed to know how much of a train wreck this guy was. "I haven't told Grandpa and I'm not going to. Can you get your guy over here?"

"One second. Brian!" I heard her call, then my dad's voice in the background. "Can you call Bernie? We need him at Dad's house." Another pause, then she came back on the line. "Your dad is going to call and send him over this morning. Tell your grandfather not to worry. Dad'll call you when he knows what time."

"Will do." I decided not to mention what had happened here last night. I hung up, topped off my coffee, and pondered my next move. I resisted going out front to see the lights for myself. The real electrician would come and take care of it. Not my issue.

My phone buzzed and I glanced down at it. Another number I didn't recognize. I tapped the message.

Maddie, it's Annie Daniels from the flower shop. We were supposed to get some tables and other items delivered for the tours and they haven't arrived. Can you help?

Guess it was time to get to work.

Chapter 17

I was starving, so I went out to the cafe and got fresh coffee and a bowl of oatmeal—Ethan handed it to me without even asking me what I wanted, adding that I should eat something other than his amazing baked goods for a change.

The place was already hopping. Ethan had started opening at seven, and our cafe was quickly becoming a place for people to come and hang out, do work, or just linger over a cup of coffee and something yummy before they started their day. I found a table in the back and tried to focus.

I went through all my texts, compiling the issues related to the event. Which included multiple things related to the bazaar tonight, along with the marketing issues I already had noted. The bazaar would take up most of the day, I figured, so I started with the marketing stuff since I was handing a lot of that off once I got it sorted.

First thing I did was go to the list my mother had given me of every business that had signed up for something during the event and reconciled it with what was on the website. I noted all the discrepancies—way more than I'd even heard about yet—and put them in an email to send to Bones once I got in touch with him later. Then I went back to the list and reconciled it with the paper copy of the map that I had. Aside from my spelling mistake, I found a few missing businesses that were going to be mad once they started paying attention. I noted those on the map and sent a note to Eva about getting the raw files so we could make the updates and send them to the printer. Then I called Annie Daniels, whose brother owned the local print shop, and explained the situation. She promised to pave the way for us to get priority as soon as we sent the right files over—once I'd promised to get her the tables she needed for the flower shop.

Getting organized was making me feel better. I stood up, stretched, and started back toward the counter for a refill. Ethan's coffee was really like crack.

But before I could get there, the door burst open and Becky flew in, looking around frantically. When she saw me, she made a beeline.

"You are never going to believe this," she said, her voice reaching a pitch I'd never heard before, as the whole cafe turned to stare at her.

I could almost see the steam coming out of her ears. I hurried toward her. "Beck? You okay?"

"You won't even believe what just happened!" Becky's voice didn't lower. Instead, it hit an even higher pitch that I'd never heard from her before. The whole cafe had pretty much gone silent, staring. I could see Ethan's concerned gaze out of the corner of my eye from behind the counter.

"What? Is everyone okay?" I felt my heart speed up, anticipating what might be wrong.

"That—that *woman*!"

I was at a loss. I took her arm and tried to pull her to the side, away from the prying eyes of everyone trying to enjoy a cup of coffee and a pastry. "Beck. Can we—"

Becky either didn't hear me or just ignored me. She snatched her arm away and paced past me, her restless energy scattering anyone unlucky enough to be in her path. A woman who had just left the counter with a mug of coffee scurried out of the way. For such a tiny person, Becky was like a tornado when she got like this. It took a lot to shake her even-keeled temperament—working in news she had to be a steady Eddie most of the time—but when she blew, look out. "That crazy woman. Do you know what she's doing?"

"I don't even know who we're talking about," I said, glancing nervously at the cafe patrons. Some, in true New England fashion, were trying to ignore the scene. Others were openly staring in fascination. Becky didn't notice any of this.

"Donna!" she screeched. "My so-called boss. Who. Has. Lost. Her. Ever-loving. Mind!"

I blinked. "If you're talking about last night, I was there, remember? Did something else happen? Come sit down."

"No. I'm not talking about that. I went over there today. Can I get some coffee?" She crossed her arms over her chest, the fight suddenly *whooshing* out of her.

"How about some tea?" I asked soothingly. I didn't really think caffeine was the best thing for her right now.

"Whatever." She let me lead her behind the counter into the back room. I looked at Ethan, silently asking for help. He nodded.

"I'll bring some tea," he told us. "Are you hungry, Becky?"

She shook her head.

I led her out back and sat her at the little table we had out there for breaks. "What happened? You went over where?"

"She called me. This morning at some ungodly hour. Asked me to come over, said she wanted to talk to me about last night. I thought that was a good thing. That she wanted my opinion or something. How could I be so stupid?" She folded her arms on the table and dropped her head onto them.

"Okay, so what did she want then?" I asked.

"So she could tell me she's going to make it official. She's going to *sell our paper* to some corporate conglomerate and start her own media company! About *cats*! Can you believe it? I mean, I'm sure you can believe it," she amended, waving a hand around at the cafe. "I guess that was a dumb question. But still. About cats. And she wants me to run it!"

I was at a loss. What she was telling me didn't even make sense. A media company about cats? I was getting worried about her.

Ethan came in with the tea and placed it in front of Becky with a little jar of honey and a spoon. "Everyone okay?" he asked.

"I have no idea." I gave him a pleading look that said, *Help me.*

He turned to Becky. "Can I do anything?"

Becky raised her head from the table. "Can you talk sense into someone who's clearly had some kind of psychotic break?"

Ethan looked at me. I could see him trying to decide if that question warranted an answer.

I gave a slight shake of my head.

"Probably not," he said. "I'm going to get back to the counter." He dashed out front.

I refocused on Becky. "Drink," I said, pushing the mug toward her. "Then you can tell me what's up because I honestly have no idea what you're talking about."

"Fine." The adrenaline seemed to have left her. She spooned some honey into her mug and stirred, then took a long swig of tea.

Ethan returned and handed me a plate of goodies and another cup of coffee, which I accepted with a silent thanks.

Becky was still sipping her tea. Now she just looked depressed. I handed her the plate.

She perked up and grabbed one of the chocolate chip cookies.

I waited until she'd eaten most of it. "Now what on earth is going on?"

She sighed. "Donna called me this morning, like I said. Asked if I could come to her house and talk."

"Her house? Have you ever been to her house before?"

Becky shook her head. "Nope. Weird, right? But I thought it was because she didn't want anyone at the office to hear us. So I said sure. When I got there, that stupid lawyer was there too."

"Brandon," I confirmed.

She nodded. "So I go over, and Donna couldn't have been nicer. Made tea, had scones, then gave me the whole sob story about how much she loves the paper and the legacy her family created, and how dedicated she is to the news and the people of the island. But newspapers are struggling right now, and she feels like she gave so much of her life to this and it's probably time for someone to come in with new blood and rejuvenate it. And then she wanted to tell me all about how she was ready for something new, how she wanted to pursue a passion project she'd been working on in her spare time, thought it was time to bring it to life, yada yada. And how she needs great people to do it. And then sketchy lawyer guy hands me this offer letter and contract. She wants me to run the thing. She offered to double my salary!" Becky sounded so indignant I almost laughed, but she probably would have thrown her tea at me so I covered it up with a cough.

"And this passion project has something to do with cats? What is the project, exactly?" I was trying to follow the threads of the gibberish Becky had spewed earlier.

"Yeah. Freakin' cats," she muttered, then remembered her audience. "I mean, no offense. You've got a rescue organization going on. That's different. She wants to start some online media company dedicated to, like, show cats or something. I don't know. I tuned out because I couldn't get past the ridiculousness of the whole idea. Can you imagine me as editor of a cat media company?" She shook her head and took a violent swig of tea.

I couldn't, actually. It might be kind of funny. "Show cats?" I repeated. "A media company?" I was lost.

"She's apparently some kind of cat-fancier type in her spare time. She started telling me about it, but honestly my head was about to explode because it's . . . weird. She's obsessed with these high-end cats who get judged in contests or whatever. But the point is, she's moving ahead with the sale to do this and she's trying to get me to come work for her! To run a cat publication. Can you imagine anything more insulting?" She grabbed another cookie and bit into it so forcefully I worried she'd break a tooth.

"And how is she getting the money to double my salary?" she went on. "They want me to travel to all these cat shows and all kinds of crazy stuff. She was trying to entice me with that, how I could get off the island more and go to nice places. Clearly she hasn't met me."

That was true. Becky was staunchly a Daybreak Island lifer. She had no interest in being off-island. I was surprised Donna didn't know that about her. College was the only thing that had enticed her away, and she'd come right back with her sights set on the job she now had. We were different that way. I couldn't wait to get out when I was younger, although now I was happy to be home. But the travel part didn't sound so bad to me—not that I would tell her that, though.

But she was right—how did a fledgling business like this offer such an amount right off the bat? I didn't know what Becky made now and I knew journalists were notoriously underpaid, but I was still willing to bet it had to be upwards of a hundred thousand.

"Yep. Isn't that insulting? They can't pay me more to tell the truth and report on actual news, but they can offer me that kind of money to do some fake editor job about million-dollar cats?"

"When you put it like that, I see what you're saying," I said. "But it's a different business model, maybe more funding, or less employees. Probably both. And more investors, perhaps." My business mind was kicking in, trying to make sense of this from a financial perspective. What did one do with an online media company dedicated to cats? "So what did you say?"

"I told them to go pound sand, basically. A little nicer than that because I need to keep the job that I have, at least for as long as it's an option before she totally sells us out. But there's no way. That's not my thing. It sounds absurd and it would completely derail my career." She slumped over the table now, all the fight seemingly going out of her. "What a mess."

"At least you know she values you," I said, trying to come up with something positive to say.

She gave me a look. "More like she's trying to get me on board so I don't tank the whole thing."

"How would you do that?" I asked.

"I don't know. Tell the staff? Have everyone quit now

so the sale doesn't go through?" Becky shook her head. "Of course I'd never do that. I care too much about the paper. But I guess I'm the only one."

"What about Rick? Does he know?" Her direct boss who reported to Donna had to be in the loop on this—right?

"I don't think so," Becky said. "But maybe they'll offer him the editor job now that I've turned it down. He's her second-in-command now. I don't know why she wouldn't bring him in the first place. He's wishy-washy. He'd probably just take the money and run. He's not overflowing with journalistic integrity." She fell silent, still seething.

I wasn't sure how to make her feel better. "How did you leave it?" I finally asked.

"That I wasn't interested. And that I was really disappointed that she's selling. What else could I say?"

"Maybe she was testing out her options," I said. "Until she signs on the dotted line, it's not a done deal. And even if she does, it doesn't mean everything is going away. Look, don't overreact. Keep Donna on your good side."

"But someone needs to shake some sense into her!" She glanced at her phone as it began to ring. "The newsroom. Hang on." She picked up, listened. "I'm on my way now." Standing, she picked up another cookie. "Gotta run. I was supposed to be back at work an hour ago. Thanks for letting me vent. And sorry for scaring your customers." With a wave, she was gone.

Chapter 18

After Becky left, I went back inside to take a shower and get ready for the day, which already promised to be long if this morning was any indication. I dressed in my glittery red sweater and a pair of jeans, which boosted my mood, then went downstairs to see what else needed to be done before I left. And maybe catch Grandpa to pick his brain about all this Donna stuff. They had been huddling yesterday, and now I was extra curious about what they'd been discussing.

I found him directing Val, Sam, and Ethan on how to best organize the Christmas tree decorations. Shoot. I'd forgotten we were all supposed to be decorating. And Lucas wasn't even here. I texted him.

On my way back now. I wouldn't miss it! he responded.

I let myself get all googly-eyed over the text, then refocused.

"Hey, Grandpa, I need to talk to you for a second."

"Okay." He looked up from his wheelchair where he'd been unwinding a string of lights.

"In here." I pushed his chair back into the kitchen, leaving my sisters fighting about which of their elementary school ornaments deserved a prime spot on the tree.

"What's up, Doll?"

"I need to get your thoughts on something. But you can't tell anyone." I filled him in on what Becky and I had overheard last night and the whole debacle she'd regaled to me this morning.

Like I expected, he didn't seem surprised. But he did look unhappy. He motioned to the coffeepot. I filled his mug while I waited for his reply.

"I'd heard rumblings that she's been in talks for a while now about potentially selling the paper," Grandpa said after a moment.

"Was that what you guys were talking about yesterday? Was she having you look into the buyer? Why didn't you mention it?"

He gave me a look. "I don't perpetuate the rumor mill, Maddie. And obviously I didn't want to worry Becky unnecessarily."

I noticed he didn't answer my question about their meeting. "Brandon Tyson was talking to her. Why would she hire that firm?"

"She didn't," Grandpa said. "Brandon's a private advisor for her. The family connection." At my blank stare, he said, "Angelo Longo is one of the paper's investors. Did you not know that?"

Angelo the co-op owner? Was an investor? "I didn't even know the paper had investors," I said. "I thought Donna's family owned it outright."

"They did. Still have majority share, but when Donna took the helm, she wanted to do some different things. Needed more money to do them and decided to get some local buy-in and commitments. Smart business lady, that one," Grandpa said, tapping the side of his head. "She does know what she's doing. The family didn't approve— but they also didn't want to be involved—so she told them tough, deal with it. She got enough investors to raise the money she wanted, but she kept the shares to a minimum. That's when Angelo bought in. He's a big proponent of the paper and what it does for the island."

"So he's been an investor for a long time," I said.

Grandpa nodded. "Twenty years or so."

"But isn't that a conflict? If Brandon is trying to get her to sell? That would mean his family gets a payout."

"Could be. Not necessarily. Depends on the terms. And when you say *trying to get her to sell*—what do you mean?"

"I don't know. I just heard bits and pieces. But he was definitely a proponent of her selling. And it sounded like she had to decide by Monday to get the full offer." I handed him his coffee and a biscotti. "Who else is an investor?"

"I'm not sure," Grandpa said. "I know there were a few. I'm sure I can find out."

"Did you know about this media company? That Donna was into this show cat stuff?"

"No. She mentioned that she's been working on expanding her media presence, but didn't get into details."

"Do you know where she's getting the money for this? It can't be cheap," I said.

"Her family has money, don't forget. Honestly, though, I have no idea."

I thought I knew the answer, but had to ask anyway. "What would that mean? If she sold it?"

He shrugged. "Depends on who's buying. Probably whoever it is would come in and restructure it. Try to make it more profitable. If that doesn't work, they'll start cutting staff."

I waited. He didn't say anything else.

"And then?" I asked finally.

"A lot of times these big corporations close the smaller operations. It's hard to predict. This is a unique place, of course, with only one newspaper. That could change things. And honestly, I don't know how profitable or not the paper actually is. I've never heard it was in any trouble, but my guess is no one would have even if it was true."

I felt like he might be trying to sugarcoat this a bit. "Grandpa. If Donna sells, what's going to happen?" *To Becky,* I thought, but didn't say that out loud.

He held my gaze. "I don't know, Madalyn," he said finally. "But we'll cross that bridge if and when we come to it. No use getting worried about something before it's even a reality, right?"

"I guess," I muttered. But there was no doubt Becky was crossing that bridge in her head right now with a million different scenarios on the other side. And none of them were probably what she wanted. "Cats," I mused. "I mean, I knew she liked cats, but did anyone know she liked them that much? And the fancy ones to boot?"

"Doll, one thing I've learned over my career is that you never know everything there is to know about anyone else. Don't forget it," Grandpa said.

Now that we could wholeheartedly agree on.

My phone buzzed, interrupting our conversation. My dad. I grabbed it, held up a finger to Grandpa, then left the room so he wouldn't hear our conversation.

"Hey Dad," I said, keeping my voice low. "Is the electrician coming?"

"Bernie is on his way now. He'll send me the bill directly, so don't worry about anything."

"Dad, you rock," I said, relieved. "Thank you."

"Of course."

The doorbell rang out front. "I think he might actually be here," I said. "I've gotta go. I'll let you know how it goes. Thanks again." I stuck my phone in my pocket and hurried to the front door.

A giant teddy bear of a guy stood on the other side. His red flannel shirt strained around his bulk. He had thick red hair and a matching beard and carried a tool bag almost as big as he was. Behind him in the driveway was a black van with white lettering proclaiming Elliott Electric—25 Years of Excellence on the side panels. A far cry from Todd's kidnapper-looking white van. Two younger guys waited by the van, giant coffees in their hands. I felt their pain.

"Hi," I said. "I'm Maddie. Thank you so much for coming."

He nodded. "Bernie Elliott. Of course. Just wish you'd all called me in the first place instead of that other guy."

"Yeah, me too. But we didn't know—"

"When someone with twenty-five years' experience puts in a bid at a deeply discounted rate and the town still goes with some new schmuck who doesn't even have a full set of tools, you know things are going straight to hell around here," Bernie went on as if I hadn't spoken. "I bet they didn't even check into that guy's license. But maybe this'll teach 'em that you get what you pay for."

"Right. Of course," I said. "I'll definitely talk to my mother about that. Should I show you where all the breaker boxes are?"

He shook his head. "Just show me what's out and we'll figure it out."

"Okay. Follow me." With a quick glance over my shoulder to make sure Grandpa hadn't come out of the kitchen, I turned the lights on and led Bernie outside to the area where the cheery colors abruptly stopped. I pointed out the extension cord and the outlets.

He started to laugh. "Is that really how he did this?"

"Is that a trick question?"

He sighed. "I got this." He waved at his guys, who

hoisted large bags over their shoulders and started toward us. "Bring a ladder!" he yelled.

"You think you can fix it by five?" I asked.

"I'm a pro," he said. "Unlike whoever did . . . this." He gestured at the pile of extension cord on the ground.

"Let me know if you need anything," I said, and headed back into the house. When I got to the door, I paused and looked back. The three of them had already sprung into action. One of the younger guys was setting up a tall ladder while Bernie walked around with some device in his hand, testing outlets.

I felt a little sorry for Eva Flores. Her first attempt at making a good impression as the new Chamber leader wasn't going so well. Rather, it seemed to be having the opposite effect.

Chapter 19

After the tree was decorated to Grandpa's satisfaction, we scattered—Val to do her last-minute event stuff, Sam to the cafe outside for her shift, Lucas back to work, and Grandpa and me to the cat cafe. I figured I'd check in to make sure everything was good before I headed out for the day.

Grandpa was ready to jump right into host mode. He loved being part of the action. When we'd concocted the idea of the cafe, I'd wondered how he would feel about his home being overtaken with cats, not to mention the general public. But he'd wholeheartedly assumed his role as co-owner and business partner and he actually spent more time in the cat cafe than Ethan or I did these days. He loved to dress up in funny clothes, usually with cats on them, and tout the virtues of all our babies. He was a skilled adoption counselor too, instinctively pairing the right cat with the right person when someone was interested in adopting. I was glad he had this to keep his mind off his ankle.

Adele and Clarissa were putting some finishing touches on the rampant Christmas spirit they'd brought to the place while Harry greeted visitors. He met my eyes when he saw me and gave me a slight nod, which I assumed meant Adele had conveyed the message about keeping extra eyes on the patrons. I knew Grandpa would be too. I could tell he felt terrible about what had happened last night.

JJ held court on the front counter where the guests checked in, another perk for visitors. He was the perfect mascot—friendly, funny, and super sociable.

The cats were excited, clearly feeling the energy too. I'd been half expecting to see them all wearing Santa hats to go with their Christmas collars.

"We've got a full house of guests lined up for the day," Adele said. "Then we close at four to do another cleaning and sprucing before the tour, in case any of the judges want to come inside."

"Awesome. Are you guys able to spare me for a bit?"

Grandpa looked at me, amused. "What else do you have to do today?"

"Just have to help Mom out with a few things for the event tonight," I said. "And, yes, I know you're all going to laugh and say I told you so."

He and Adele looked at each other, then burst out laughing. "Harry owes me ten bucks," Adele declared.

"What? You're placing bets on me?" I couldn't believe them.

"Course we are," Adele said with a wave of her hand. "Harry thought Halloween would keep you out of the mix for a while. He doesn't know you well enough yet."

I glared. "I'm glad you all have nothing else to do but make fun of me."

"All in good fun," Grandpa said. "Also, you're predictable."

Before I could protest to that, Adele cut in. "Speaking of predictable. There was another flyer outside this morning when I came in."

"You're kidding." I looked at Grandpa.

"I wish I was," she said. "You think it was the thief?" Her eyes flashed angrily at the word.

I had no idea. It was brazen enough to break into a former police chief's home. Even more brazen to pause to tape a flyer to the telephone pole while you were doing it. But these people sure had some nerve, whoever they were. "Could be," I said. "I'll call Mick."

"Excuse me. Do you have any kittens?" A young woman who had come in with her boyfriend came up to us, almost bouncing with excitement.

"We do," I said, pointing her toward the back of the room. She grabbed her boyfriend's hand and made a beeline in that direction. I watched as her partner picked up one of the feather toys we left out for people to play with the cats, and the kittens were jumping and falling over each other in an attempt to catch it. Good. Maybe they'd take two.

"No kittens," a young mother who had come in with her son, who was probably five or six, warned him as he followed my gaze to the feather-toy play. "We're getting a nice, calm adult cat."

The little boy seemed fine with this. "That one," he said, pointing to Rory, who lounged on one of the kitty shelves on the wall.

"Rory is a lovely cat," I told them. "She's very calm and very sweet. Why don't you go over and see if she'll say hi to you?"

The little boy's eyes sparkled with excitement as he approached. I was pleased to see he didn't try to grab her or pick her up. Instead he sat on the floor under her perch and waited for her to come to him—which she did, pretty quickly. I had a feeling Rory might be going home, which I had to admit made me a little sad. While

I knew I couldn't keep all of them, sometimes it was hard to let them go.

"They're all so adorable," a woman's voice behind me said.

I turned to see who was speaking. The woman who had just come in looked familiar, and it took me a minute to place her. Then I recognized the long-in-front haircut. The woman from the tree farm whose husband had gotten into it with Angelo stood at the counter. Camille Billings. The one who was giving my mom a hard time about the event.

JJ had perked up at her arrival, sniffing at her like she smelled better than anything he'd ever smelled before.

I managed to keep my pleasant smile in place. "They are, aren't they? Have you been here before?" I got ready to launch into my spiel again, but she smiled and held out her hand.

"I have," she said, gazing around, taking in the decor. "It's such a cute place." She paused. "Camille Billings. I don't think we've met, but I know your family."

I nodded. "So good to meet you."

"I've heard so much about you. And your cats. The pastor at our church adopted from you all and raves about the place."

"Oh. Well, that's lovely," I said. I studied her. She didn't look like a nightmare, but as we all knew, looks could be deceiving. Camille stood much shorter than me, even though I was only wearing sneakers today. I had to look down to speak to her. But what she lacked in height, she made up for in style. She wore jeans with an orange blazer in kind of a tweed style, and a multicolored scarf around her neck that looked so cute I felt like I needed to ask her how to tie my own scarves so they looked like that. She appeared to be somewhere between my parents' age and my grandparents' age, though I couldn't put my finger on it with any certainty.

"So, are you here for a cafe appointment?" I asked.

"Nah, she's here to scope the place out."

Chapter 20

We both turned to find Grandpa, who had wheeled him-self over.

Camille laughed. "Well, of course I am, Leo! Competi-tion doesn't wane as we get older. I'm sure you know what I'm talking about."

It was Grandpa's turn to laugh. "I sure do. How are you, Camille?"

"Doing well, doing well. Sorry about your ankle," she said, gazing at the offending leg.

He waved her off. "So are you intimidated by my lights?"

"Of course not," she scoffed. "Mine are better." Her eyes were twinkling and their banter was friendly, but I didn't actually get the sense they were joking. "Espe-cially since yours are still under construction."

I cringed. This lady had just outed me with Grandpa.

His eyes narrowed, but he didn't comment on that. "Well, it helps that you got the tree you wanted," he said instead. "At least I hope you did after the scene yester-day."

To her credit, her face reddened just a tad at that. "My

husband is very protective. He always wants me to have what I want. Sometimes he can get . . . carried away."

"I'll say," Grandpa remarked.

She turned to me. "We do this all the time," she explained. "We're old friends. I was part of the garden club with your grandmother for a few years too, although she was much more of a green thumb than I ever will be. And my first husband, Jerry—he died a few years ago—was good friends with Leo here."

"I'm sorry for your loss," I said.

"Jerry was a good man," Grandpa said.

Camille nodded. "So is Ray. They are very different, but both good men. I'm lucky."

Grandpa gave a noncommittal nod. "I have to go see to our guests. Good luck tonight."

"Oh, I don't need luck," Camille assured him.

Grandpa laughed and wheeled himself away, leaving me with her.

"So. You came by to see if our lights were any good," I said. "Anything else I can do for you? Otherwise I have to get back."

"Actually, I did come to see you. I'm working on the Christmas celebration. I don't know if your mother told you." At my nod, she went on. "I'm on the committee leading the events, which after tonight consists of the bazaar and the tree lighting. And also I'm biased because I'm organizing my church's participation in the bazaar. So I have a multipurpose interest in making sure things go off without a hitch. We have amazing handmade items that our parishioners make to help us fundraise."

I didn't respond. I didn't really care about her personal interests in making sure the event went well.

"Anyway, your mother mentioned this morning that you were helping us out with a few things. So I wondered if we could chat for a minute." She glanced around. "Alone?"

I hesitated. "I'm supposed to meet with Eva first . . ."

"It'll only take a minute." She clearly wasn't taking no for an answer.

"Well, I—JJ, stop sniffing her!" I exclaimed, as JJ doubled down on whatever he smelled on her arm, his nose going a mile a minute.

She laughed. "I had a smoked salmon bagel sandwich right before I came over."

"That'll do it." JJ loved seafood. Damian had spoiled him by bringing him all the seafood scraps from the Shack pretty much daily. I took a look around the cafe. Everything seemed to be under control. May as well get this over with. "Let's go outside to the coffee shop," I said.

"Wonderful."

We turned toward the door, but then I heard Grandpa call my name. And he sounded mad. He crooked his finger at me in a *Come here now* gesture.

I excused myself and hurried over. "What's wrong?"

"Why did my competitor just point out to me that my lights weren't fixed yet?" he demanded.

I cursed Camille again in my head. "Don't worry, Bernie Elliott is here right now," I said, pointing toward the window, although no one was visible at the moment. "They're taking care of everything. I just didn't want to worry you."

He frowned at me. "You're keeping things from me because I have a sprained ankle? This *is* my house, you know."

I tried not to take that personally. I knew this had been a tough week for him. Grandpa Leo wasn't used to being out of commission in any way. "Grandpa. I didn't think you needed the extra stress," I said, keeping my voice even. "I told you I would handle it and I am. Trust me, okay?"

His bluster immediately faded away and he sighed. "Of course I do. Sorry, Doll. I just want everything to be . . . normal."

I patted his shoulder. "I know. Don't worry. I'll let you know when it's all set and you can check on it before they leave, okay? I'll be back in a few."

After I was sure he was placated, I led Camille outside. But as we headed to the garage, she paused.

"I see you're having a problem with your lights," she said, her tone a little triumphant, waving at Bernie's truck.

I gave her a sideways glance. "No. Just getting some tweaks. Grandpa likes perfection."

"Humph," she said, as if she didn't believe me. "Well, that's actually one of the things I wanted to talk to you about."

"Bernie? Why?"

"Not Bernie. But that's part of it." She paused as we got to the door leading into the food area. "It's the whole contract process. I'm worried about the method they used to put these people in place."

"What people?"

She huffed out a breath. "People like that incompetent electrician, Mr. Banks. And his wife. That new president of ours at the Chamber . . . she's allowing things to become very slipshod. And frankly, I'm concerned about it. I need your help to figure out the next best move."

I needed more coffee already. My mom was right—she was definitely trying to influence whatever was going on here. "Let's get something to drink before we talk." I opened the door and motioned her inside.

Camille paused, looking around. "It's very busy in here."

She was right. The cafe was packed. Sam was behind the counter, making coffees like a boss. I remembered her first week here when she could barely make coffee, and felt proud. Ethan and two other people worked the register, served food, and helped with coffees. Everything looked under control, which was good.

I spotted a table in the process of being vacated in the corner. "Over there." We made a beeline to it. "Sit," I told Camille. "What can I get you?"

"I'd love a coffee and one of those lovely doughnuts," she said, eyeing the pastry display.

"You got it." I went up to the counter and got two coffees and two doughnuts.

Ethan gave me a look as he handed me the plate. "What is this, coffee number eight so far?"

"Don't start with me," I said. "I'm having a bad day."

"Caffeine and sugar won't help you get through it," he chastised. "You'll just crash and be worse off."

I bared my teeth and him and carried the food back to the table. "So what's up?" I asked Camille.

"I'm worried about the influence this woman is having on the event," she said.

"Which woman?" I asked, already exhausted from this day.

"Eva Flores. The Chamber president."

"Well, she is running the event," I pointed out. "That means she's influencing it."

"Incorrectly! Letting people who aren't up to snuff be responsible for things that are important. Like the lights."

"Okay. But what can I—"

"Your mother is part of the advisory committee. But she's not advising," Camille said bluntly. "And Donna

Carey's sponsorship money, combined with Eva's do-gooder mentality, is ruining things."

At my surprised expression, she softened her tone. "Don't get me wrong. Donna is a lovely woman and a dear friend. But just because she has this business to flaunt, it doesn't mean she should be taking over."

I wasn't sure how sponsoring a town event was taking over, but I kept my mouth shut.

"And that Banks person could very well have cost me the contest if I hadn't made alternate arrangements. He came to help out at my husband's behest and made a complete mess of things."

I sat back in my chair. So this wasn't about the town. It was about her. "Look, Camille, I don't know what I can do about any of this."

"I need you to talk to your mother. Someone needs to rein in the people who think that they can just change things without others' input."

"My mother is simply advising. The Chamber is running the event, and they get final decision-making ability. You need to talk to Eva." I pushed back my chair to stand.

"I can't. She doesn't understand how to put on an event this size," Camille insisted.

I sat back down. "Camille. You said you're heading up the events committee?"

"That's right."

"If I recall, my mother said there were some problems related to the bazaar too," I said pointedly.

"Absolutely. And I was going to ask you to help with that also. Your mother did say you were an event ninja."

At this, I burst out laughing. "An event ninja? What exactly does that even mean? Also, are you sure she wasn't talking about my sister? She's the event planner."

Camille shrugged and went back to her doughnut. "I

don't know. Someone who gets it done. And we don't need an event *planner*," she added. "*I'm* the planner. We need a manager." She pulled some papers out of her purse. "This is the diagram of the gymnasium, where the bazaar will be held. But no one has cleaned out the room yet or brought in the tables and other supplies we asked for."

"Who was supposed to do it?" I asked.

"I have no idea. The school, I would guess."

"But . . . as the event planner, wouldn't you have nailed that down?" I asked, truly baffled at this conversation.

She waved me off. "Those are just details. I'm not a details person."

I pressed a hand to my forehead. *Maddie, Maddie, Maddie,* that little voice in my head chided. *You can never leave well enough alone.* "Kind of important details, no?" I asked. "Since the bazaar starts tonight?"

"Exactly!" she said triumphantly, as if I was finally getting it. "I have no idea where we can get the supplies we need on such short notice. The church doesn't have them. I have other things to take care of, and we have people heading over there at three to set up for a five p.m. start time. We *have* to be open." She looked at me imploringly. "So can you help?"

I glanced at the diagrams. "You need the room set up for vendors," I confirmed.

She beamed. "Yes! Your mother said you were good at this. Here, take this. It tells you how many vendors there are and the sizes of the tables they need. These doughnuts are so good. Are there more?" She turned, craning her neck to see what was in the pastry case.

"I'm sure there are. And the Chamber doesn't have access to this stuff?"

"Great question," Camille said. "The answer is no. They haven't done an event this large. So they've been trying to cobble a solution together. Why they waited so long to realize they had an issue I have no idea." She shook her head. "See what I mean? There are serious problems here."

She was right about that.

"I'll see what I can do to help with the bazaar setup," I said. That seemed like an easier problem than whatever this infighting was. "I'll let you know what happens. Do I have your number?"

Camille recited it and I saved it in my phone. "Thank you, Maddie." She clasped her hands together in front of her chest. "This takes such a weight off the rest of us."

"Happy to help," I said through gritted teeth. I needed an Advil.

Chapter 21

Friday
1 p.m.

I left Camille to her doughnut—she'd gone back for a second—and headed to the house, my mind making a plan for how to tackle the rest of the day, of which I suddenly felt like I'd lost control. I needed to talk to my mother, stop by the Chamber, and then figure out how to get a hundred or so tables to the high school gym in time for said hundred or so vendors to be all set up for an event that started in, like, four hours. I couldn't believe no one had addressed this before today and that somehow I was the one on the hook for it now. But before I got to the house, a shout from the front lawn made me snap my head around.

"What do you think you're doing?" a man's voice rang out.

I came around the front of the house and saw Todd Banks' van parked haphazardly, half on the lawn. Two guys who looked kind of sketchy waited next to it, both smoking cigarettes and watching whatever was going on in my yard. Todd himself stood in front of Bernie's ladder in that obnoxious coat—wasn't he freezing?—glaring up at him.

"Oh, for the love of God." I made an about-face and

headed over to them. Was I really going to have to stop
two grown men from fighting over some Christmas
lights? Then again, I'd witnessed two other grown men
fighting about a Christmas tree yesterday. So much for
the Christmas spirit.

I grabbed Todd's arm and pulled him aside, waving
apologetically at Bernie on the ladder. Bernie gave me
an amused look in return. I pulled Todd into the front
yard, away from any staring cafe patrons. His forearm
was surprisingly muscular given his overall scrawniness.

"I was coming back to finish the job," Todd said
through gritted teeth.

"I know. Thanks for coming back, but we've got it covered. And please don't throw your butts on the ground,"
I snapped at his guys.

They both backed off, heading toward the van.

Todd didn't. He glared at me, opening his mouth to
protest.

I bit back all the angry words that were still on the tip
of my tongue when I thought about how this could have
turned out and managed to paste on a smile. "This is a
contract with the town, right?"

"Well, yeah, but—"

"So that means you're getting paid anyway. Don't
worry about it." I could hear the edge creeping into my
own voice. "Bernie's almost done, we need the lights on
today, we're good."

We stood there, facing off for a long moment until
Todd broke eye contact with me, gave Bernie one more
glare, then turned and flounced back to his truck, lighting a cigarette of his own as he went. His dramatic exit
was marred by the fact that his long, silly jacket got
caught in the door when he slammed it shut and he had
to open it, free the offending material, then slam it again

before he attempted to roar down the street. His truck only managed a weak engine rev, but we got the point.

As he turned the corner, I looked at Bernie. He looked at me. Then we both started laughing.

Grandpa waited at the door.

"What did Camille want?" he asked.

"Something about the event. Why?"

He frowned. "She's here because she wants to win the contest. I don't want her taking any last-minute ideas and copycatting." He leaned forward. "I know she's been snooping around at night when the lights are on, too. She wants to see everything."

"Well, how am I supposed to stop that?" I asked, ex-asperated. I was getting sick of Christmas lights at this point. "You know what, never mind. I have to go."

I left him staring after me and went in search of my sister. I tracked down Val on the fourth floor. She'd turned one of the extra rooms into an office, and she was in there poring over some lists when I knocked and stuck my head in. "I need help."

She looked up. "With what?"

"I need tables and I guess chairs and whatever else vendors need to set up shop in the high school for the bazaar."

She cocked her head. "The bazaar that's starting in a few hours?"

"That's the one." I went all the way into the room and sat on the floor since she had no chairs. "I can probably cobble some stuff together, but you're the events person. Figured you might have a ready-made solution."

"I do, actually. How many tables do they need?"

I pulled out the diagram and showed her. She stud-ied it, made some calculations on a piece of paper, then nodded. "Let me make some calls. I'll let you know what I come up with."

"Thank you." I wanted to kiss her. I stood to leave. "Why are you so calm? The party is tonight."

She grinned. "Because I don't leave anything until the last minute, remember? My stuff was locked last week. I'm just tweaking last-minute stuff now to make it even better."

"Why didn't they ask you to do this?" I grumbled.

"I'm doing it anyway," she pointed out.

"True." I headed down to my room, shut the door and called Bones, my web guy.

"I need help with a website," I said when he answered.

"Send it over." Bones was a man of few words. He was also a professional hacker, which I kept in my back pocket in case I needed it. I didn't necessarily want to get involved in hacking anything. I preferred to think of it that if I needed information, I had a way to get it. He'd helped me out on a few occasions in the past. Nothing really illegal. At least, I didn't think so. Either way, it was nice to know the option was there.

By the time I'd sent over the info about the website, Val had texted me: *Tables and everything else you need will be there by two. Can you meet them?*

You bet. Thank you! I texted back, relieved. Maybe this wouldn't be so bad after all.

I slid behind the wheel of Grandma's old car, crossing my fingers it would start. I really needed to get a car soon. None of us had wanted to part with this one, and it was convenient having it here. But it was old, and lately it was hit or miss whether it would run or not, which wasn't great, especially in winter.

But it started, thank goodness. Maybe that meant the day was turning around. As I drove, I called the Chamber marketing person and had her send the map files to the cat cafe email address; then I called Clarissa, our marketing volunteer, and asked her to handle the edits, which I'd already put in a file on our shared drive. She promised to have the updated map to the printer in thirty minutes.

Confident that was handled, I pulled into the high school parking lot and slipped in the main doors of the school and headed down to the gymnasium. It always felt so weird being back here. It felt so far away that it was like stepping back in time.

I reached the double doors, but before I could push them open, they opened from inside and I came face-to-face with Brandon Tyson. We both jumped back, surprised.

"Hey," I said finally, when he didn't say anything. "Are you helping with the event too?"

He snickered. "No. Dad—Angelo—is. He's in there." He waved vaguely behind him.

"Thanks," I started past him, but he blocked the door with his arm.

"Excuse me," I said, trying to maneuver around him.

"You're friends with that newspaper chick, right?"

I narrowed my eyes at him. I didn't like his tone. "That *chick*. You mean Becky Walsh?"

"Whatever. You should tell her to mind her business."

I turned so I was face-to-face with him once more. "I'm not sure what you're talking about, but I don't love your approach, Brandon."

"Don't play dumb, Maddie," he said, mimicking my tone. "I'm talking about Becky butting in where her nose doesn't belong. Having opinions where she shouldn't."

"If you're talking about the newspaper—which you probably shouldn't be talking about, since I assume it's confidential—I hardly think she doesn't belong. She's the managing editor."

"Doesn't matter. She has no ownership. Donna has a decision to make and she doesn't need any do-gooders influencing her. This is business."

"It's definitely her decision," I agreed. "So I would think lawyers with some sort of self-interest shouldn't be influencing her either."

Brandon didn't react to that. Instead he said, "She's taking the offer. It's not on the table long. And it's very generous. She just has to make it official. But it's done."

I shrugged. "That's Donna's prerogative. And Becky's reaction has nothing to do with me. If you want to discuss it further, you should call her."

He regarded me for another long few seconds. "Just give her the message. Might do more good coming from a friend." He nodded at me, then brushed past, his fancy shoes clicking against the floor as he strode down the hall.

I watched him go. Why did Brandon care so much about what Donna did with the paper? Was it really because he cared about the island like his father-in-law? Or did he have another stake in the game, like perhaps his family—he, Angelo, and Molly—stood to make a nice paycheck if she decided to sell? Given that they were investors, I could safely bet that was the case.

So why would Donna seek out his advice, then, instead of a neutral third party?

Chapter 22

Still annoyed about my interaction with Brandon, I pushed through the doors into the gym. The familiar smells of sweat and old sneakers mixed with some kind of holiday-scented cover-up hit me in the face, taking my breath away for a second. The room was mostly empty, save for a giant banner with the event name and all the sponsors on it. I saw the newspaper logo front and center—Donna's platinum sponsorship. That wasn't unusual—the newspaper always sponsored big town events—but I remembered how Camille had specifically mentioned it as a problem. Which seemed like an odd perspective, since the sponsorship dollars were likely footing the bill for most of this. The town had a budget for events but it wasn't much, and even though they tried to earmark funds specifically for Christmas, there usually ended up being less than anticipated. So sponsorships literally made this possible. Especially if there was a cash prize.

But, not my problem. I just needed to get some tables delivered, make sure people could set up, then figure out what other help I needed to provide for this shindig.

I looked around to see if anyone was here to give me some idea how they wanted this done, but no one was in sight. Annoyed, I pulled out my phone to text Camille when the woman herself walked out from the locker room area. Apparently she'd torn herself away from the doughnuts and found her way over here.

"There you are!" she exclaimed. "You have tables?"

Before I could answer, Angelo Longo rushed in, pausing when he saw me. He grinned happily, the dimples in his cheeks becoming more pronounced, his gray mustache lifting with his smile. That was how I remembered him, as a pleasant, happy guy. Not the possessive, angry person I'd seen acting erratically yesterday. "There she is. Our event ninja." Despite being on the island for as long as I could remember, Angelo still had a slight Italian accent that gave the words a pleasant lilt.

The title was cracking me up. I wondered who had come up with that one.

"Good to see you," I told him, then turned to Camille. "I was just about to text you. The tables are handled. They're on the way."

She clasped her hands together. "You are *wonderful.*"

"You're making her do your dirty work?" Angelo thundered at Camille, his face flushing red. Whoa. He did have a temper.

"I offered," I interrupted before Camille could shout back, hoping to smooth over the tension. "I didn't know you were working on the committee too, Angelo."

He glared at Camille a moment longer then turned to me. "Yes, well." He shrugged. "I always try to help if I can. They said they could use extra hands this year." His eyes darkened. "Probably because no one else is using their hands."

Camille bristled. Before she could jump in, I said, "The tables should be here any minute. I need to let them in. Just wanted to make sure everything was unlocked."

"I'll go open the bay out back," Camille said. "I finally

got the keys from the school staff." She waved a key ring at me. "You know where the door is?"

"I do. I went to school here," I reminded her. "I know all the nooks and crannies."

She nodded and walked past me. A minute later I heard the heavy double doors leading to the back parking lot shove open.

Angelo sighed. "This event has been stressful."

"Camille told me," I said. "Sorry about that. These things always are tough."

He snorted. "That *soggettone*."

I knew that was Italian but wasn't sure what it meant, although it seemed safe to assume it was an insult so I didn't ask for clarification.

He didn't seem to notice. "These things should not be this complicated! This"—he indicated the gym—"was her responsibility. She pawns it off on you. And I have my own business I need to set up here, and now I'm in charge for it to be running right. She lies. About everything. Never again will I be on these committees. Everyone is . . ." He drew a line across his throat.

Lies? "What do you mean?" I asked.

"He's just mad about the contest," said a voice from behind me.

I turned and found Molly, his daughter, grinning at me. She looked like she'd just come in from outside. A sparkly pink hat with a pom-pom covered her hair, and she was pulling off a pair of gloves. "Oh, hey," I said. I wondered if she'd come here with Brandon.

Angelo frowned at his daughter, but a smile pulled at his lips. "You have a big mouth."

Molly grinned. "It's true, Dad. He doesn't like all the competition this year. And he's still mad about the tree," she explained to me. "Not to mention—"

Angelo's face reddened. "Molly Jane," he warned.

"What? Dad. Maddie was there. She saw the whole thing," she said with an eye roll.

Now Angelo looked at me, shame washing over his face. "You did?"

"I was with Grandpa. I didn't really catch the whole thing," I said evasively. "Anyway, who's going to show me where the tables should go?"

"Camille should. She won't decorate, at least she can oversee." His eyes narrowed thoughtfully. "You'll help decorate?"

"Decorate?" I said, alarmed. "No. I told her I'd arrange the tables, but I have other—"

"The band needs to know where to set up. That will dictate the layout of the room. Come." He took my arm and led me back into the gym.

"The band?" I hadn't heard about that.

"Yes, yes, the band. Christmas music! We need a space for them."

"Thanks for letting me know before we set the tables up," I said, only a little sarcastically, taking note that the only Christmasy object so far was an artificial tree in the corner with a sad offering of decorations. Half the lights were also out. "And it looks like you need to *start* decorating, never mind finish."

Angelo frowned at me. "Which is why we need help."

I watched my plan of being in and out fade into the sunset and sighed. "I can stay for a bit," I said. "Make sure things get set up correctly."

Angelo excused himself, leaving me with Molly. "Did you get roped into this too?" I asked.

She laughed. "Always. I'm usually on the hook to help with whatever my dad signs up for."

Sounded familiar.

"By the way, I'm sorry about my dad's behavior lately. He's been a little stressed."

"About the event?" I asked. "That seems to be going around."

She shrugged. "That and some other things. He's just . . . anyway." She shook her head, changing her mind about whatever she was going to tell me and looked up with a smile. "He's a good guy. And a really good dad. I wouldn't want you to think otherwise."

I assured her I didn't—I really didn't think about him much at all, but didn't tell her that.

"It's good you're jumping in, though. Those two will kill each other if they have to be in the same room for long," she said.

"You mean him and Camille?" At her nod, I smiled a little. "I can see that. Are they really that competitive about the contest?"

"You don't know the half." Then she seemed to catch herself. I could see her about to exit the conversation, so I jumped in and changed the subject.

"How's Brandon?" I asked casually. "I just saw him on my way in."

She glanced at the doors to the gym as if she expected to see him there, a shadow passing over her face. "He's fine." Her tone had turned clipped.

"Still at the law firm?"

"Yeah. He's about to make partner."

"Really? Congrats!" That sounded big.

Molly didn't seem to share my enthusiasm. "Yeah. It's great. Anyway, I should . . ." She motioned to the space around us."

"Right. Same." I glanced at my phone as it buzzed. The tables had arrived. I excused myself to let them in while Molly turned back to the business of Christmas-ing everything up.

Chapter 23

The rest of the afternoon passed in a blur of getting all the tables and other necessary items into the gym, setting everything up, and checking vendors in. The tables hadn't arrived much before the vendors, and in some cases we were simultaneously setting them up when people were trying to unload their wares.

But most people took it in stride. At least not everyone seemed to have been robbed of the Christmas spirit.

As for the committee, a few other volunteers had shown up to hang garland and snowflakes from the ceiling. It wouldn't win any contests, but the place looked pretty good once they'd gotten going. Someone had come to the rescue with a new string of lights for the tree, and Ellen, the librarian, had even brought some decorations that were much better suited to the vibe we were going for.

Once I got over the initial panic of the empty gym and the ticking clock, I relaxed into the role of event ninja and took charge. I don't know why I fought it—I liked being in the middle of things, contributing to town events and seeing things run smoothly. And I liked being part of the things that were bringing more people to the island during these cold, sometimes lonely months.

Quite possibly I liked it too much, because I totally lost track of time until Lucas texted me to ask where I was. We had been planning to come back tonight as actual bazaar-goers with Becky and Damian anyway—although we'd made those plans before Becky had retreated into her funk—but even if we did make it back to enjoy everything, it now appeared I would be wearing the event ninja hat too.

Still here, I replied to his text. My eyes widened when I realized it was nearly four thirty. A lot of the vendors had streamed in and were deep in the setting-up process. I hadn't seen Camille at all after she'd opened the back doors. She must've slipped out from there. Angelo's table was set up, but he was nowhere in sight. Neither was Molly. There were other people from the store putting some last-minute touches on the decor, which looked pretty great, and heating up the hot cider they were selling.

I called Camille, who really should have been back by now. Her phone went straight to voicemail. I left a terse message that I needed to leave soon then called Lucas. "Do you want to meet me here? Or wait for me?" I looked doubtfully down at my jeans that were now dusty, and my sparkly red sweater that had somehow gotten grease stains. "I can't find anyone who's supposed to be running this thing. Also I haven't heard from Becky at all." I needed to fill her in on the weird conversation with Brandon, too.

"See if you can get out of there by five? Otherwise we'll meet you," Lucas said. "I can check in with Damian."

"Thank you for being so understanding," I told him. "I'll call you back in a bit." I disconnected and looked around again, hoping to see someone in charge. I didn't. Molly wasn't even at the co-op's booth. I made my way through the maze of tables one more time, checking to see if anyone needed anything.

Half an hour later, neither Angelo nor Camille had resurfaced. I texted Lucas and told him to just meet me here and to bring an outfit for me to change into. Even if someone showed up soon, it would take more time to go all the way home and come back. Luckily, he was good at that kind of thing, so I didn't worry about ending up with half an outfit or no shoes. Even so, I spelled it all out just to be safe. Then I tried calling Becky to tell her the change of plans. She didn't pick up.

I stopped back at the co-op table. Two of the regular staffers were working. No sign of Angelo or Molly. I got a cup of hot cider, then walked out of the fray. I waited near the door, sipping my cider and delighting in the taste. The whipped cream was melting in and gave it a nice texture. Hot cider was one of my favorite things.

I figured I'd give it until five thirty before I called my mother or Eva to ask for a backup for the evening. I realized I'd also never made it to the Chamber to talk to Eva, which I really needed to do tomorrow. But at five twenty-eight, Camille rushed through the gym doors, which I'd propped open for shoppers to come in and out more easily, with a stack of towering boxes. Her hair, which had been perky earlier, looked a bit limp, like it had had a long day.

She barreled past me, not even noticing, and I had to hurry to catch up with her as she zigzagged through the crowd, coming to a stop at a table about halfway down the right side of the room. The banner hanging in the front read "United Methodist Church of Turtle Point." A man and a woman sitting behind the table glanced up, relief in their eyes. "Camille! We were getting worried."

"I'm sorry. I forgot the scarves and had to go home and get them." She deposited the boxes unceremoniously on the table. Fabric spilled out of the open one on top.

The woman jumped up and opened the top one, pulling out some beautiful handmade scarves and beginning to arrange them on the table.

"The place looks wonderful!" Camille exclaimed, turning to me.

"Thanks. Where did you run off to? You missed all the decorating fun," I said pointedly.

She winced. "I know. I'm very sorry. I got tied up."

Yelling at someone, I imagined. Maybe getting Todd Banks fired, or Angelo kicked off the committee. "I'm not going to be staying much longer," I said.

"Don't worry, dear. Go do your thing. Thank you for bailing us out today."

"No problem." My gaze fell on the scarves again. I couldn't help it—I reached out to touch one. It was incredibly soft and the colors were vibrant. I made a mental note to come back and get one for my mother for Christmas. She loved scarves.

"On sale," the lady said with a wink. "Buy one, get one free."

What the heck—one for Mom, one for me. I picked out two and handed over my credit card, accepting the bag she handed me. Then I went out to the hallway to get away from the crowd and wait for Lucas. I watched the people stream happily in, the excitement of holiday shopping and a festive evening with friends and family making everyone cheerier than they usually seemed. They had no idea about the underlying drama that had gone into this up until an hour ago. As it should be.

I saw Craig and his girlfriend, Jade Bennett, walking in and went over to say hello. As I made my way over to them, I almost bumped into Angelo, who was hurrying in with the crowd.

"There you are," I said. "I've been looking for you."

"Maddie. I apologize, I had to run out and get more supplies," he said. "You could've had Molly text me."

I sighed. "I can't find her either."

"What do you mean? She should be here." He looked concerned, then shook it off. "Anyways, I'm back for the night. Thank you again." He patted me on the shoulder and hurried toward his table.

"Wait," I started to call out. He didn't have anything with him. Maybe he needed help bringing stuff in. But he was already too far away to hear me.

Oh well. Not my problem. I turned back to go talk to Craig and Jade.

"How are you? I heard about your grandfather," Jade said, giving me a hug. "I hope he's back running around town very soon." Jade ran the bar Jade Moon, which had become the town hotspot over the past couple of years. She stayed open all year-round, which naturally attracted a lot of our younger crowd. Plus, her vibe was fun.

"Thanks for asking. He's good," I told her.

"You're not working this thing, are you?" Craig asked.

"Just helping out a little," I said.

He laughed. "What happened to not getting involved in this one?"

"Yeah, yeah." I waved him off. "Go shop. I'll be joining as a civilian as soon as my change of clothes arrives."

They headed into the gym just as Lucas texted me

that he was on his way in. A minute later he and Damian came into view. Lucas had a bag of clothes with him.

"You're the best," I said, taking the bag and giving him a kiss. "I'll meet you inside once I change. Nothing from Becky?"

Damian shook his head. He looked worried. "I haven't heard from her at all. You?"

"I tried calling before but nothing. I'm sure she's just head down at the paper. You know how she is."

"I know, but she's been in such a bad mood after last night. We should go by the office and see if she's there."

I guessed she had told him after all. "She'll be okay. She's going to fixate on it for a while, and whatever's going to happen will happen anyway. We'll deal with it." I patted him on the shoulder and headed for the bathroom, hesitating before heading inside. I hated school bathrooms. Especially since this one probably hadn't been upgraded since I'd graduated twenty-something years ago. I poked my head cautiously inside. It still looked the same, but didn't smell as bad as I remembered, which was something. I went into the larger stall on the end and started to change, careful to make sure none of my clothes touched the floor, the walls, or the toilet. Yuck.

I was just pulling on my knee-high boots when my phone vibrated on top of the toilet paper holder, the buzzing nearly making it jump off the ledge. I snatched it up before it fell into the toilet, relieved to see Becky's name on the screen.

"Where have you been?" I demanded. "We're all here at the gym. Are you coming over?"

"I need you to come to Donna's house. Now," she said, and her panicked tone made chills run up my spine. Becky never sounded panicked.

Also, I was confused. "Donna who? Donna like your boss?"

"Yes!" she snapped.

"Why? What's wrong?"

Silence. Then Becky said in a choked voice, "She's dead."

Chapter 24

I froze, feeling my heart start to pound uncontrollably in my chest. Still, I tried to force my voice to sound normal since Becky sounded so freaked out. Both of us freaking out wouldn't be good.

"What are you talking about? How can she be"—I dropped my voice to a whisper—"dead?"

"She's . . . outside on the ground. Not moving. There are"—I heard her draw in a shaky breath—"lights wrapped around her neck. Christmas lights."

What?

"Becky. You're not saying . . ."

"Can you just come?" Her voice hit a pitch that made me pull the phone from my ear.

"Me? Why me? Did you call nine-one-one?"

"Of course I called nine-one-one! But I don't know what else to do." Her breath hitched and I knew she was on the verge of hysteria. "I mean, I tried to check her pulse but I didn't feel anything, and anyway, I have no idea how to check a pulse so I don't think I did it right anyway, and then—"

"I'll be right there," I cut into her babbling, suppressing my questions. Why was she at Donna's house? Did this have something to do with Brandon and the offer? I thought back to my conversation with him earlier. The thinly veiled threatening tone his words had underneath them. And what *exactly* did she mean that there were lights wrapped around her neck? Like, she'd gotten tangled in them? Or someone had wrapped them around her neck and choked her with them? I didn't really want to ponder that theory for very long.

But I didn't say any of that. "Craig's here. I'll bring him," I said instead.

"Thanks." She hung up.

I threw my stuff in the bag and burst out of the stall, texting Craig as I headed for the door.

I need help. Women's bathroom.

Less than a minute later I heard footsteps running toward me. I stepped into the hall. He slowed when he saw me. "What's wrong?"

"I just got a call from Becky. She's at Donna Carey's house." I took a breath. "She found Donna outside in the yard. She says she's dead."

"Dead," he repeated, his voice flat.

"Dead," I confirmed, lowering my voice and glancing around. "With lights wrapped around her neck. Can you take me over there?" I hoped he would agree. I hated to ruin his evening, but he was a newly minted detective and I was betting that he would want to be in on the action.

"Wait." He held up a hand. "Lights around her neck? What do you mean?"

"I'm not sure," I admitted. "Like, Christmas lights I think. I'm just telling you what she told me."

His jaw set. "Why do these things always happen when you get involved in something?"

"What am I involved in? All I did was answer my phone!!"

He gave me a skeptical look but let it go. "Did she call nine-one-one?"

"She said she did."

"I'm on my way. But you don't need to go over there."

"I do," I insisted. "At the very least I need to take her home. She's distraught."

He glanced behind him as if calculating what that would mean for his evening, then nodded with barely a hesitation. "Fine. But you're staying in the car. Let's go." He called Jade as we walked out, telling her to meet us out front.

I had to tell Lucas and Damian, but I didn't want to worry them yet until I knew what was really going on. Instead I texted Lucas and said Becky had called and I had to go get her, and that I would be right back.

We piled into Craig's car and he pulled up in front of the door just as Jade came out. "What's going on?" she asked.

"Emergency," Craig said tightly. "You should probably stay here, but I'm not sure when I'll be back."

She nodded, like she was used to this. She probably was, being with Craig. Especially when I was around. "Be safe," she said.

"Don't mention anything about an emergency," he told her.

"Got it." With a curious look at me, she turned and went back inside. I hoped she didn't think there was anything weird about me going with him. Then again, she knew my history with police investigations.

"You sure Becky didn't give you any other details?" Craig asked as we sped toward Turtle Point.

"Just what I told you. Maybe it's not . . . maybe she's not dead," I said, trying to convince myself. "Maybe she just fell or something." *Right, and then some Christmas lights accidentally ended up around her neck.*

He glanced at me, his expression skeptical. "With everything else she said? Sounds peculiar."

That was one word for it. I couldn't comprehend that this could even be happening. How on earth could Donna be dead? I'd just seen her last night.

At the newsroom. Arguing with Brandon. And Becky had just seen her today. They'd been arguing too. This whole potential newspaper sale had gone beyond contentious.

I hadn't realized how far down the rabbit hole my thoughts had gone until Craig said, "How did she happen upon this festive scene?"

I had no idea how to respond.

"Maddie? Why was she over there?"

Well, that was the million-dollar question, wasn't it? "I'm not sure," I said, which wasn't entirely true. I mean, I didn't know for sure, but I had an idea. I just didn't want to say it until I *did* know for sure.

Thankfully there was no traffic, and Craig pulled up in front of Donna's house barely fifteen minutes after we'd left the high school. The ambulance was already there, parked at the curb, silent but lights flashing. I could hear sirens in the distance. Police cars on their way, probably.

"Stay here," Craig told me, and got out of the car.

I waited until he was far enough away, then pushed my door open. I slipped into the yard before he could see me and stop me. I registered that half the lights on the house and the yard decorations were out. Which seemed . . . unconscionable given that tonight was the judging contest. Looked like Todd Banks hadn't come through after all. Again.

I paused, the reality of that thought flooding over me. The judging contest. Oh, God. What if the limo with all

the judges had come by already? What if they'd seen . . .
what Becky had seen? Or what if they came now, during
this chaos? That would be bad. If they'd come already,
they may have missed it. But now, it would be like a train
wreck you couldn't look away from.

And then the next thought—Todd Banks. She'd been
yelling at him in her backyard just two days ago. About
Christmas lights. Now hers were still out, and she was
dead with lights strung around her neck. Coincidence?

I saw Craig and the paramedics standing over by
the side of the house, but none of them were near
Donna. There was at least ten feet of space between
her and them. Craig was on the radio. A gurney was
parked in the snow next to the paramedics, and a
person sat on the edge of it while they seemed to be
checking vitals. My eyes widened when I realized it
was Becky. She'd said she wasn't hurt . . . so what was
going on? Were they just being cautious?

I started over there when something small ran in front
of my feet, startling me. I jumped back, pressing a pounding hand to my chest.

Then I peered more closely at the creature, which was
frozen in fear and staring at me, and I realized it was
Donna's cat, the one I'd seen yesterday—Simon. "What
are you doing outside?" I asked, crouching down and
holding a hand out for him to sniff. He shrank back,
keeping his eyes on me.

I knew there was another cat. Were they both outside?
They hadn't seemed like outdoor cats. How had they
gotten out? I reached for him, wondering if he would
run, but he let me scoop him up. "It's okay," I told him.
"I'll bring you back inside."

Simon snuggled against my chest. I could feel his
hairless body shaking in the cold. I stood again, looking

around. I didn't see the other cat anywhere. I tucked Simon in my jacket and made my way over to the small group on the lawn.

Craig was talking to the paramedics. Becky still sat on the gurney, purposely not looking at the scene in front of her. They seemed to be done with her. Her head was bowed and she looked like she was crying. I risked a glance at the still form lying in a melted, dirty puddle of the recent icy snow.

Donna was on the ground, blond hair fanned out and floating in the small puddle, the color faded to a dirty brown from the muck. She wasn't wearing a coat or shoes, and her jeans were soaked through from the water underneath her. A few feet away, her red eyeglasses lay in the snow, like a splash of blood on the pure white.

But none of that stood out like the string of blinking, multicolored Christmas lights that were around her neck—a macabre necklace highlighting her unseeing eyes.

Chapter 25

"Maddie!"

I jumped, nearly dropping Simon when Craig barked my name. His phone was in his hand mid-air, as if he'd been making a call. He must have seen me creep around the side of the house and was trying to ward me off.

"Why aren't you in the car?" he hissed, grabbing my arm with his free hand and roughly pulling me away from the scene.

I was still trying to process what I'd seen, but managed to choke out, "The cat," shoving my jacket at him so he could see the creature huddled up inside it.

Craig eyed the cat, then shook his head and pointed to the car. "Go."

"The cat needs to be put back in the house. And I need to see Becky," I protested. "I told you."

"You *need* to stop tramping around on a crime scene. And you need to stay far away from what's going on over there. It's not safe."

His words ping-ponged in my brain. *Crime scene.* Yes. If nothing else, I'd seen for myself that the lights around Donna's neck erased all of my hopeful theorizing about her falling and hitting her head, or having a medical emergency. Unless she'd been trying to wear those lights as a necklace and it had gone horribly wrong, which I doubted. But what did he mean, *not safe*? I swallowed hard, not really sure what to do next, when Becky saw me and rushed over.

"Oh, thank God," she said, throwing her arms around me.

I met Craig's eyes over her head, stopping the protest that was forming on his lips. "Are you okay? Are you hurt?"

"I'm not hurt. They were just checking to make sure I . . ." She faltered at the look on Craig's face. "Just checking me out," she finished lamely, and I knew there was more to the story. She stepped back, pulling my coat with her and letting out a little gasp when she saw the cat snuggled inside. "Oh, you got him," she said, reaching a shaking hand out to stroke him. "I saw him bolting through the yard earlier, but I couldn't catch him. They're not supposed to be outside. I figured Donna would be"— she choked up—"really upset if something happened to them."

She was shivering. Probably in shock.

A patrol car pulled up to the curb and two cops, a male and a female, got out just as Craig's phone began to ring. "Stay right here," he warned us both, then walked a few feet away to take the call.

The paramedics were still waiting for direction on what to do next. The whole scene seemed frozen in time, those blinking lights on the ground—on Donna— that I could still see out of the corner of my eye a silent reminder of the horrible sight just a few feet away.

"Did you find the other cat?" Becky asked, her voice shrill.

"I haven't seen the other cat yet. But it's okay. We'll

get her. But Beck . . ." I hesitated, something inside me dreading the answer I would get to this question. "Why were you here?"

Becky's eyes moved back to where the paramedics stood over the body. "Donna called me a few times after I left her house earlier. She knew I was upset. I ignored her call. I was working. But then I started to think it probably wasn't such a good idea to ignore the boss for too long. When I tried her back she didn't answer. I figured I'd come by and try to smooth things over before I met up with you guys." She paused, taking a deep, shuddering breath. "When I got here, the door was open. I stuck my head inside and called her, but she didn't answer. Then I figured maybe she was outside and accidentally hadn't shut the door all the way. So I went out and looked around and saw one of the cats. I followed him . . . over here"—she swallowed—"and saw her. She was like that and didn't move when I called out to her."

She drifted off into silence. I saw Craig huddling with the patrol cops, giving them direction, probably on securing the scene. Lights were starting to come on in neighboring houses now, and a few brave souls ventured out into the cold night air, huddled in coats hastily thrown over pajamas, to see what was going on.

I turned away. "You didn't see anyone when you got here? No other cars?"

She shook her head. "Nothing." Her eyes finally met mine and they were full of fear. "Those lights. Around her neck. Someone . . . did that."

I nodded grimly. "Yeah. Seems so. And why were they checking your vitals? Do you need to go to the hospital?"

"No. I'm fine."

She didn't sound fine. "Becky, do you think—"

"Mick is on his way," Craig said, coming back over

to us. "And the coroner. Becky, why don't you come with me so I can get your statement. Maddie, go back to my car."

"I need to find the other cat," I insisted stubbornly.

He looked like his head was about to explode. "This is a crime scene. Did I not mention that? We need to check for footprints and other evidence. So unless you want to be a suspect . . ."

"Fine," I muttered. "Can you tell me when I can go look for the cat? Or if you guys find her?"

He didn't bother answering me. Instead, he took Becky's arm and led her toward the patrol car, which the other cops had left running. She glanced over her shoulder at me, her eyes pleading. She'd never told me why they'd been checking her out. I didn't know how to help her. And I didn't want Craig mad at me. He wouldn't tell me anything if he was. But me being here wasn't the only reason why he'd be mad. He'd brought me, after all. He knew I was about as likely to just wait in the car as I was to join a convent.

Trouble had seemed to follow me ever since I'd moved back to Daybreak, and he and Mick never hesitated to point that out. It wasn't my fault, exactly. I just seemed to attract it. But I was worried it was rubbing off on my friends and relatives. And at this point I figured the police would be happy if I left town.

I watched them get in—the front seats, thank goodness—then headed slowly back toward Craig's car. But as I reached it, another car pulled up in front. Mick, in his unmarked car.

He got out, his gaze taking in the scene, then he turned to me. "What the hell happened?"

I lifted my shoulders in a defeated shrug. "No idea. Becky found Donna dead in her yard."

"With Christmas lights around her neck? Did I hear that right, or did I just have too much eggnog tonight?"

I knew Mick didn't drink, so he was clearly being sarcastic. "Go see for yourself."

He sighed, loud and long. "Why was Becky here anyway?"

"She works for Donna—worked," I corrected myself.

"So they hung out together?"

"No. But they had been having some . . . discussions of late. They had a couple of meetings today." It sounded kind of lame even to me.

"What kind of discussions?" There was an edge to Mick's tone. "I know the news doesn't sleep, but what kind of discussions had to happen on a Friday night at the publisher's house?"

"Look, Craig's talking to her now. You should go ask her. But listen, Donna has—had—two cats." I pointed at the still-shivering Simon in my arms.

Mick squinted at the odd-looking creature. "That's a cat?"

"Yes it's a cat," I snapped. "The other one might be out here somewhere. I need to find her."

"I'll let you know when you can look." Mick started to walk away, then turned back. "Are they supposed to be out?"

"No."

"Do you know how they got out?"

"Becky said the front door was open a little when she got here."

He nodded and walked away, toward the spot where Donna's body still lay in the snow.

I was cold, but I didn't want to get in the car. I glanced around, trying to determine my next best move.

An older man crossed the street from the house

directly across from Donna's, approaching me. "Excuse me, miss," he called. "Do you know what's going on over here?"

I glanced around to see if anyone was watching me. Mick was occupied with the body and everyone else was crowded around him. Craig and Becky were still in the patrol car. I turned back to the man. "Not really. I just came to pick up a friend," I said evasively. "Did you happen to see anything odd going on out here earlier?"

He blinked, his eyes runny with the cold. "Odd how?"

"I don't know . . . like any strange vehicles or people?"

He shook his head slowly. "No, but my wife and I were at the church setting up the Christmas displays until just a little while ago," he said. "Is Ms. Carey alright?"

Luckily I didn't have to answer that because one of the patrol cops came over. "Excuse me, sir, I'm going to have to ask you to clear the yard," she said briskly. "And Ms. James, Lt. Ellory said if you'd like to wait in the back of the patrol car you're welcome to."

Funny. I glanced at Mick, hoping he could see my dirty look under the streetlight. *Back of the patrol car, my—*

Sweeping headlights pulled up on the street next to the plethora of emergency vehicles, illuminating the chaotic scene. We all turned, shielding our eyes, to see a big black stretch limo pulling up behind the line of official vehicles on the street, the windows already rolling down, replaced by gawking faces.

Great. The judges had arrived.

Chapter 26

Mick strode toward the limo, uttering a string of creative curses that I could hear all the way over where I stood. He pointed at the driver, then back down the street. "You can't be here. Move the car now!" he yelled from the edge of the yard.

No one moved. I could see the limo driver frozen in shock, unsure what to do next, knowing he had a car full of the town's elite waiting to look at some Christmas lights.

Mick turned to the cop standing next to me. "Get rid of them!" he barked.

She sprang to action, heading over to the limo and motioning for it to move. The car didn't. She went around to the window and leaned in. It appeared that the driver wasn't backing down easily. If the situation hadn't been so dire, I would've laughed a little. Clearly the police didn't realize how seriously this contest was taken. Those judges had a job and by God they were going to do it.

While she was arguing with the driver, one of the back doors opened and a figure jumped out. With a sinking heart I realized it was my dad. In all the chaos, I'd kind

of forgotten he was a judge. And anything with an ambulance involved would peak his interest, since it would
typically mean a trip to the hospital.

Although in this case, the hospital wasn't needed. The
morgue was more like it.

"Madalyn!" he shouted, heading over to us, dodging
the other cop, who tried to do an evasive maneuver on
him.

Mick stepped in front of him. "Mr. James—"

"That's my daughter," he said, stepping around Mick
until he could see me. "What's going on?"

"Dad. I'm fine." Still carrying the poor cat, I hurried
over to him.

He gazed at the cat, whose ear was clearly visible
sticking up out of my coat, but didn't ask. "What are you
doing here? Who's hurt?"

"Mr. James," Mick said more firmly. "Maddie's fine.
She's a . . . bystander. Who happened to get involved
somehow," he added with a sidelong glance at me. "But
I'm going to have to ask you to step off the property."

Before my dad could respond, another figure scram-
bled out of the car. Eva Flores. Oh, man. I forgot she and
Donna were friendly.

"Donna?" Eva asked frantically, rushing over to me.
"Where is she? What's happened?"

Mick stepped in front of me. "I'm sorry, I'm going to
have to ask you both to please get back in the car."

"Give me five minutes," I told my dad. "I'll come talk
to you."

Mick shook his head. "This limo is leaving. There's
no five minutes. Sorry, but I have a crime scene here and
I can't have everyone staring at it."

"Crime scene?" the elderly neighbor who I'd nearly
forgotten about yelped. I hadn't even seen him come up
behind me. "What do you mean, a crime scene?"

Eva burst into tears. "What happened?" she wailed again, louder this time.

"I have to echo this man's question," my dad said. "What crime scene? Madalyn?"

Mick's gaze turned toward the sky, as if asking for otherworldly help in dealing with his life right now. He pulled out his radio. "I need extra patrols at 101 East Bay Road." Once the dispatcher had confirmed his request, he put the radio back in its little holster on his shoulder. "Okay," he said, his tone leaving no room for argument. "I need everyone off this property now."

"Dad, it's okay. Go. I'll call you later," I told him.

My dad looked like he was about to argue, but he finally nodded, took Eva's arm, and led her back to the limo. The neighbor shuffled slowly—much more slowly than when he first came over—back across the street.

Mick looked at me.

I pointed at the cat. "Should I put him inside?"

"Sure. Let me take you in. While we're in there, I can make you some tea too," he snapped. "Would that be good?"

"I don't know why you're mad at me. I didn't kill her," I shot back.

Mick sighed, the fight going out of him. "I know. It's just . . . this is gonna be a cluster."

"I know. I'm sorry," I said.

"The house is off-limits for now until I get a sense of what was going on here. It could be part of the crime scene."

I shivered involuntarily. "Mick. Was she . . . strangled with those lights?"

His gaze moved to the street, following the new van that had just pulled up. "Coroner's here now. We need to do an autopsy, and hopefully we can get it done fairly soon. We'll know more then. You know this, Maddie."

He was right. I was, unfortunately, much too aware of
the protocols for a murder on the island. The medical
examiner had an office on the mainland. I knew from
previous experience if the body was taken over on the
ferry tomorrow, depending on the backlog and the ur-
gency, they would probably have an answer early next
week. He turned back to me, his gaze intense. "I get
the feeling you're not telling me something about why
Becky was here."

I sighed. "She was here earlier this morning because
Donna offered her a new job. I don't know why she came
back."

"What kind of a new job?"

I felt like a traitor, but he would know in the next fifteen minutes anyway. I gave him the elevator speech
about the offer for the paper, Donna's proposed new media company, and the role she'd had in mind for Becky.

"So what did Becky decide?"

I looked away. "She said no. But Donna called and she
came back," I reminded him. "Maybe she changed her
mind." I doubted it, but I couldn't read Becky's mind, so
so I couldn't say for sure. Maybe she had given it more
thought.

"Why'd she say no the first time?"

"Because Becky is a journalist. She reports on the
news. Reporting on cats didn't seem like her thing."

He nodded. "Understandable. What was her mindset
on all of this?"

I shrugged, avoiding his eyes. "She was processing it."

"Which means she was mad," he said.

I said nothing.

He turned to walk away.

I grabbed his arm. "Mick. She didn't do anything. You
know that."

He regarded me for a long moment, then shook his head. "Go away, Maddie. I have work to do." He turned and started to walk away.

"What about Becky?" I glanced over to the police car where Craig had brought her.

"I still need to talk to her, so she's going to be here for a bit."

I stood my ground. "I can't go. You told me I could look for the other cat. And who's going to take care of them? Does she have an emergency contact?"

"I don't know. We haven't checked her phone for that yet. Maybe you can take the cats back to the cafe," he suggested.

"I will, if there's no one else. I feel like there has to be someone in her family who would want them." Did Donna have a partner? I realized I had no idea. Other than her professional life, I didn't know much about the woman at all.

"No idea. I'll find out when I reach whoever I can reach, and let you know." He jerked a thumb in the direction of the coroner's van. A woman had just gotten out and was making her way over to him. "Now, do you mind if I go try to do my job?" He strode away without waiting for my response.

I watched him walk over and say something to her, then he rapped on the window of the cop car and motioned toward me. A minute later, Craig got out of the police car and came over.

"I'm going to bring you back to the high school," he said. "I'm going to be tied up for a bit. Would you mind giving Jade a ride home?"

I considered arguing, but I knew Craig pretty well. The more I pushed, the more he would dig in. Understandable given the chaos of the moment and the adrenaline he was probably feeling. Mick was watching too. So I figured I'd play my cards right and let him take me back to the high school so I could get my car.

Then I'd turn around and come right back. Someone had to be there for Becky, after all. I still had a cat stuffed in my coat and another possibly running loose outside somewhere, so that had to be dealt with too. And if I could catch Mick or Craig when they weren't so focused, I'd get better answers out of them. And maybe offer up some helpful theories of my own that could send them in the right direction to figure out who had killed Donna.

I just needed to figure out what those theories were.

Chapter 27

I got in the car to wait for Craig, extracting Simon from my coat and placing him on the seat next to me. He snuggled against my leg, shivering. Poor guy. He must be really confused. I pulled out my phone to text Becky and realized I'd missed a million texts from Lucas. Shoot. I responded, telling him I was on my way back to the high school. Then I texted Becky that I had to go get my car but I'd be back soon.

It took Craig another ten minutes to join me. When he did, he just slid in, started the car, and drove. Neither of us spoke—only Simon punctuated the silence with some dramatic meows—until he pulled up in front of the high school.

"Do not talk about this," he warned.

"I won't. But you know a car full of Christmas contest judges will be desperately trying to figure out what happened."

"Don't remind me. You'll bring Jade home?"

I nodded. "Don't worry. Will you please keep me posted?"

He gave a noncommittal grunt. Better than nothing, I supposed.

I tucked Simon back into my coat and we got out of the car. Craig sped off, back in the direction of Turtle Point.

I watched until his taillights disappeared before I went over to my car and found one of the spare cat carriers I usually kept in the trunk. You never knew when a cat would need rescuing. I put Simon inside with a blanket, then placed him in the back seat. He dug a little hole in the blanket and curled up. I promised I'd be back soon, then headed inside.

I had to tell Lucas what was going on. And Damian. He was going to want to run right over there and collect Becky, and I had to convince him that was a bad idea. I planned to ask the guys to bring Jade home anyway so I could go back.

I texted Lucas as I got back to the gym entrance. The place was packed—I could barely see anything beyond the crowd of people. The Christmas music—a lively rendition of "Jingle Bell Rock"—booming out from the open doors seemed like a stark contrast to the scene we'd just left behind.

Damian and Lucas waited by the door. Lucas pressed a cup of cider into my hands and I took it gratefully, letting the hot liquid warm me. I thought of the first cup I'd had earlier, when my biggest problems were finding tables, bad decorations, and missing event organizers.

"What's going on?" he asked in a low voice, turning slightly away from Damian. "Your texts have been a little cryptic. And I know something's up. There's an undertone in here, like some news is being passed around."

I groaned. "Already? That was fast. Listen." I tugged him out of earshot, holding a finger up to Damian. "Someone killed Donna Carey." I filled him in on what Becky had found and what I'd seen. His face got whiter the more I told him. "They're talking to Becky right now and I'm a little concerned given . . . what was going on."

"Oh, no way, Maddie. I'm sure they're just talking to her because she was there." He hesitated. "Why *was* she there?"

If one more person asked me that question . . . "I don't know. She said Donna called her to come back. But also, Brandon was here earlier. And he said I should tell Becky to basically fall in line with the sale idea."

"Do you think he called her to go back there?"

"I have no idea. She didn't mention him, but she was also in shock. I need to talk to her." I told him what I needed him and Damian to do while I went back to Donna's.

He didn't ask, or protest, or suggest an alternate course of action. He just nodded and gave me a hug, promising to take care of it.

I loved that man.

Damian politely waited for us to finish talking before he came over. "Where's Becky?"

"I have to go back and get her. She got hung up," I said.

"Hung up? On what?"

I ignored his question. "I need to go pick her up, but I need a favor."

"I can come with you," Damian said. "To get Becky."

Lucas cut in. "What do you need?"

"Jade needs a ride home."

"We're on it," he said, looking at Damian for confirmation. I could see him really wanting to protest and demand answers, but his Midwestern politeness took over and he nodded.

"Thanks. I'll meet you at home," I said to Lucas. "And Becky will call you soon," I added, shifting my attention to Damian. I took a big gulp of my cider, noticing my hand holding the cup was shaking, and pulled out my phone to text Jade.

Damian hesitated. "Is there something you're not telling me?" He scrutinized my face. "Are you sure Becky's okay?"

"She's fine." I really hoped I wasn't lying about that. "But I don't want to leave her waiting, so . . ."

He nodded. "Go."

"Thanks." I kissed Lucas, fired off a text to Jade that she should come find Lucas at the door for a ride home, then went to the ladies' room. The place where it had all started a few hours ago.

I took my time, needing a minute to myself to try to calm down and think. I couldn't wrap my mind around what had happened here. I kept hoping I'd wake up and find out it was all just a mistake. Or a bad dream.

Becky hadn't responded to my text, which probably meant she was still taking them through what had happened. Craig and Mick were super-thorough cops, I reasoned. They'd want to go through the whole thing step-by-step to make sure no details were missed. After all, they'd learned from the best—Grandpa.

Grandpa. I should call him. I was sure he'd heard already. Maybe he'd even heard some kind of theory. Or could tell me if Becky really was a suspect.

I finished up, debated going for another hot cider, then decided against it and headed out to the car. I got in, cranked the heat for Simon, and scrolled to Grandpa's number on my phone. When he answered, I blurted out, "Donna Carey is dead."

The heavy silence on the other end told me all I needed to know. Grandpa knew already. It figured.

"I heard the chatter about her address," he said finally.

Grandpa still listened to the police scanner religiously. He had one down in his office, and he must've had someone bring it to his room for the duration of his stay on the main floor of the house. He'd recognize her address and the code that they would use to communicate that there was a murder. "They have a method?"

"They haven't said yet."

I backed out of my parking spot and drove around the back of the high school to the other exit. It was a shortcut to the main road that would lead me back to Donna's. I took the turn around the building probably a little fast and had to jam on my brakes to avoid hitting someone hurrying across the lot to the back door. "Jeez," I muttered, then squinted when I recognized the cute newsboy hat and braids peeking out from under them. Molly Longo. She gave me an apologetic wave. Probably packing up. The bazaar was shutting down. I drove more slowly until I reached the road so as not to hit any other vendors, then hit the gas.

"And how exactly did you come to know about this? I heard there was a civilian on scene. Was it you?" Grandpa asked.

"No. Well, I was, but later." I filled him in on how the whole thing had gone down.

"So Becky found her," Grandpa said.

"Yeah. And then the contest limo showed up. Mick was apoplectic." I winced, remembering my dad and Eva jumping out of the car. Eva's hysteria. And God knew who else had been in that limo. I wasn't even sure who was on the judging committee this year. The mayor, surely, along with other town officials and bigwigs. And they tended to have the biggest mouths of all. This story was going to spread like wildfire.

I wondered if my mother knew yet. She hadn't called,

so maybe not. I hadn't heard from my dad either. He was going to be tied up with this thing for the better part of the night, between the press that would likely descend on the hospital and the contest itself. Murder or not, there were a bunch of other houses that were in the running for the title of Best Christmas Lights this year, and no one would let them out of doing their job. If anything, some of the more contentious competitors might look at this as less competition, at least for tonight. They could be sad tomorrow.

Or not.

They could be happy that one of the top contenders had been eliminated.

I remembered Angelo fighting with the Billingses over the tree. And Camille coming to the cafe to look at our lights. And how beautiful Donna's display had been.

No, I chided myself. No one would kill anyone over a lights display.

But Becky had said someone had been disqualified for sabotaging someone else's lights. Was murder that far beyond? It seemed cold and calculating to think that a person's death would matter less than a made-up award but, unfortunately, human nature continued to surprise and disappoint.

"You said there were Christmas lights around her neck?" Grandpa asked.

I wondered if his brain was going straight where mine was. "Yeah. Grandpa, this contest . . . it seemed so contentious this year. You don't think . . ." I let the words trail into the ether. The whole dynamic of the contest had changed this year. It was no longer for fun now that there was money involved. And twenty thousand dollars could definitely be a motive for murder, whether or not there was an unspoken rule that the winners were strongly encouraged to put the money back into the town coffers. We both could vouch for lesser motives for murder, that was for sure.

Grandpa heaved out a heavy sigh. "I'd love to say no way, but stranger things have happened. You don't know that the lights are what killed her though."

"No. They didn't say yet. But it's a weird coincidence, yes? Although it's hard to imagine that any of our old-timer islanders would care that much about the money. They've been doing this for years because they love it. Isn't that why *you* do it?"

"Of course it is," he said. "But you have to remember, our community is expanding, Maddie. There are new people here who don't have the same attachments we do."

"It does seem like a statement, doesn't it," I said.

"Anything is possible. We have to be careful not to jump to conclusions," he reminded me. "That's a big leap. And there are other things going on with Donna right now."

"Yeah." The newspaper drama. Despite Donna's insistence to us that the potential sale needed to be kept quiet until she'd made a decision, I couldn't help but think perhaps more people knew than she'd let on. "Speaking of that, I'm on my way back to her house to get Becky. Grandpa, do you think she could be . . . in trouble? Given the whole sale thing and everything? I'm kind of worried they're going to fixate on that."

"Why would she be in trouble, Madalyn? A fight is one thing. Murder is quite another."

"I guess," I sighed.

"So do you know why she was there?" Grandpa asked.

I repeated what she'd told me.

"Don't worry, Doll. We'll figure it out."

I really hoped so. Either way, we had another murder on our hands. The last thing we needed around here. At Christmas, too. The Chamber of Commerce was going to have to work a lot harder on their tourism campaigns if this kept happening.

Chapter 28

When I arrived back at Donna's, the activity was still in full swing. The coroner's van, police cars, and Craig's car still crowded the street. Becky's car was still there too. That was a relief. Mick's was gone, though. I wondered if that was a good thing or a bad thing. There was also a white van that I recognized. Elliott Electric. What was Bernie doing here?

Spotlights shined over the yard, lighting it up only a notch or two below Fenway Park during a night game. The crime scene techs were standing by. The paramedics were also standing by. *Why hadn't they taken her away yet?* I wondered. Two patrol cops stood out front, probably to keep away onlookers. Crime scene tape was strung up from the front steps all around the side of the house.

I pulled up behind Craig's car and called Becky. Still no answer—straight to voicemail. I sighed and got out of the car, leaving it on so Simon would still get the blast of the heater. I still had to find his sister. I glanced around. There were lights on up and down the street, and I could see people peeking out behind various blinds and shades. I felt exposed out here.

I headed into the yard, but one of the cops veered over as soon as he caught sight of me.

"Sorry, ma'am, but no one is allowed beyond this point."

The front door opened, and Craig came out onto the front stoop. I froze, hoping he wasn't going to throw me out.

"It's okay," he said to the cop. "She's with me." He motioned for me to come forward. The cop gave us both a skeptical look, but stepped aside.

"Have you seen the other cat?" I asked.

He shook his head. "No. But I've been a little busy."

"Where's Becky?"

He avoided answering. "Did you check in there?" He shined his powerful Maglite into the heavy shrubs lining the front of the house.

I peered into the light. No Becky. No cat, either. "There's nothing there. Can I just check inside? She could be hiding."

"Fine. Make it quick." He led the way up the front steps. He wore gloves and still moved gingerly as he opened the door, although I could see fingerprint dust smearing the doorknob and the frame.

Inside, I paused and looked around. We were in the kitchen. It felt cozy and lived in, like Donna had just stepped out for a moment and was coming right back. Which I'm sure had been the case many hours ago. The room looked like it had been recently upgraded—it didn't match the older vibe of the house. The cabinets were light wood and shined with new polish. An island with matching wood and a sleek, marble top resided in the middle of the room, a stack of mail piled up on one side. A tea kettle sat on the stove. I wondered if Donna had been about to make herself a cup of tea before someone knocked on her door. Or maybe she'd heard something and went outside to investigate.

In the living room to my right, I could see the Christmas tree in all its colored glory, standing in the big picture window. She'd chosen colored lights, and her ornaments were an eclectic mix of sleek silver and delightful kitsch, including a squirrel with a Santa hat, what looked like a handmade Grinch, and two personalized Sphynx ornaments with her cats' names, which she must have had done recently. It was beautiful.

I felt my chest constrict like I was about to cry and turned away. I hadn't known her well, but just the idea that someone's life could end so abruptly was shocking and sad.

"Why haven't they taken her away yet?" I asked.

"Just covering all our bases," he said.

"Why is Bernie Elliott here?" I asked.

"Look for the cat," was all he said.

"Did you guys ever find an emergency contact?" I asked, swallowing the emotion.

Craig nodded. "Her brother. But he's in North Carolina. He can't get here until Monday."

So the cats were definitely coming home with me. "How did he react?"

Craig shrugged. "It's what you'd expect. Her brother was shocked. Said their parents aren't alive, so it's just his wife and daughter and Donna left. They're coming out to take care of things."

"I'll take the cats home until they come," I said. "So where's Becky? You never told me."

He hesitated.

"What?" I demanded.

"Mick took her to the station. To get her statement."

I stared at him, my heart starting to pound again. "Why?"

"What do you mean, why? She's a witness. She has to make it official. You know the drill, Maddie."

I did, but when it was my best friend, it was different. "She couldn't make it official here?" At his stony non-reply, I blew out a breath. "Why didn't she call me?"

"Mick was in kind of a hurry. She didn't have a chance."

"So I need to get her at the station."

"Mick will drive her back."

I shook my head. "She'll want me to pick her up." I didn't know if that was true, but I really wanted to talk to her. "Why were the paramedics checking her out?"

"She was in shock. They wanted to make sure she wasn't injured at all. She declined to go to the hospital."

I studied him. It was a reasonable explanation. Kind of. "Why would she have been injured?"

"They didn't know what had happened here. Better to be on the safe side."

We stared at each other for a full minute until Craig spoke again.

"Jade get home okay?" he asked.

"Lucas took her."

"Thanks. Look, if you want to look for the cat, let's go. I need to finish up here and lock up."

I started my trek through each room, peering under furniture and inside any cubby hole I could find. Craig was on my heels the whole time.

"So, did you find anything interesting?" I asked casually, once I'd cleared the living room, kitchen, and bathroom.

"Not a thing. No fingerprints, no signs of a struggle. Seems like she went outside, either on her own or because she heard something."

"But she left the door open. Which meant she must've been in a hurry. Otherwise she'd have noticed it hadn't closed. She wouldn't have wanted the cats to get out."

Craig nodded. "That's what I thought too."

"Do you know how . . ." My fingers went up to my neck inadvertently, remembering the grotesque sight of a string of blinking lights around Donna's neck.

Craig shook his head once. "Not yet." He must've known he was being much more close-lipped with me than usual, because he added grudgingly, "But it doesn't seem like she was strangled."

My eyebrows shot up. "No?"

"No. There weren't external signs. Some marks on her neck, but not severe enough to suggest that's what happened. And no sign of hemorrhaging. And that's not for anyone else's ears," he warned.

"I know. Of course. So what do you think happened?" I started up the steps, glancing over my shoulder at him.

He opened his mouth, closed it again. We eyed each other.

"Come on, Craig. You know I won't say anything."

"Aside from Becky, do you know anyone who had an issue with Donna?" he asked instead of answering.

The hairs on the back of my neck stood up. "Becky didn't have an issue with her, per se. She had an issue with the idea of her selling the paper. But Brandon Tyson seemed to have an issue with her *not* selling it." I filled him in on what I'd overheard in the hallway of the newspaper offices last night.

At the name, Craig made a face. "She was using *him* as an advisor?" The way he said it made it sound like using Bernie Madoff would've been a better choice.

I smiled a little, remembering Craig beating him up as a kid. "That's what I heard, yes. But also, Brandon's family has a stake in the paper. His father-in-law is an investor." I went into a bedroom. Donna's, from the looks of it. I really wanted to snoop, but Craig was watching me like a hawk.

"Angelo," Craig said slowly, leaning against the door-jamb while I got on my hands and knees and looked under the bed. "That's right. I forgot Brandon's married to his daughter."

"Yeah. And Brandon actually cornered me today. Told me to get Becky on board to make things easier." This house was too darn clean. There was nothing to even see under the bed.

Craig frowned. "Like, he threatened you?"

"Not with anything in particular, but he definitely was trying to strong-arm me." I backed out and sat back on my heels, glancing at him in time to see a muscle in his jaw clench at that.

"So Donna hadn't made up her mind, then."

"It didn't sound like it. But I guess offering Becky a job at this new media company kind of hinted that she had." I got up, grabbing on to the nightstand to haul my-self to my feet. As I did, my hand landed on a piece of paper that looked familiar. And realized it was the same flyer that Katrina had been waving around during her rant about breeders and designer cats.

Had Donna been looking at these insanely expensive cats too? I supposed it was possible since she needed hy-poallergenic breeds. Maybe she wanted more than two.

But then I remembered Sam's phone conversation with the person. The eighteen-thousand-dollar price tag. Could Donna afford that? Maybe she'd be getting enough from the sale to splurge. I wondered what she'd paid for Simon and Sheila.

"What?" Craig asked, noticing my attention had shifted.

"Nothing. Tired," I said, realizing it was true as the

adrenaline rush of the last few hours started to subside. "The lights, though. Do you think it had to do with the contest? Cash prize and all that?"

Craig scrubbed his hands over his face unhappily. "Mick mentioned it, yeah. Which means we're going to have to look at everyone on the roster. See if there was any unfriendly competition going on behind the scenes. But that seems . . . I don't know, obvious."

"I guess, but why else would there be Christmas lights around her neck? What else would they possibly symbolize?" I asked, frustrated. *Unless* . . . I stood up straight. I'd almost forgotten about it until now, but the answer might be right in front of us. I couldn't believe I hadn't thought of it sooner, especially with Bernie's presence. "The electrician."

"Huh?"

"The electrician who has the town contract for the Christmas lights. Todd Banks. He's . . . not so good. He messed up our lights and Grandpa got zapped. That's how he fell off the ladder. And I saw him here. The same day Grandpa fell off the ladder. Lucas and I came by to bring Donna flowers. They were out back arguing. She sounded really mad."

I could see Craig's ears perk up. "They were arguing?"

I nodded. "Eva Flores was here too, but she didn't seem to be involved in the argument. However, Eva had pushed for Todd to get the contract, from everything I've heard, and she would have the power to take it away. And one of the committee members, Camille Billings, was really mad about some of the contract stuff, including the electrician. I think he may have messed up her house too, so it was definitely self-serving. But she was also pushing to get him fired. Even badmouthing my mother in the process. Anyway, maybe when Donna got in his face it was the last straw."

Interest had brightened his eyes now. "Did she have any other connection to this guy?" he asked.

"I have no idea. He and his wife are hosting the party for the judges tonight. All I know is that Eva Flores insisted that they give other people a chance to work this event."

Craig pulled out his phone. "Are we done? I have to make a call."

"There are two more rooms," I said.

He gestured for me to go. "Hurry up," he said, then disappeared into the other room with the phone in his hand.

Chapter 29

I walked slowly out of Donna's house with Sheila huddled in my coat. I'd found her at the last possible minute
before Craig threw me out. The cops didn't pay attention
to me this time when I walked by them. The investiga-
tors had wrapped up in the yard, and the patrol cops
were taking down the lights. The neighbors were probably happy about that. Those things were bright.

The night felt cold and still around me, as if the whole
town had been frozen. I could see the frost in the air in
front of me as I breathed. Somewhere in town there were
probably still festivities going on, but it felt pretty heavy
and not so joyful right here.

Donna Carey, as much of an island institution as her
newspaper, had been murdered. And whether or not it was
the weapon, someone had rubbed salt in the wound—
possibly literally—by wrapping a string of Christmas
lights around her neck. A final *screw you* if I ever saw
one. On the surface, it seemed like an obvious nod to
the contest—someone hoping for the cash prize who
thought Donna was going to keep them from getting
it, perhaps. Someone who, if this was the right theory,
had no intention of donating the money back into the

community coffers. It had to be someone who wanted it. Or needed it.

But Craig could also be right about this being *too* obvious. Someone who knew about the contest, knew the stakes were high or could be high for someone, and tried to make it look like that was the motive. Classic re-direct.

Which also meant the crime had been premeditated. No heat-of-the-moment stuff. I wish I knew how she'd actually died.

Premeditated would not help any case against Becky, if they were trying to build one. And at this very moment she was at the police station going through her story for the umpteenth time about how she felt about Donna since finding out about the potential sale. Since she'd been the one to have stumbled upon her boss's dead body and all. Which, in the privacy of my own mind, I could admit that it didn't look great for her. And I still hadn't heard from her.

But the Brandon Tyson angle couldn't be overlooked. I hated that Angelo would, by default, be part of that possible equation, but who knew what was really going on there? I wondered if Angelo wanted her to sell or not. If he and Brandon were on the same page.

And on the third hand, there was the notorious Todd Banks, who'd definitely had his manhood challenged by Donna just a couple of nights ago. Plus, he kind of looked like a serial killer with that stupid coat and hat. Maybe he'd failed to fix the lights again after their confrontation on Wednesday. Or failed to return at all. Maybe she'd called him back over here the night of the contest with the threat of destroying his reputation along with pulling his contract. She'd heard his van pull up and gone out to meet him, and they'd gotten in an altercation about the lights.

Maybe he killed her in the heat of the moment.

It was a better theory in my mind than the focus on Becky and the newspaper sale. Granted, I didn't know if they were actually worried about Becky as a suspect, but they were asking a lot of questions about the current state of her relationship with Donna. Todd Banks could easily be a person of interest, though. Although if he wanted to make a name for himself on the island, he couldn't exactly go around killing his customers when they were unhappy with his work. Unless he was mentally unstable or something—which of course was entirely possible. And if it was the case, very unlucky for Donna.

I got in the car and transferred Sheila to the carrier with her brother. Simon was huddled in the back, the blanket around him like a cocoon. When Sheila arrived, he immediately started licking her and they snuggled up together.

At least they were happy, for the moment.

As I drove down Donna's street, my phone started vibrating. I'd had it on silent this whole time, figuring it would be ringing incessantly as word started getting around. As I picked it up to see who it was, a tow truck lumbering through its turn nearly sideswiped me. I leaned on my horn, shooting the driver a dirty look. "So not in the mood," I muttered, accepting the call. It was Becky.

Finally.

"Can you come get me?"

"On my way."

When I pulled up in front of the police station, Becky was waiting outside. I could see her shivering even from in the car. "Why were you outside?" I demanded when she got in.

She jerked a shoulder. "I didn't want to be in there anymore." She stared straight ahead, but I could still see her eyes were red from crying.

I cranked the heat as high as it would go and pulled out, heading toward my house. "I'm going to take you home with me. You can stay with us tonight."

She didn't argue. Not a good sign.

"Damian's been calling. You should call him. He's probably frantic," I said. I'd also had a bunch of missed calls from Lucas, my dad, and my mom.

She didn't answer.

"What took so long?" I asked. "What did they want?"

"Mick was full of questions," she said, her voice bitter. She finally turned to look at me. "I think he thinks I killed her."

I forced a laugh, the sound high-pitched and foreign to my own ears. "That's crazy."

"It's not. I was publicly fighting with her. Then I'm the one who 'finds her dead'?" She used air quotes around the words. "Not even just dead. Murdered. I'd probably suspect me too. Plus I was alone for most of the afternoon. I didn't go back to the office after that meeting. I worked from home the rest of the day, and I didn't talk to anyone."

"Not even any reporters?" I asked. That wasn't good.

She shook her head. "Raoul was in, so he was handling the daily stuff." Raoul was the city editor. He mostly worked with the reporters on individual stories, while Becky oversaw the bigger picture of the paper and jumped in on anything front page or more sensitive.

"It doesn't matter," I said, although I wasn't sure that was true. "Donna wasn't having the best week. She had a fight with the electrician too. I saw that. So at least you have some competition." I was only half joking, but she didn't need to know that.

From the back, one of the cats let out an ear-splitting meow that made Becky jump. "What the . . ."

"Donna's cats. I'm taking them home until we figure out if her family will take them."

"Oh God." She closed her eyes. "I feel so bad. How could this happen, Maddie?" Her voice broke and she buried her face in her hands.

"I don't know, Beck," I said grimly. "Someone had to be pretty mad at her."

"Do you think it's because of the newspaper?" she asked, her voice muffled. "Do you think . . . it was Brandon?"

"Why do you think that?" I asked, tensing up.

"Because he was super involved. Taking his role so seriously. He was getting really pushy this morning about Donna making a decision by Monday, and trying to get me to sign the offer. Said if I was in place, it would speed things up once she sold. She finally got annoyed and asked him to leave the room so we could talk."

"How did he feel about that?"

"He was mad. But he went. I assume he listened from the next room."

"Was he still with her when you left this morning?" I asked.

"Yeah. They were probably debriefing on what to do about me," she said bitterly.

I opened my mouth to tell her about Brandon accosting me in the gym today, wanting my help to get her on board, then closed it again. No need to fuel that fire, and I'd at least let Craig know.

The car fell silent except for the soft mewling of the cats from the back seat.

"What do you think is going to happen now?" she asked finally.

I had no idea. "Mick and Craig will figure out who did it," I said.

"How?" She sank lower in her seat. "What if they don't look anywhere else?"

"They are. And maybe we can help. Starting with when you got to Donna's today. This morning, not . . . tonight. Was the electrician there?" I asked. "A guy in a white van? Probably wearing a long leather coat?"

"I didn't see a van or anyone around."

"How long were you there?"

"I don't know, an hour and half? Two hours? Why?"

"Trying to see if this guy was still coming around. If he had screwed something up that bad and couldn't fix it, I'm wondering if there was some kind of altercation."

She shot me a look of disbelief. "You think he murdered her over Christmas lights?"

"It's better than them thinking you did it," I shot back. "Is there anyone else who had a problem with her that you know of?"

"She was the publisher of a newspaper. Tons of people had a problem with her in varying degrees." Becky drummed her fingers on the armrest. "She did get a call while I was there this morning. Stepped out to take it. I was distracted by Brandon's hammering me, but I did hear bits and pieces. Sounded like someone was upset with her, because she had that voice, like she was trying to smooth something over, you know? But I couldn't hear much."

"Was it about the sale?"

She looked at me, helplessness written across her face in the glare of the streetlights we drove under. "I wish I could tell you but I don't know."

I put a brave smile on and patted her arm. "Don't worry. The cops will pull her phone records and figure it out."

Chapter 30

When we got back to the house, the first thing I noticed was that the Christmas lights were still on. Miraculously, none of them were out. And there was a giant, illuminated sign on our front lawn that proclaimed our house as the winner of the annual Daybreak Island Christmas Lights Contest.

Wow. We'd won. The instinctual elation gave way to an irrational worry almost immediately, though. On the off chance that Donna's murder had been related to the contest, I hoped whoever it was wouldn't come after Grandpa for revenge or something. As long as that didn't happen, the news was a little piece of happy after a crappy couple of days. Grandpa would be very pleased, although Donna's death had certainly put a damper on the whole experience.

The second thing I noticed was Damian's car out front. He wasn't letting Becky get away with not talking to him tonight. Good. I hadn't wanted to press her too much tonight, but was worried she was going to stonewall him because she didn't know how he would react.

I unlocked the front door, trying to be quiet, motioning Becky ahead of me and hoping the cats wouldn't scream. But I didn't need to worry—no one was asleep anyway. Grandpa, Damian, Lucas, Ethan, and Val were all waiting in the kitchen even though it was after midnight. JJ and the dogs too. Everyone looked pretty wound up, but Damian looked absolutely frantic. He jumped out of the chair, went straight to Becky and hugged her, then led her out of the room to talk.

"Poor guy," Lucas remarked after they'd left the room. "He was worried."

"I know. She didn't want to call. She's worried everyone thinks she killed Donna."

Val gaped at me. "Why on earth would anyone think that?"

"Long story," I said wearily, setting the carrier down on the floor. JJ immediately went over to investigate. "Donna's cats," I explained. "Figured I'd bring them here so they wouldn't be alone. So what happened at the party?" Val and Ethan had been working the party at Todd Banks' house the whole night, which meant they'd had a front row seat for everything that had happened after the limo full of judges returned.

Ethan let out a low whistle. "Man. It was mayhem. Everyone was freaked. It took a lot of convincing to get them to settle down and vote. Your dad was really upset, Mads. And Eva couldn't stop crying."

I winced. My poor father. And of course he'd had to see me in the middle of the whole thing.

"Maddie. You can't just drop that on us without telling us what happened," Val jumped in. "Why would Becky be a suspect in a murder? Do they know it's a murder?"

"They do." I didn't elaborate. "Was Todd at the party?" I asked.

"I don't think so," Val said. "I never saw him."

I hoped he hadn't jumped on a late ferry and left town. Normally there wouldn't be ferry service in the evenings in winter, but with the holiday event, they'd added two extra runs per day. The last one left the dock at nine.

I met Grandpa's eyes. We'd talked about the Christmas lights being the possible motive, but the Todd thing had hit me later. I didn't know if I should mention it to everyone yet.

He read my mind. "Why don't you all go off to bed," he suggested, looking at Val. "It's been a long night."

"Want me to get the cats settled?" Lucas asked. He was so good at knowing what I was thinking. And right now, I wanted them all to clear the room so I could talk to Grandpa.

"That would be amazing. You can put them upstairs in the—" I'd been about to say Frederick's room, which reminded me that he was still missing. Could this week get any worse?

Of course Lucas didn't need me to finish the sentence. "Got it." He picked up the carrier and headed upstairs.

Ethan and Val both gave me a hug and followed him. Becky still hadn't returned from talking with Damian, but I could hear the low hum of their voices in the next room. It was just Grandpa and me.

After making sure the kitchen door was shut, I sat back down at the table.

"What's on your mind, Doll?" Grandpa asked.

"I was thinking about the lights. I know we talked about the actual contest being a motive, but then I had another thought." I told him about Donna's altercation with Todd and my theory about why he could've been mad enough to kill her. "You have to admit, he seems like a weird dude."

Grandpa thought about this, drumming his fingers on

the arms of his wheelchair. "That's interesting that he was involved with her house," he said. "You heard them fighting about the lights?"

"I heard her say she hired him for a job and he screwed it up. Half her lights were out tonight. We know his work was shoddy at best." Although her lights hadn't actually been out the other night when he was at her house.

He nodded slowly. "I'll see what I can find out about him."

"Good. Also, do you think it's time to tell me what you and Donna were working on?"

He smiled a little. "I figured you'd be asking." He reached into the pocket on his wheelchair and pulled out a notebook. "After all the talk about the sale, I did a little digging."

"And?"

"Angelo Longo bought out the rest of the paper's investors over the past two years."

I stared at him. "Why?"

Grandpa spread his hands. "I assume because he wanted a larger share. Or maybe because he was trying to hedge against something like this happening. Newspapers are a tough bet these days. He might have been trying to protect his assets."

"Did Donna know?"

"The board would have approved it, but yes, she would know."

"So . . . he would've had to approve the sale?"

Grandpa shook his head. "Even with the other shares, he would only have forty percent ownership. But he might've seen it as more leverage, and also a way for him to make some money back if something like this did come up."

"Then Brandon's efforts to get Donna to sell might

have gone against his father-in-law. Unless . . ." I said slowly.

"Unless Brandon had convinced him that selling was in his best interest," Grandpa finished. "She told me Angelo asked Brandon to advise her. And put it in front of the board first, so saying no would be harder for her. I don't think she trusted Brandon. She also told me that she had been trying to buy back the shares that other investors held."

I sat back in my chair. "Wow. So she and Angelo . . ."

"Weren't exactly friends," Grandpa said. "But they had to have a cordial relationship because he was so involved. He got the jump on her and bought out a few of the other investors. She wasn't happy about it."

"When was all this?"

"Over the last couple years or so. I suspect Donna has been thinking about an exit for a while and was just trying to decide the best way to do it."

"She's been planning this?"

Both of us whirled around to find Becky in the doorway, face pale. Neither of us had realized she'd come back into the room. Damian must've gone home.

"I don't know for sure," Grandpa said, holding up a hand. "Just surmising."

"God. I feel like a fool." She sank down into a chair and dropped her head into her hands.

"Why?" I asked. "She wouldn't have been telling her employees anyway, Beck. There's no way you could've known."

She didn't reply.

I turned back to Grandpa. "So this is what you were working on with her? Was it about the sale?"

"Not exactly. She came to me a few weeks ago because she was getting threats."

"Threats? What kind of threats?" I asked. This was new. And sounded important.

Becky's head shot up too as she waited for Grandpa's answer.

"They were somewhat cryptic, but had been escalating. The last one threatened to burn her house down," Grandpa said. "That's when she came to me to see what I could find out."

Burn her house down? Woah. "When did they start?" I asked. "Did she have a theory on what they were about?"

Grandpa sighed. "She was a newspaper person. Unfortunately that happens to people in the media."

Becky looked at me. "Told you."

It was true—she'd just mentioned in the car that newspaper publishers got a lot of flak.

"I get them all the time," she said.

"You do? You've never mentioned that!" I guess I shouldn't have been surprised.

"Donna said she's been getting threats on and off for years," Grandpa said. "People who don't agree with the direction of the reporting, or editorials, the whole drill. So at first she wrote them off. But they were going to her house, not the paper. Which also didn't alarm her at first because again, small town, small island, right? People know you and can't help but know where you live."

"Right," I said, even though it still sounded a little scary to me. If I'd been getting threats for years I didn't think I'd be so blasé about it. Although if it was an ongoing thing and nothing had happened yet, maybe she'd let her guard down.

"Did these particular ones start when she got the offer?" Becky asked.

"Or when the Christmas event kicked off? Was there a catalyst?" I added.

"That's what we were exploring. Unfortunately all these things kind of happened at once."

I was quiet for a minute. "Do you think the threats really were from the murderer?"

"Could be," Grandpa said grimly. "At first it was all about ruining her reputation, that kind of thing. The burning the house down was the last one, and as far as I'm concerned, a whole other ball of wax." He turned to Becky. "Did she tell you anything else that could help figure out who did this?"

Becky hesitated.

Grandpa and I both saw it.

"What is it?" Grandpa asked. "Now isn't the time to be worried about confidences. There's too much at stake."

"I know. I don't even know if it means anything."

"Go on," Grandpa prompted.

"The new media company. She told me it wasn't just fluff. I think she knew that's what I thought, even though I didn't say it out loud. She said that she wanted to be doing investigative reporting. That there were a lot of things about that world that were sketch." She met Grandpa's eyes. "And that there was something potentially tied to our island that she was homing in on that would be her go-live story."

Chapter 31

"Wait. What?" I wasn't following. "Like what kind of sketchy stuff?"

"Like stolen show cats and questionable breeding practices," Becky said.

"Stolen show cats? What does that have to do with the island?"

"Aha. I'm surprised you don't remember this." She pulled her phone out of her pocket and typed, then held it out to me.

I leaned forward and scanned the page. It was a story from our newspaper. A female cat named Jasmine, who was apparently something called a Rustic Rosette Lynx, had vanished from the Airbnb property where her family was staying in Daybreak Harbor. The family swore the place had been sealed up tight and Jasmine was in her crate when they'd gone out. She was gone when they returned home.

That was wild enough, aside from the fact that I'd never heard of a Rustic Rosette Lynx. But the part that had my mouth falling open was the owner's insistence that Jasmine was worth one hundred thousand dollars.

They'd contacted the police, canvassed the area, and

put out pleas for her safe return. They even offered a reward of twenty thousand dollars for anyone with any information. Two pictures of a beautiful, exotic cat accompanied the photo. At first glance, she looked like a pretty regular cat. But the side profile photo gave her the appearance of a small leopard with perfect spots that were more reddish orange than brown.

It had happened in late August, which explained why I hadn't paid enough attention for it to be seared into my brain. August had been one of our busiest months at the cafe, and even though I'd never tell Becky, I didn't actually read the paper every day. But now that I was reading the story, it rang a bell. Someone had mentioned it to me, I was sure of it. Which wasn't actually surprising. People naturally wanted to fill me in on anything cat related.

I glanced at the byline and was surprised to see Alice Dempsey's name. Alice had been writing for the paper for a while, it was true, but she usually wrote obits and her helpful household tips column. Becky had never mentioned that she had been branching out to other things, but it must be part of her new role supporting Donna directly. Although now she would no longer have that gig.

"Alice?" I asked.

Becky nodded. "Donna's got her dabbling in writing too."

"I wonder if she has any other info she's sitting on," I said.

"Could be," Becky said. "I'll ask her. Donna told me she's been investigating this and other things possibly related for a while. She told me she's really close to breaking the story."

Bells were going off in my head now, though. "You know, I did see that same flyer at Donna's last night," I said.

"Flyer?" Becky asked.

"The one that's been showing up all over town, offering exotic cats. The one that showed up on our telephone pole again after someone broke in and stole the cat. Don't even ask," I said, holding up a hand when Becky's mouth fell open. She hadn't even heard that story yet. I'm surprised her cops reporter hadn't picked up on it, but maybe Mick had asked them to stand down. "Do you think her having a flyer from an expensive breeder had anything to do with the story? Or do you think she was just looking for more cats for herself?"

"I have no idea," Becky said.

"Why hasn't she broken the story yet?"

"She probably had a few loose ends to tie up. She was trying to sell me on needing my help. Alice has been working with her, but she hasn't broadened it out because she's trying to be discreet about this. But Alice is pretty new to investigative journalism so she said she could use someone like me since she didn't want to give anything away by getting directly involved in speaking to people herself. Honestly, I wasn't sure if she was just trying to get me on board any way she could."

"Oh, she was serious," Grandpa said.

I glanced at Grandpa. "You knew about this?"

He nodded. "I was getting to it," he said, when he saw my mouth open to ask why he hadn't said anything. "She mentioned some recent reporting that could have perpetuated the threats last time we met. Which was right before this stupid accident." He gestured to his leg. "I told her to get me whatever she had and I'd look into it. When I saw her the day I came home from the hospital I asked her where it was and she said she felt bad throwing that at me when I was recovering. I told her to stop being silly and get it to me, since I had nothing but time to work on it. I wanted to see if I could track it to the threats."

"And did she?" The party had been Thursday. After she'd left our house, she'd been back at her office, which was where Becky and I ran into her and Brandon. Had she had time to put it together before she was killed the next night?

Grandpa shook his head. "I haven't gotten anything from her."

"How would she have sent it?"

"Probably email. But I never got one from her after . . . that last time I saw her."

"You're sure?" I asked. "You checked your spam folder?"

That earned me another *Do you think I'm stupid* look. "Yes, Madalyn."

"I'm just asking." I slumped in my chair. "Did she share any of the reporting with you?" I asked Becky.

Becky shook her head, looking chagrined. "I was too busy dismissing everything she was saying. And then Brandon came back and she clammed up. She definitely didn't want him to hear what she was telling me. I got the sense she was keeping this new venture very close to the vest."

"And no names, I'm guessing."

"Nope."

"Awesome. So now we have four motives for why she was killed." I held up as many fingers. "The possible sale, the contest, the electrician, or a cat exposé." I wished I had a whiteboard like the cops did on all the TV crime shows.

"What contest? The Christmas lights?" Becky asked.

I nodded.

She burst out laughing, which I thought was more from nerves than actually finding it funny. "Are you serious?"

"There was money involved," I said with a shrug.

"Not even just the money. It's prestigious." Grandpa sighed and rubbed a hand over his face. "It's a stretch, but it's possible. She was definitely in the running for the top slot. Hopefully they don't think *I* killed her." He said it tongue in cheek, but now I was paranoid.

"Don't even joke."

"What about the people who got caught sabotaging another contestant's house?" I asked Becky. "Any update on them?"

"They're waiting to see if the person is pressing charges. I think they left the island for the winter, though."

"And it wasn't Donna whose house got sabotaged."

She shook her head no.

"Did anyone else know about the threats?" I asked. "Did she report them to the police?"

"She didn't. But she did tell me Angelo knew."

"How?" I asked.

"She told him. He came to her office to talk. She dropped that bomb on him kind of unexpectedly to see his reaction. She said he seemed genuinely surprised."

Angelo again. He kept popping up in this thing. Coincidence? He was generally a nice guy with a good reputation. But he had a temper—that was obvious. He was also a top contender in the Christmas light contest, and he took it seriously. The tree farm fight with Camille Billings and her husband showed that, not to mention his attitude toward her at the gym during setup. He seemed fine later in the night, though.

Later in the night. After he'd returned from wherever he'd disappeared to.

"Grandpa," I said slowly. "Angelo was at the high school with me yesterday for a while setting up. But when things got busy and the tables were delivered and the vendors came, he disappeared. I didn't realize it until I'd gone looking for him when I was leaving."

"Did he come back?" Grandpa asked.

I nodded. "Before the bazaar got started—and right before Becky called me. He said he'd gone to get more supplies, but he was empty-handed."

"So we need to know where he was for certain," Grandpa said. "And Brandon, for that matter."

"Maybe I can talk to Molly. Angelo's daughter." She was caught in the middle of this thing between her husband and her father. I just wondered if she'd be open to talking about any of it.

But something told me that talking to me might be more appealing than talking to the cops.

"And the electrician," I added. Since he hadn't been at the party at his own house, his whereabouts were currently unknown as well.

Grandpa nodded. "Yes, talk to Molly. I'll see what I can find out tomorrow about how Donna died. Or how they think she died." Which was an important distinction because it would be a couple of days at least until they had the final verdict from the medical examiner. But they'd be working the case based on their theories in the meantime, and method would play into theory. "And what the current theory is on a motive."

"We should try to find her computer," I said to Becky. "Or any files she had on this stuff."

"If she had a computer at her house, I'm sure the cops grabbed it," Grandpa said.

"But maybe not files." A plan was blooming. Maybe I could go back over there under the guise of picking up something for the cats and see what I could find.

Becky was reading my mind, because she was nodding. "I can see if I can check her office at the paper too," she said. "I'm sure I can weasel my way in there."

"Just be careful," Grandpa warned. "Both of you. You can push the limits, but don't make enemies of the police. They won't share what they have with us."

"You got it," I said.

"Good. I'll call Mick this morning. Clue him in about the threats and see if that gets them going," he said.

I nodded, hoping it would get them pointed in a different direction than Becky.

Chapter 32

I probably got two hours of sleep before I was shaken awake at what felt like an ungodly hour. I sat straight up, disoriented, to find Becky holding on to my arm. Her eyes were dark, and her curly hair was pulled up into a messy ponytail. She looked like she'd slept even less than me.

"You have to take me to my car. I have to go to work," she hissed in a loud whisper.

"Right now?" I searched blearily for a clock, blinking at the numbers. It wasn't even seven a.m.

"We have to put something out on Donna. Before the Boston papers get a hold of the story. We have to be the first one to report this. It's her news outlet. How would it look if we didn't? Also my boss just called me. Freaking out. There's an emergency management meeting at eight." She leaned in conspiratorially. "I also want to check her office for anything on the cat stuff and I'll be able to do that more easily if not that many people are around."

Right. That was important. I forced myself awake, since there'd be no convincing her to get back to bed. Becky was wound tight about work on regular days. She'd be an absolute nightmare to go up against today. Lucas was still asleep next to me, so I threw the covers off and followed her into the hall. I had a splitting headache and definitely needed coffee.

Once we were in the hall with the doors closed, she turned to me. "Also, someone leaked the news about the potential sale. Rick just told me. He's kind of shocked. About both things, of course, but the sale threw him for a loop. Guess she really hadn't told him."

"Wow. Who do you think did that?" We both looked at each other and said in unison, "Brandon."

"I wouldn't put it past him," she said. "It might force her brother into making a quick decision to offload it. He's the only family she has."

I knew Becky hadn't killed Donna, but at that moment I wouldn't put it past her to murder Brandon.

"When you drop me at her house to get my car, you think you can get inside to check for . . . anything?"

"I'll do my best. Give me five minutes." I didn't bother changing out of my flannel Scottie dog Christmas jammies. I brushed my teeth, splashed water on my face, and put my hair in a bun. Ethan, beautiful man that he was, had set the coffee on a timer for six this morning just in case anyone was crazy enough to be up after going to bed in the middle of the night, so there was coffee in the kitchen. I poured it into the biggest travel mug I could find and pulled on a pair of UGGs, and we headed outside.

I pushed open the door to the porch and nearly screamed when I came face-to-face with some guy I'd never seen before. Becky ran into me from behind, causing coffee to splash out of the top of my travel mug all over my pajamas and onto the porch. The guy was startled too—he dropped the tape measure he was holding with a clatter.

"Whoa. Sorry, miss," he said, holding up a hand. "Didn't mean to disturb. We wanted to get the banner up."

"No problem," I said, pressing a hand to my pounding heart. "What banner?"

He gave me a funny look. "The winner's banner. For the lighting contest. It's a new thing this year," he explained. "The winner gets a banner to display." He picked up his tape measure and nodded at the front of the house. "So, any preference on where you want it?"

Becky made a frustrated noise and pushed past me, hurrying out to the car.

I shook my head. "No. Wherever you think. You're the expert."

He gave me a funny look, but shrugged as if to say, *Whatever, it's too early for this.*

I felt his pain. I pulled the door shut behind me, making sure it was locked, then joined Becky. She waited outside the car, hands shoved in the pockets of her puffer coat, shoulders hunched miserably against the cold. It had gotten colder overnight, a warning of what was to come as we got further into December. I shook the excess drops of coffee off me and unlocked the doors.

We got in and I blasted the heater. The car was slow to start. I really had to look into getting another one soon.

"Do you think the cops have her computer? She probably had a lot of audio files. So they're probably in the cloud somewhere if we can't find it." Becky didn't look up from her phone, where she was texting or emailing the whole drive.

I was slugging what was left of my coffee, needing to chase this headache away so I could think clearly. "Don't forget to check with Alice," I said.

She nodded. "I'll keep you posted on what I find out." She glanced up as we pulled in front of Donna's house. Then she sat up straighter. "What the . . ."

I searched the street, looking for whatever had caught her attention. It took me a second to realize I wasn't looking *at* something. It was the absence of something. Becky's car, which had been parked in front of Donna's, was gone.

Becky swore under her breath. "Where's my car?"

I scanned the street as I pulled over on the opposite side. Aside from a couple of cars at neighboring houses parked in driveways, the street near Donna's was empty of vehicles except for a police car. "I have no idea."

We both pulled our phones out at the same time. I had a sudden flash of recognition in my newly caffeinated brain of seeing a tow truck pulling onto the street last night. And Craig's sudden insistence that I hurry up and leave at the end of the night. I thought it was because he wanted to leave himself, but he must've known the tow truck was about to arrive and didn't want me to see it. I texted him.

Where's Becky's car?

I impatiently waited for the dots to appear signaling he was answering. I wondered if he'd still be asleep. I shouldn't have worried. Murders usually meant the couple of detectives on the force didn't sleep much.

It's at the station's impound lot.

My eyes almost popped out of my head. I glanced over at her. She'd called Damian to ask if he'd picked it up for her, from what I could tell from her side of the conversation, and he of course had just told her he hadn't.

WHY?????? I texted back.

Standard procedure, he returned. *All non-resident cars near the scene were towed. We'll let her know when it's released.*

Once again, I had so many questions. But not with Becky sitting here. "I found it," I told her. "It somehow got towed to the police station. They'll release it later, Craig said."

"What?" she screeched. "Why?"

"They were getting rid of the non-resident cars on the street," I said, trying to make her feel better.

She wasn't buying it. She stared straight ahead, a muscle in her jaw working. "Can you just take me to work?"

I did as she asked since I didn't think I'd be able to sneak into the house with the patrol car parked out front anyway. When I pulled up in front of the newspaper building, there was a whole shrine of pictures and candles and other tribute paraphernalia on the sidewalk in front. A few people lingered, heads bowed.

"Thanks," she said, reaching for the door handle, but I grabbed her arm.

"Wait. Should I come with you to check her office? It's so early. Probably no one is around."

"Brilliant," she said. "Let's go. Park around the corner so no one sees your car."

"Good idea." I found a spot in the alley two streets away and parked. We got a couple of strange looks from the people at the vigil, probably because of my pajamas, but we hurried past them. Becky let us in and we took the stairs to the executive floor.

"Wait here. I'll be right back." She raced up the rest of the stairs to the newsroom. True to her word, she reappeared two minutes later and motioned me to follow her.

We slipped into the hall where we'd been the other night, listening to Donna and Brandon. Everything was quiet, the kitchen area dark and all the office doors closed.

"Who else has offices down here?" I asked in a whisper.

"HR, the billing people, the head of ad sales. No one will be here today." She marched purposefully down the hall to Donna's office.

"Will you be able to get in?" I asked.

"You mean do I have a key? No. But I have Rick's." She grinned and held up a bunch of keys. "He always leaves them in his desk."

"Nice."

"Let's go. He'll be here any minute." She unlocked the door and went in. I followed, locking it behind me.

Becky flipped on the light and grinned. "Laptop is here. She must've left it when she was arguing with Brandon that night and never came back Friday. I know that aside from meeting with me she was taking the day off anyway. She said she was still prepping for the contest." She opened the laptop and powered it on.

Of course, it asked for a password.

"Crap." She flipped through some papers and Post-its on the desk.

"You think she wrote it down?" I asked.

"No, but you can hope, right? Shoot." She slammed the lid.

"I expected that," I said, holding out my hand. "Give it to me."

She stared at me. "You want to take her computer?"

"Yeah." I had a plan. "I can bring it back in a bit. But I think I know how I can get us into it."

"I don't want to know. I could be in enough trouble already." I could see the mental ping-pong going on in her head: Take it? Leave it? Finally she turned away. "Take it, but I don't want to be involved."

I grabbed it and slid it into my bag as she started checking drawers in the desk. I didn't expect her to find much in there, but the computer had to be a goldmine.

Unless there was a personal computer that was actually missing. "Do you think she just uses this for this job?" I asked, tapping my bag.

"I have no idea, but she has this computer." Becky motioned to the Apple desktop. "And an iPad. If it was at her house, the cops probably have that."

"Okay, let's see what I can find out," I said.

"Well, I hope you find something because there's nothing here." She slammed the last drawer in frustration and turned to the file cabinet. It was small, a slate-gray two-drawer version with no lock, which wasn't promising—it meant she didn't care if people got into it. Becky took the files from one drawer, I took the files from the other. The only things in there were newspaper-related contracts and other administration stuff. Nothing even related to the investors. No offer letter from the mysterious company that wanted to buy the paper.

Just normal everyday paperwork.

Becky stuffed the files back in and closed the drawer. "That was kind of useless."

"Let's see what we have on the computer first," I reminded her.

"I'm dying to know how you're going to get into that. But please don't ever tell me." She glanced at her phone as it vibrated. "Shoot. Rick just texted that he has coffee and is on his way upstairs. I have to get his keys back in his drawer before he gets here."

She motioned for me to go and shut the lights off.

We froze as voices filtered down the hall.

"Crap! Hide!" she hissed at me.

I stared at her. "Where?" There was literally nowhere to hide in here.

"Under the desk," she said. "Go."

Jeez. I hurried over and crawled into the little space under Donna's desk, hoping my jammies weren't visible, since the bottom frame didn't reach all the way to the floor.

Becky held still at the locked door, holding her breath. The voices got closer—a woman's and a man's.

"Let me just find my keys," the woman's voice was saying. "They're right . . . oh, shoot!"

I tried to strain my ears to hear better. The voice sounded familiar. Was it Alice?

"I'm so sorry," I heard her say. "I left my other key ring at home. I'm going to have to track down another set of keys. I'll just be a minute. Why don't you come with me and I'll get you some coffee? It's so early."

"Thanks. Sure, that will be great." The man's voice rang clearly through the door and I felt my stomach twist. Craig.

The footsteps receded and the voices faded away. Becky waited a minute, then another, then opened the door and peeked out. The hall was dark and quiet.

"Let's go," she hissed, and I crawled out and hurried out after her. She locked the door and we raced down the hall, pausing to check the elevator bank and stair landing before busting out. Coast was clear.

I turned to go down the steps. Becky turned to go up.

As I hit the landing and went to open the door to the street, the door to the reception office on the bottom floor opened, scaring me half to death. I froze, praying it wasn't Craig. He'd be super suspicious about why I was here so early.

But Alice Dempsey was smiling at me. She was alone. "Use this door, hon," she said, pointing to the door that any member of the public had to use to get in. "Looks less suspicious if anyone sees you."

I breathed a sigh of relief. "Thanks, Alice. Where's—"

"Don't worry about it." She winked.

I wasn't about to look a gift horse in the mouth. Especially since I had Donna's laptop, which felt super conspicuous in my bag. I slipped by her gratefully and hurried to my car, happy that Becky had had the foresight to get me to park out of sight. Otherwise, Craig would definitely have seen my car and been on the lookout for me.

Chapter 33

Back in my car, I blasted the heat, looked around to make sure no one was watching me, then pulled the laptop out and shoved it under my seat. I had a stop to make, and I couldn't have it in my bag when I did.

Because I was still thinking about Becky's car being taken to the police impound lot, even if it had seemed to slip her mind, at least for the moment. Had they really taken all the cars—I hadn't even noticed if there were others—or had they taken *her* car? I needed to talk to Mick.

Before I drove over there, I took out my phone and texted Bones.

Call me. ASAP.

I shook off the guilt of what I was about to do—really what we'd already done by taking potential police evidence out of Donna's office, even though I planned to return it as soon as possible. Although I wasn't sure how I would do that without arousing suspicion given that Craig would have already been in the office and not seen the computer. For it to miraculously reappear, well, we'd have to think about that. But I had a hunch I could tap into Alice for that one. She had clearly saved our butts by diverting Craig so we could escape. I'd forgotten how good Alice was at keeping secrets.

I didn't expect to hear from Bones for a while—it was still basically the middle of the night in California—so I tucked my phone in my bag and drove to the police station. I parked haphazardly out front and marched inside with a confidence that belied my coffee-stained Scottie dog pajamas, which I'd forgotten I was still wearing until I saw the cop behind the bulletproof glass at the front desk staring at me and glanced down at my own outfit.

"What?" I snapped. "Everyone goes out in pajamas these days. Especially at Christmas. I need Mick Ellory."

He didn't even argue with me. Probably because he thought I was crazy. Instead he picked up the phone, spoke for a moment, then buzzed me in. They knew me well here. I wish I could say it was because of Grandpa. It partly was. But it was mostly because of all the stuff I happened to get involved in.

I knew where Mick's office was and headed down the hall. Just as I reached it, a giant redheaded man in a flannel shirt emerged, pulling the door shut behind him.

"Bernie," I said, surprised. "What are you doing here?"

Bernie Elliott broke into a grin and reached out to pump my hand. "Your granddad won the contest," he said by way of greeting. "That made my day. I was happy to help. I like to think I pushed it over the edge for him." He leaned in conspiratorially and said, "I had some extra lights in my truck and I did a little something-something for him to make it really pop." He gave me a thumbs-up.

"Thank you. Yes, he was happy. But what—"

"I had to consult on something. And give an expert statement." He looked proud of himself. "The lieutenant there asked me to come in and look at some evidence." He jerked his thumb toward Mick's office.

"Maddie." Mick was suddenly in the doorway. "You needed to see me?"

"Yeah," I said.

He held the door wider. "Come on in. Thanks again, Bernie," he said, clearly dismissing him.

Bernie gave a sheepish wave, then hurried out.

"What was that about?" I asked. I trusted Mick to bring me in as much as he could on this. He was still a by-the-book cop, of course, but there had been instances where he'd bent the rules a bit. At first he'd not wanted me involved in any parts of his investigations. But now, he'd started bringing me into the fold if a situation called for it. I wouldn't say he treated me like a partner—maybe a subordinate. But that was fine with me, as long as I could be part of the solution if I had anything that could help.

Mick sat down behind his desk and motioned for me to take a seat. I could see him looking at my outfit with some amusement.

"Don't say anything," I warned before he could comment.

"I have nothing against Christmas pajamas," he said with a shrug. "Maybe I'll get Katrina a pair. Where did you get them?"

"Don't be cute. Why was Bernie Elliott here? Something to do with Donna?"

"I'm guessing that's not why you came by, since you wouldn't have known he was here," Mick said dryly.

"It's not, but I'm still curious."

He said nothing.

"Fine. Why did you impound Becky's car?"

Mick sighed, scrubbing his hand over his face. He looked like he'd been up all night. "Maddie. I'm investigating a murder. Any car that was part of a crime scene needs to be looked at. That neighborhood has strict parking rules anyway."

Because of the beach. That was true—but it hardly applied in winter. I sat down heavily in the chair across from him. "You really think Becky had something to do with this? That's insane, Mick."

"I didn't say that. But we have to look at every angle." He spread his hands wide. "Her livelihood is at stake. That's a pretty big motive, wouldn't you agree?"

"Well, killing her boss wouldn't make it any less at stake," I pointed out.

He inclined his head in acknowledgment. "Possibly true, but in the heat of the moment, that's not really what angry people think about. And you have to admit, she doesn't have a great alibi. Home alone working is hard to verify."

"What are you looking for in her car? A signed confession?" I asked, exasperated. "You don't even know how Donna died yet."

He said nothing.

That surprised me. "Do you?" The coroner's office wasn't that fast. Especially since they needed to do the exam off-island since they didn't have an actual morgue here.

"You're too close to this one, Maddie. I can't discuss it," he said.

"Too close?" I laughed. "Really? Just because she's my friend? Come on, Mick. She would never. Have you talked to Todd yet? That's who you should—" I leaned forward. "Is that why Bernie was here? Something to do with Todd?"

Mick glanced at his watch. "Anything else? Because I've got a lot on my plate today."

"You're really not going to tell me anything?"

"You're not a cop, last I checked," he said, exasperated. "When we talk about cases, it's because it's beneficial to me. Not because I'm that into sharing."

"It can be mutually beneficial," I insisted.

"Really? How?"

"Because I heard Donna talking to—no, yelling at—the other electrician. Didn't Craig tell you?"

Mick nodded. "He did, actually. That was good information. Thank you."

I hissed out a frustrated breath. "Brandon Tyson in his starring role as advisor on this sale? His father-in-law, Angelo Longo, also an investor in the paper?"

He was looking at me with some amusement. "Got all that too. Thank you."

"Okay, then." I crossed my arms over my chest. "What about the cat scandal?"

Now he cocked his head at me. "Excuse me?"

"The cat scandal. A big story she was about to break on her new media platform."

"Whoa. Back up. New media platform?"

I smiled triumphantly. "See? Mutually beneficial."

He sighed. "Tell me."

"Will you tell me what the deal is with Todd if I do?"

"There is no deal with Todd. We'll question him today. So tell me about the cat scandal."

I gave him the elevator speech of what I knew from Becky about Donna's new venture. But I was disappointed when he didn't look impressed.

"Interesting, but not as high on my list as a motive,"

he said. "Her actual newspaper business seems like much more high stakes to me."

I didn't disagree, but I was worried about tunnel vision. Which I didn't want to say out loud because he'd be insulted and probably throw me out.

"Okay, but I wanted to share. Full transparency," I said.

"Right," he said with a small smile. "Thanks."

"And I'm guessing you already heard from Grandpa?"

"He called, but I haven't talked to him yet," Mick said. "Why?"

"He has information. He was working with Donna on something," I said.

"On what?"

"He'll have to tell you. Also, Becky mentioned someone called Donna during their conversation yesterday morning, and said it sounded like Donna was trying to smooth something over. I'm guessing you're checking her phone records?"

"Gee, I hadn't thought of that," Mick said snarkily, standing up. "Thanks for the visit, but I have to get back to work. If that's okay with you," he added.

"Fine." I shoved my own chair back and stood. "Do you know around what time she died?" I asked.

He frowned at me. "If I tell you, will you leave?"

"Promise."

"Initial thoughts are somewhere between four thirty and six thirty."

I filed the information away in my brain as I turned to go, then glanced back at Mick. "Don't fixate on Becky. Look at all these other people and things going on in Donna's life. She was a busy lady. And it sounds like she was definitely ruffling a lot of feathers."

"I got it," Mick said with a dismissive nod.

I paused at the door. "Any luck on the catnapping?"

"No. And you know I have to shift my focus now to this."

Of course I'd known that, but it made me super unhappy to hear it. I didn't bother responding. I shut the door behind me a little harder than necessary.

Chapter 34

Saturday
7:45 a.m.

I left the police station with as much dignity as my Scottie dog jammies would allow and headed to my car. When I got out to the parking lot, I saw Bernie Elliott's van still parked at the far end. I hadn't noticed it in my mad rush when I'd first arrived. I changed course, went over, and peered inside. Bernie was doing something on his phone. I reached out and knocked on the window.

He glanced up, then grinned and rolled the window down. "Everything alright, Maddie? Need more lights set up?"

At least he liked his job. I nodded. "Fine. Just curious about what they wanted you to consult on. I'm so fascinated by people who get asked to help with police investigations!" I put what I hoped was just the right amount of gush into my voice. I didn't want to sound over the top. But I guessed that Bernie couldn't resist talking about it either. He seemed to take great pride in his work and being recognized as good at it.

I was right.

"Well . . ." He peeked into his rearview mirror as if he thought Mick might storm out and yell at him. "It's about this murder." Bernie dropped his voice lower and leaned forward emphatically. "That poor lady. Donna. They think someone rigged her lights."

"Rigged her lights? What do you mean?" I wasn't following.

"You know. So she got electrocuted."

My eyes widened. "What?"

"Yeah. They think that's how she died." He looked positively excited at the news.

I thought about Grandpa's zap and subsequent fall from the ladder and shuddered. "Then wouldn't it be an accident?"

"Well, it coulda been. If the brand-new wire hadn't been frayed so neatly." He looked triumphant at that little bombshell.

My face must've shown my confusion. He held up a finger, then reached into his passenger seat. I could see a giant mess of tools, wires, and other electrician-looking paraphernalia jumbled together—one pile on the floor and another on the seat. Bernie tossed a few things aside before he pulled out a string of Christmas lights from the jumble on the floor.

"So this is a busted set. This is my trash pile," he explained, waving at the floor. "But you see here?" He showed me the bottom of the lights where the plug was. "See how it's flat?"

I nodded.

"Okay." He grabbed another piece of wire and showed me the end of it. "Now see this?" He pointed at a small piece where the outside coating was gone, showing me the guts of the wire.

I nodded again.

"So if this happens down here"—he held up the Christmas lights and pointed at the bottom part—"and it got frayed like that, no one would even notice it. So if you go to plug it in and your feet are wet, boom. You're a goner."

I totally wasn't following. "I don't see how—"

"Donna was in a puddle of water and her hand was still holding the plug," Bernie explained. "And it appeared that the lights were new. So the only way they could be frayed would be if—"

"Someone did it on purpose," I finished grimly.

"Right." He nodded. "Now you got it. First, weird that there's a puddle of water right there and nowhere else in the yard. The snow was pretty icy and wouldn't have melted on its own."

This was sounding more sinister all the time. "You think someone, what? Melted the snow so there would be water there, knowing she would come out and see the plug on the ground and go plug it in?"

"Bingo." Bernie pointed at me. "So she's just focused on the lights being out, the contest is starting, she sees the plug and picks it up. Then she plugs it in, and there's probably no GFI protection since it's an old house." He shrugged. "Boom. Seen it happen a hundred times."

"GFI protection?" I asked.

"Ground fault interrupter. Basically, it grounds the electricity so it doesn't shock you. But she didn't have that."

"So she got the shock."

"Sounds like," Bernie agreed.

That sounded terrible. "And then, what? Someone wrapped the working lights around her neck?" I asked. "If she was already . . . she was on the ground. How could they?"

Bernie shrugged. "Not hard. They could've picked her head up and slipped them on."

"Wouldn't they have gotten zapped too?" A thought struck me. "Becky. She touched her when she got there. She told me she felt for a pulse. How come she didn't get zapped?"

"Good question!" He looked proud. "That power source was disconnected."

I frowned. "How?"

"Seems like after they knew she was dead, they killed the power. No pun intended. You know, to prevent someone else from getting hit. Considerate, I guess," he said. "Clearly they didn't want anyone but her to get hurt."

"Isn't that complicated?" I asked.

He guffawed. "You just turn the breaker off. Only complicated thing is figuring out where the box is. The electrical box," he said at my blank look. "Where all the breakers are. And if you have any sense in your head, all your breakers are labeled."

So someone had shut the breaker off to that particular power source—once they knew she was dead. "Is that why the lights on that whole side of the house were out?" I asked.

"Bingo," he said.

"But then how were the lights around her neck on?"

"Different plug, different breaker," he said.

"That's why your van was there," I said, that connection finally dawning on me.

"Yup. They needed someone to make sure it was safe before they went near the body. The paramedic spotted the wire in her hand and alerted the police. They called me." His chest puffed out a little with pride.

I let that sink in. Talk about premeditation. Anyone with that cool of a head, to go in search of the breaker box and switch it off to prevent any other injuries, had to know what they were doing. And definitely had thought ahead. "So are they looking at . . . anyone in particular?" I asked. "Like the other electrician? Wouldn't he be the obvious offender? He would know how to do that."

Bernie's expression turned dour. "They weren't telling me none of that. But honestly, you don't need an electrician to do that kind of thing. You take a little knife like this"—he scanned the cab of the van then pulled a pocketknife out of his cupholder—"slice off half an inch of wire, and you're good to go. My five-year-old nephew can figure that out from watching YouTube." He rolled his eyes at this. "It's no wonder so many people get killed trying to do electrical work. Think they can watch a couple videos and they're a master electrician all of a sudden," he grumbled.

"They're sure it was tampered with?" I said dubiously, knowing the question would make a whole lot more sense without the necklace of Christmas lights. "I mean, it could've been a bad set of lights. And if Todd Banks had brought them over, who knows, maybe they weren't even new? He was there working on her stuff. I saw him."

Bernie cocked his head at me. "He was? You sure about that?"

"I saw him at her house. She was yelling at him about a bad job."

"Hmm. I don't think that's why he was there, because she never uses anyone but me. Listen, I'd be happy to sign that guy's license revocation myself. But the string they showed me looked pretty new. Gotta follow the story chapter by chapter."

"Yeah. I guess you do." I wanted to ask him more, but I caught sight in his rearview mirror of two cops walking out of the building. They both glanced at us curiously as they headed to their cars. It could have been my pajamas, but I was feeling kind of exposed. I didn't want Mick to see us talking. "Thanks, Bernie," I said. "And thanks again for helping at the house."

"No problem." He waved and drove out of the lot.

I got back in my car and sat there for a long time. This whole thing was just weird. And kept getting weirder. Craig had totally kept this from me last night, although I understood he had been concerned for everyone's safety when he'd come upon the scene. I wondered how he'd known what they were walking into. And no wonder Becky had to be checked out. She was really lucky that the power source had been disconnected when she went to check on Donna. He must have told her not to say anything about it, even to me, because it might be the detail they were holding back from the press. Although she was the press.

But then I realized with a sinking feeling in my gut that maybe that looked even worse for her. They would wonder if it had been sheer luck the power wasn't on—or if she had known it wasn't on. Although my best friend did not have any electrical knowledge that I knew of, nor would she have any reason to know where Donna's electrical box was. But Bernie had said a five-year-old could go on YouTube and figure some of this stuff out, which also wasn't very reassuring. And most people's breakers were somewhere in the basement. It probably wouldn't be hard to find, especially if it was an unfinished basement.

The other odd thing I'd picked up from Bernie was that it sounded like he didn't think Todd had been doing electrical work for Donna. But Todd had been doing some sort of job. What then? Landscaping? Maybe setting up the rest of her decorations? What else could he have been doing for her?

I needed to talk to Eva Flores. She was at Donna's the night Todd was there. She had to have known why Donna had been so angry at him.

Chapter 35

Since I couldn't go see Eva in my pajamas, I figured I'd go home first and get ready. I also had to call my mother for clarification on the Todd thing. Because I remembered now that when I'd mentioned Todd doing work for Donna, my mom had seemed surprised. She and my dad were probably worried anyway.

When I pulled up in front of the house, I was surprised to see so many cars and so much activity. It was only eight thirty on a Saturday morning. The cat cafe didn't even open until nine, although Ethan started selling coffee and food at seven, which drew a lot of people these days.

But then I remembered that in normal people's worlds who weren't dealing with catnappers and murder, today was a big, festive day. The tours started tonight and tourists who were here for the whole weekend of fun— including the tree lighting Sunday—would be trying to get their visits in before they left the island. Not to mention the regulars who were now coming here for their morning coffee, regardless of whether they were visiting cats or not.

Adele's and Harry's cars were here, which was good.

The cafe was covered, despite the fact that I was running around town in my pajamas. And I'd never checked on the maps, or the website. Everything else had flown out of my head after that call from Becky had come and I'd rushed over to Donna's. But at least that gave me a reason to show up on Eva's doorstep—the meeting we were supposed to have yesterday that I'd never gone to because I'd been setting up the gym and then, well, everything had gone sideways.

Although I hadn't gotten any texts from any upset vendors or event participants, which maybe meant that things on that front had been sorted out.

I fished the illicit laptop out from under my seat and shoved it in my bag. I'd need to hide it from Grandpa. He wouldn't take kindly to me removing evidence from a police investigation. Before I went inside, I opened my phone to the newspaper website, figuring the news about Donna had probably spread like a California wildfire in September.

I found a short, just-the-facts-ma'am update on the home page that the newspaper's publisher and founding family member had been found deceased at her home last night. There was a very brief mention that she had been in talks to sell the business at the time of her death, but that was it per strict orders from Mick. Then I checked the *Boston Globe* and sure enough, there it was on the front page: "Newspaper mogul found dead, foul play suspected after potential sale talks."

Ugh. I clicked off the website. Becky would have her hands full today. And Donna's relatives would be here soon. I wondered when the cause of death would officially be released. If we had to wait until the coroner released a report, it might be a long few days.

I wondered who would take over the paper as publisher until . . . whatever happened next. What *would*

234

happen next? Would this push the sale forward, or stop it in its tracks? Too much to think about so early in the morning. I headed inside. The main house was quiet. I poked my head in the kitchen. No one in there, but there was fresh coffee, so that was something. I poured a mug and went upstairs to shower. I found Lucas, who looked like he had just vacated said shower. His hair was still wet but he was dressed and doing something on his laptop. He glanced up when I came in and smiled.

"Hey, gorgeous." He got up and came over to give me a hug.

I laughed. "You're sweet, but seriously?" I looked down at my outfit. "I can't believe I went out like this."

"You look great." He kissed me. "Where'd you go so early?"

"I needed to bring Becky to work." I left out the car impounding and the laptop theft portion of the morning. He was a good sport, but there were probably limits.

"Ah. The news never sleeps. I bet she's got a long day ahead of her." His face turned serious. "How's she doing?"

"I think she's still in shock, honestly." I decided to also leave out my visit to the police station and subsequent conversation with Bernie until I had processed it. I was still trying to put everything together in my head. "They ran the breaking news last night. But they have to do a longer piece today, and of course a tribute to her and her family. It's her paper. I mean, talk about when the newspeople become the news, right?"

"Terrible," Lucas agreed. "And she was a really nice lady."

I glanced at him. "Did you know her? I don't think I realized that."

"When I saw her the other day in the window I thought

she looked familiar. Then I remembered she'd been in the salon a couple weeks ago. She was looking at sweaters for her cats. I had no idea she was the newspaper lady, but the name wouldn't have triggered that for me anyway. By the way, I took care of the new residents in the guest room."

"Thank you. Must have been when she first got them?"

He nodded. "I think she said that. And she thought they'd be cold. Said her house was old and the windows needed an upgrade, so they needed sweaters since they had no hair."

That made me sad. The poor cats. The fact that they'd come from a breeder wasn't their fault, and it seemed like Donna had loved them very much. "Sweet," I murmured.

"It was," Lucas agreed. "And she got them cute sweaters. I remember that because Caro said we needed to order more of them. She actually made a comment about having to keep extras in stock because of all the hairless cats we've seen."

"You're kidding," I said.

"Nope. She placed a bigger order the same day." He shrugged. "Guess more people have allergies these days."

"I guess," I said thoughtfully. "Aside from hairless cats, have you guys seen any other exotic breeds?"

"I'd have to check my roster," Lucas said. "Honestly I've been doing more of the dogs. Caro has taken any cats that have come in. She's also more knowledgeable about cats and breeds. I just think they're cute."

His other groomer was definitely super into cats. She came by the cafe at least once a week to visit with our babies. She had three cats of her own, and I had a feeling she was getting ready to add a fourth.

Lucas leaned over and gave me a kiss. "I've got to run. Appointments," he said, pointing apologetically at his watch. "Want me to bring the dogs?"

"Would you mind? I won't have a lot of time to spend with them today. I'm sorry." I looked over at both of them, snuggled up on the bed. Ollie had one eye open and on us, as if he understood we were making plans for the day. Walter's little tail wagged hopefully as he waited for some attention.

"Of course. They love hanging at the shop," he said.

I went over and sat with them while Lucas finished getting ready, kind of wishing I could chuck the responsibilities of the day and just play with the dogs and cats all day. But there was a Christmas event that still needed attention, a missing cat to find, and a murder to solve— one for which my best friend might be a suspect. It was enough to make me want to go back to bed.

But I couldn't do that. Instead I tucked Donna's laptop into my sock drawer and covered it, then called my mother.

"I need to ask you a question," I said when she answered.

"Good, because we're almost to your house. Are you okay, honey? I've been so worried!"

"I'm fine. And that's perfect. I'll see you when you get here."

I got off the phone and took a scalding hot shower that I stayed in way too long. Then I got dressed, put some curl product in my hair—crossing my fingers that it would dry without turning into a frizzy mess—then went looking for JJ. It was no surprise he was hanging out in the new kitties' guest room. He must've followed Lucas in there earlier. When he saw me from his perch on the bed where he was overseeing the newcomers' kingdom, he squeaked but didn't move.

"Hey, don't get up," I told him. "Just making sure these guys are okay." I looked around for the cats. Simon and Sheila were nowhere in sight. I got on my stomach to look under the bed. They were huddled under there. "Hi," I said.

They blinked at me, but didn't move. Poor things were probably traumatized from last night. And now they were in a whole new, unfamiliar place. It didn't look like they were coming out any time soon.

I sat back on my heels, thinking about them and about poor Frederick. I reached for the vet papers Katrina had sent with him, which included a picture of his sad little face. He kind of looked like the cat in the newspaper article. But that had been a girl. Jasmine. And also that would be too convenient that a stolen, super-expensive cat with a reward out on her would show up behind a dumpster.

But what if Jasmine had been stolen and bred?

I sat up and snatched my phone from the nightstand where I'd put it and called Katrina. "What did you and Sam decide about meeting up with that breeder?"

"She's supposed to call him back today about when to meet. She texted me that she's on her way to your house right now and will do it after. Why?"

"She's coming here? Perfect. Can you come over too? We have to talk."

Chapter 36

I headed downstairs with JJ on my heels. Katrina had promised to be here in ten minutes. I could hear chatter coming from the kitchen so I veered into the room, where I found Grandpa with my parents and Sam.

"Maddie!" My parents both jumped up and tried to hug me at the same time, my dad's lasting longer than normal. "Are you doing okay?" he asked.

"Hi, Dad. Hi, Mom. Yeah, I'm fine."

"I can't imagine," my mother said. She looked as exhausted as I felt. "And Becky? How is she?"

I shrugged. "Working. You know Becky."

"What a tragedy," my dad said. "I can't even imagine who would do this. Did you talk to the police at all?"

"I did," I said carefully. I didn't want to say too much right now. "They're still trying to figure everything out." The understatement of the year.

"What about you, Dad?" My mother turned to Grandpa. "Did your contacts tell you anything?"

But this time Grandpa shook his head. "Haven't really talked to anyone yet. This darn leg is throwing me off." He glared down at his offending ankle in its brace.

Which I figured meant he didn't want to talk about it

with anyone yet. Aside from me, of course. And with all the theories on the table, it made sense.

"Did you know Donna was looking at selling the paper?" I asked my dad.

He shook his head. "No. I had no idea until this morning."

"Someone leaked it. That's why Becky went into work this morning despite . . . everything."

"Who wanted to buy it?" my mother asked.

"Not sure," I said. "But she had an offer that she was supposed to decide on by Monday."

"Wow. Do they think that's why she was killed?" Mom looked at Grandpa.

"Honestly, Soph, there are multiple theories floating around," Grandpa said.

"Yeah. And this electrician is moving to the top of the list," I said, turning to my mother. "When I told you about Donna's fight with him the other day, you looked surprised. Why?"

"Because she wasn't on the list to have him do anything for her."

"What list?"

She rummaged in her giant purse and pulled out an iPad. "We created a list of all the homeowners in the contest, and asked them to come through the Chamber to schedule work with him. We were tracking the work to see if the proposal was in range, and what would be extra billing." She flipped the cover off and tapped her screen, scrolling while she talked. Finally she flipped the device around so I could see it.

I came closer. It was a spreadsheet. The first column listed names and addresses for all the houses that had registered to be part of the Christmas light contest. The second column noted which ones had asked for help putting lights up. The third column noted what kind of

help—just hanging, electrical, additional decorations—
and the fourth column indicated whether the work had
been completed and when. I thought they probably
needed to add multiple columns for callbacks, but didn't
say it. "So this is every house that was part of the contest."

My mother nodded.

I scrolled through the list to find Donna's name. All
the columns next to it were blank. I looked at my mother.
"Weird. You're sure she didn't just reach out on her own?"

"No. We told them specifically we had to coordinate
through a central system."

"Donna and Eva were friends, though. Maybe she did
a workaround. It happens," I said.

My mother looked doubtful. "Eva probably wouldn't
have done that, because the town was super clear that
they weren't paying for anything that wasn't properly
documented. She wouldn't want the Chamber to be on
the hook for anything that could get expensive."

I scrolled through the rest of the list. Our house was
on there, per the work order my mother had put in on
Grandpa's behalf. Lilah Gilmore's house. Angelo Longo's. There were a number of residents that had been
using Todd in some capacity, although I noticed that
more than half were for help with putting up decorations
rather than actual electrical work. "Could people on
this list hire anyone they wanted?" I asked, thinking
of Bernie.

My mother sighed. "We asked them not to. We wanted
to keep the playing field level. I know, it's silly," she said
when I opened my mouth. "But again, Eva was adamant
that we had to make things . . . more accessible for new
people."

I understood what she was saying despite her attempts
to be delicate. Daybreak Island was an old-money New

England place. For as much talk about diversity that had ensued over the past few years, a lot of the older, white, rich people around here preferred that things stay the way they were. It was a hard truth, but it was a truth. And a young Latina like Eva Flores coming to town would certainly see the job of the Chamber as one that helped make everyone get on a more equal playing field.

But I also remembered Bernie saying Donna only used him. It was possible she had followed the rules on this one, but honestly unlikely. She was sponsoring the event. She could do whatever she wanted.

"Can you send me this?" I asked my mother.

She nodded, touching her screen. I heard my phone signal an incoming email a moment later.

"Todd Banks was doing something for Donna," I said. "I saw him at her house. She was telling him he did a bad job. Given his track record with electrical work"—I motioned to Grandpa as the example—"I figured that had to be what he was doing for her."

"Maybe he was," my dad said. "Just a different job. Maybe it was a bigger thing than Christmas lights. Her house is older. Maybe she needed an upgrade to the whole system."

"I thought he was just basic maintenance," I said. "From what I saw, it would be highly unlikely he could handle a whole system upgrade."

My mother nodded. "That's true. He doesn't actually bill himself as an electrician, although he has a license. I'm not sure how much experience he has with big jobs."

She was clearly being kind. I wasn't sure how much experience he had, period.

"What about the tree lighting?" I asked.

She held up crossed fingers. "The lights have been tested, so I think we're okay. But I don't want to jinx anything."

The doorbell rang. "That's Katrina. I'll get it. Hey Sam, can you join us?"

"Sure." My sister followed me to the front door.

Katrina waited impatiently, shifting from one foot to the other. I held the door open.

"Any news?" she asked immediately, although she would've heard before me, I was certain.

"No. And Mick said he's putting Frederick on the back burner with the murder and all."

She sighed unhappily. "I was afraid of that. I'm glad you called though because we have to get this thing set up with that breeder. I'm hoping that might lead us to him. And good, Sam's here. You're still in, right?"

"Of course," Sam said.

"I need Grandpa for this conversation but he's with my parents." I glanced at the kitchen door, hoping they were going to wrap it up soon.

"Leo? Why? What's going on?" Now Katrina looked interested.

"It's something I learned last night about Donna Carey." I broke off as the kitchen door swung open and my parents stepped out.

"There you are! We have to head out," my mother said, coming over to give me a hug. My dad did the same.

"Stay out of trouble," he warned us, giving the three of us a look in turn.

"Us?" Katrina asked innocently. "We never get in trouble."

"Mm-hmm." With one last skeptical look, my dad led my mother out the door.

I locked it behind them. "Grandpa," I called as we headed into the kitchen. "We need your help with a plan."

Chapter 37

"So you're trying to figure out how to approach this breeder," Grandpa said. "Because you think they stole the million-dollar cat and are breeding it? Right here on the island?"

"It's not the wildest theory I've ever heard. Especially if you look at the stolen cat." Katrina swiveled my laptop around on the table. Sam, Grandpa, and I leaned in to look. She had pulled up the photos of Jasmine, the missing show cat. She didn't look exactly like Frederick, but there was some similarity. I thought, anyway.

"But what are you hoping to get from the conversation?" Grandpa persisted. "You think whoever it is is going to confess to stealing a hundred-thousand-dollar cat, and maybe the cat that was staying here, and Mick will jump out of a hiding place and arrest them?"

I giggled. I couldn't help myself. Just the idea of Mick participating in a cat sting was funny. Also unrealistic given that he was working on a murder.

Katrina gave me a dirty look for humoring him. "I really just want to see who shows. Then I can figure out my next move. Like check on licensing, do an inspection, whatever."

Grandpa looked skeptical. "And tip them off if they really are doing something like that?"

"Well, how else am I supposed to figure it out?" Katrina asked, the frustration apparent in her voice. "I need to just get a sense of what I'm dealing with."

Grandpa spread his hands as if to say, *And then?* "It's not like you can arrest them for breeding cats, unless there's a violation like one you just described. But I'd be willing to bet they wouldn't leave a lot of other evidence around if you were coming in to look around."

"I know." She sighed. "I don't know what else to do though."

Sam, who had been listening to the exchange silently, said, "Why don't we just make it like I'm getting a Christmas present for someone, and I want to do the deal at the tree lighting? And I'm interested in one of the new, so-called exotic breeds. Because I'm really into one-of-a-kind things. I'll tell them I'll have cash as long as the paperwork is all in order, and that I want to see the parents too."

We all looked at her.

"That's not a bad idea," Grandpa said finally.

"Aren't you afraid that this person will recognize Sam, though?" I asked. Good, bad, or indifferent, my family was well-known around the island. Chances were that even if we didn't necessarily know someone, they would know us.

"I'm going to change my appearance," Sam said, as if that should have been obvious.

I eyed her. Sometimes I couldn't tell if she was serious or not. "You are?"

She nodded. "I have a red wig from a thing I did last Halloween. And glasses. No one will ever know."

I had to laugh. "A red wig, huh?"

"Yep." She held up a finger and raced upstairs.

"We'll all be there, of course," Grandpa said.

"We will?" I asked.

"Definitely," Katrina said. "That was the plan all along."

Sam came back into the room. At least I thought it was Sam. A woman with thick red hair that reminded me of Tawny Kitaen from the old Whitesnake video and cat-eye glasses stood in front of me. Katrina and I looked at each other and burst out laughing. Grandpa just shook his head.

Sam didn't look offended at all. "It makes me feel more confident," she said with a grin.

"Hey, whatever works," Katrina said. "So go ahead, Sam. Call." She motioned to Sam's phone.

"Should I be the same person as the other day or a new one?" she asked.

"The same. Especially if you're using the same number," Katrina decided. "Linda, was it?"

"Yup. Linda. Okay, here we go." This time she didn't even ask for a script.

We all huddled around the phone as it rang. The same male voice answered as the other day.

"Hi there. This is Linda, I called you the other day about a cat?"

"Oh yes! Hello there, Linda." He sounded super cheery.

"I've been thinking about what I want, and I'm leaning toward a very one-of-a-kind cat for a Christmas gift for my daughter," she said. "Your flyer said you had unique cats?"

"We certainly do. We've got some mixes from breeds that are *very* had to come by," he said.

"Okay. My price range is about fifty thousand. I need a snuggly, friendly cat who is very people-oriented. What do you have that fits the bill?"

Katrina and I looked at each other. I didn't know whether to laugh or what. My sister sounded so in control of this that it was pretty funny. On the other hand, I hated to think about these poor cats.

The guy was rattling off some options. I noticed he wasn't offering up breed names, but he seemed to have a lot to choose from, starting around forty thousand and going up to fifty-five.

"I had a fun idea," Sam said. "I want to give her the cat tomorrow night. At the tree lighting. Do you think we could meet there before the festivities start so I can pick from the three you mentioned? And I'll also want all the paperwork available, including for the parentage."

We all held our breath.

The guy hesitated for a moment, then said, "Of course we can do that. I think I can get us into the community room at the Methodist church to meet, if that works for you?"

Sam agreed. They exchanged a few last pleasantries and then Sam disconnected, grinning at us. "How was that?"

"Amazing," Katrina said, high-fiving her.

"So what happens tomorrow, then?" I asked.

"I have no idea," Katrina admitted. "But at least we can get a sense of who we're dealing with and if they're falsifying cat lineages."

I wanted to ask how exactly she was going to determine that, but decided against it. I had other problems to focus on. Katrina could take the lead on this one.

Chapter 38

I needed to shift into event mode. Eva had texted me this morning looking for the maps, which Clarissa had confirmed were done and just waiting for me to pick up at the printer and deliver them to the Chamber. I needed to go there anyway to see Eva. Clarissa had also delivered the updated version to Bones so he could put it on the new and improved website, which looked incredible. He'd rebuilt the whole thing in mere hours, and it was fabulous. And he hadn't just put up a downloadable pdf of the map; he'd made an interactive one that was animated and highlighted the nearby sights for each area. And best of all, the only text I'd gotten so far that was event related was a string of hearts from Ellen, whose library events were prominently displayed on the new website's front page.

Bones was a true rockstar. I still hadn't heard from him yet, though. Which meant he was asleep, but I couldn't wait any longer.

I called him. After four rings he answered with a grunt.

"It's Maddie. I need your help. Did you see my text?"

"Too early."

"The event website looks amazing," I added.

He grunted again.

I could tell he was about to hang up, so I rushed to add, "Someone's been murdered."

A pause. "And how am I supposed to help you with that?" he asked finally.

"I need to access a laptop."

Another pause. Then, "Hold on."

I used my waiting time to lock my bedroom door—just in case—and pull the laptop out from my sock drawer.

He came back a couple of minutes later and sounded more awake. "Okay. Tell me what you need."

I gave him a very brief overview of Donna's murder and her investigative reporting adventures into the world of cats. "Basically I need to see if there's anything on her computer that has anything to do with cats: show cats, breeders, anything in that world. Also anything about threats she'd been getting recently."

"I'm assuming there's a password on the computer."

"Yeah."

"What's your Wi-Fi network name and password?"

"I'll text it."

"No. Tell me. I don't want it in writing."

"Right. Sorry." Hacker rules. I gave him the info.

"I'll get back to you," he said, and disconnected.

"Okay, thanks," I said to the dead line.

I sent a quick checking-in text to Becky before I headed out but got no reply. She must be super busy. But I was dying to know if she'd found anything out. I put the phone down and grabbed my shoes. JJ looked up from where he was relaxing on my bed.

"You want to come?" I asked. I figured he was feeling a little neglected.

He squeaked out a yes.

"Let's go, then."

We headed to the printer, where he got treats and I picked up the maps. Thankfully everything looked right this time. And the new design Clarissa had created was great. Pleased, I put the boxes in the car and we drove to the Chamber.

The place was hopping. I stepped up to the front desk and smiled at the young man sitting there. He reluctantly put his phone down.

"Can I help you?" he asked. He had a hoop dangling from between his nostrils. Half his head was shaved; the other half sprouted green hair. I did love how the faces of the Chamber had changed with Eva's arrival.

"Hi. I'm Maddie James. I have the corrected maps." I held up the box. "Where should I put them?"

"Oh, great. I'll take them." He sprang from his chair and reached for the box. "Thanks so much."

"You're welcome. I also need to speak to Eva."

He nodded. "In her office. Right that way." He pointed down a hallway. "Last room on the right."

I thanked him and headed down. Eva was working on the computer. She looked ten years older than when I'd seen her earlier this week, and her eyes were puffy from crying. But when she saw me, she jumped up. "Maddie! My little lifesaver," she declared, coming around the desk to envelope me in a crushing hug.

"Hi," I managed once I could breathe again. "I just dropped off the maps."

She sighed. "You are the best, I swear. That website." She brought her fingers to her lips and made a kissing sound. "Perfection. I will never let an event happen without you involved again. And what a difference you made during such a . . . difficult time." She swallowed as tears clearly threatened to well up in her eyes again.

"Oh. Well, you're very kind," I murmured, hoping she wouldn't cry.

"I'm not. You're just amazing."

"I can't take the credit. I have a guy." I thought a little guiltily of Bones, probably sitting in a dark room uncovering Donna's deepest secrets right now.

"Well, whoever did it, it's all because of you. Please, sit." She motioned to the cushy chair in front of her desk.

I sat, taking in the office. It was way different from the last time I'd been in here. The former president had been a seventy-something Irish man. The office had reflected that, with a fancy mahogany desk, a leather couch, and paintings of Irish landscapes on the walls. Eva had transformed it into a colorful oasis—lavender walls, bright abstract art, lamps with different-colored bulbs. Lively music—flamenco, perhaps?—played in the background. The desk was light-colored, smaller, and looked like it could transform into a standing desk. The old leather couch had been traded for a scattering of different types of chairs, all comfy, all different styles—from a beanbag to a velvet chair that looked like it belonged in a living room—all in vibrant jeweled tones.

I kind of loved it. "It looks great in here," I said.

She nodded, looking around proudly. "Thank you. I've got a lot planned for the rest of the space this year. It's going to look a lot different when I'm done. A whole new place, just like I promised the community."

I nodded. "We need it, that's for sure. So . . . I wanted to say how sorry I am about Donna."

Her eyes filled with tears again. "Thank you."

"How long have you known her? She brought you here, right?"

She fiddled with a pen sitting on a notebook as she nodded. "Yes. We'd been friends for a long time. Went to college together. She wanted to help move this island into the new century, you know? It took a lot of convincing, but I'm glad I came. I just hope I can do her proud."

"Well, you're off to a great start," I said encouragingly.

"Thank you, sweetie."

"I am curious, though," I said. "The other night when I stopped by Donna's and she was having that argument with Todd Banks. Do you know what it was about?"

I could see the change in Eva's demeanor. Her back went straight, pulling her slightly away so there was a tiny bit more distance between us. "Just some work Todd had done for her," she said. "Why?"

I leaned forward, resting a hand on her desk. "Eva. Look. I know you wanted to give Todd a chance at this job, but . . . he didn't seem to be very good at it. He messed up lights at our house. My grandpa ended up getting zapped and falling off a ladder. I'm sure my mother told you."

She said nothing.

"So if he had screwed up Donna's lights and she was mad, maybe threatened to get you to cancel his contract, I'm wondering if he . . . hurt her."

Eva had gone wide-eyed at my theory. She shook her head vehemently. "Of course I want to know who killed my friend," she said. "But I think you're barking up the wrong tree, Maddie. Todd may not be the best electrician I've ever known, but he's no killer. I've known him and his wife for a long time. Besides, he wasn't . . ." she trailed off.

"Wasn't what?" When she didn't answer, I leaned forward. "Look. My mother showed me the list that kept track of who was using him for contest stuff. Donna wasn't. Do you know what he was doing for her?"

"She just . . . needed a few things fixed. Her house is old, as you know. I'm not really sure."

She was lying. But why would she be protecting him?

Eva pushed her chair back and stood. "Thank you so much for the maps. I appreciate all your help. Hopefully I'll see you later tonight at the bazaar. And I have a visit scheduled for the cat cafe too."

She walked me out of her office, then went back inside and closed the door behind her.

Chapter 39

I called Grandpa as I left the Chamber.

"What's up, Doll?"

"Eva's hiding something. She knows why Todd was at Donna's but won't tell me. Did Donna mention anything about either of them to you?"

"No, she didn't. What do you think it has to do with?"

"I have no idea. But I need to find out. Any other updates?"

"Mick released Becky's car."

I breathed a sigh of relief. "Does that mean she's not a suspect anymore?"

"It means they didn't find anything in the car."

"He tell you anything else?"

"No. He had some questions about what I'd found about the threats. They went back to her house and combed through it again, but couldn't find the letters anywhere. Same with her office. No laptop either."

"Bummer," I said, pushing the guilt away.

"They're going through her iPad now. And I took photos of the letters, which I sent, but I don't have the originals."

"Well, maybe they'll they find something on her iPad," I said.

"Where are you off to now?"

"I wanted to stop by the co-op. See if Molly Longo has any intel on her husband. Or her dad."

"Right. Keep me posted. And be careful."

"What are you doing?" I asked.

"I've got a few things I'm looking into on my end," he said. "Stay tuned."

He hung up before I could ask what they were.

I pulled into the co-op parking lot. I almost couldn't find a place to park, it was so packed. Our town was really hopping for this event, which would be so great if there hadn't been such a tragedy to kick things off.

I finally got lucky and snagged a spot that someone was pulling out of, and we headed inside. JJ trotted beside me happy as a clam. He knew this place. It was one of his familiar haunts. Another place where he got spoiled with treats.

I stepped into the store, which was as packed as the parking lot. Customers browsed the aisles, exclaiming over the fresh produce and herbs, the local selection of coffees and teas and baked goods. It was a homey little store, even though they'd expanded over the years from the original. Now there was a seating area and everything for people to get some tea and eat some of Angelo's homemade baked goods before they tackled their grocery shopping. Today, Christmas music played over the speakers and the cashiers all wore Santa hats. A tree decked out all in silver stood front and center. A small table near the front door was stacked with muffins and other baked goods. An employee was pouring cups of coffee and hot cider for patrons as they came in, exclaiming over the goodies. It was lovely, but at the same time jarring, given the events going on in town.

I got in line for fresh hot cider before I did any snooping, hoping to just "bump into" Molly and start an innocent conversation.

As JJ and I waited, I heard a low, angry voice coming from the little office area to the right of the makeshift cafe where I stood.

"No, Dad. I can't believe you did that. There's no excuse for that. And you're just hurting me." A door banged open and Molly exited, pulling on a metallic silver puffer coat that I did pause to admire for a second.

Angelo rushed out behind her, holding a tray of doughnuts. "Molly! Come back here right now and let's talk about this."

She ignored him and cut through the line to get to the front door faster. The small crowd's festive chatter paused as they watched her shove the front door open and run out into the parking lot.

Angelo looked like he was about to follow her, but then he glanced down at his doughnuts and the apron covering his short-sleeved shirt and sighed. He deposited the tray unceremoniously on the table out front, earning him a startled stare from his employees, then went back into the room from which he and Molly had just emerged.

Slowly the chatter started back up. I watched out the window, trying to get a glimpse of Molly outside.

"Miss?" The woman behind me tapped me on the shoulder. "Are you ordering?"

"Sorry. Yes." I stepped up to the counter, my mind still on Molly. And also on the doughnuts. Angelo's hot cider doughnuts were incredible. I ordered one along with my cider, accepted some treats for JJ, and pondered my next move. Did I wait for her to come in, or go out looking for her? Maybe if I caught her outside, she'd speak more freely.

I picked JJ up and headed outside, hoping she was just cooling off and hadn't left the premises altogether. I doubted it. She worked here most days of the week, and I couldn't see her vanishing on a Saturday, especially during such a busy time.

I was right. When I rounded the corner of the building, I found her huddled beside the dumpster, smoking a cigarette and texting furiously on her phone. I had no idea Molly smoked.

When she realized I was standing there she glanced up, then stood and flicked the cigarette onto the ground, stepping on it to put it out. "Hey," she said a little guiltily, like I was about to bust her.

"Hey," I said. "Everything okay?"

She waved a dismissive hand. "Fine. I know it's a filthy habit, but I've had a hard time staying at my same weight since I don't swim anymore. Smoking helps. I need to figure out a better way so I don't die of lung cancer, but it also helps with my stress."

I blinked, realizing she was talking about her smoking. "No, I meant with your dad," I said with a little smile. "You certainly don't have to explain yourself to me."

"Oh. Right." She stuffed her phone in the pocket of her coat. "Yeah. I'm fine. Just a spat. Can I say hi to your cat?" She reached out a hand to JJ.

"Of course." I put him on the ground, wrapping his leash around my wrist. She dropped to a crouch, rubbing behind his ears.

I watched her, trying to decide how to play this. In the end, I decided honesty was the best policy. "Molly, can I ask you something?"

She glanced up, shielding her eyes from the sun. "Sure."

"You heard Donna Carey was found dead last night."

She went still. "I did, but I didn't hear what happened."

"Someone killed her," I said.

Molly wobbled in her crouch, reaching behind her for the wall to catch herself. When she was steady, she rose slowly to her feet. "You're kidding."

"I wish I was. Thing is, there was all this drama swirling around the past few days. Related to the newspaper and the offer she got to sell it." I trailed off awkwardly, trying to figure out how to ask my next questions. I didn't want the assumption to be that her husband or father were under suspicion. "Anyways—I'm wondering if you'd heard anything from your dad or Brandon about what was really going on with the sale."

Molly didn't speak, eyes on me. I waited. JJ sniffed around the dumpster at our feet.

"And you think they would know because . . ." She waited.

"I know Brandon was advising her. And I know your dad's an investor."

"Ah." She smiled a little. "How do you know all this?"

"I heard Brandon and Donna talking."

"And why are you involved?" she asked.

"Because my best friend may be a suspect. Becky Walsh. She's the editor at the paper. But also because . . . Brandon was advising her and he sounded a little"—I pondered my word choice—"intense about the outcome. He was also pressuring Becky to back off on her protests that Donna retain ownership."

That seemed to surprise her. "Becky? She wouldn't kill anyone. She's really nice. Intense, but nice. Wow." Molly shook her head, looking into the distance. Finally she pulled another cigarette and a lighter out of her pocket. "You mind?"

I motioned for her to go ahead.

She lit the cigarette and took a drag. "And you're going to do what with this information? I know your grandfather is a PI. Are you helping him?"

I nodded. "We're just trying to help Becky."

Molly stared at me for a long time, her gaze intense. Out here in the bright sun, her eyes were even more blue. Her cigarette burned, unattended. Ash that she hadn't flicked away from her cigarette fell onto her boot. She kicked it off. "I guess it doesn't matter. The cops are going to be looking at my husband soon enough."

Chapter 40

Molly said the word *husband* like one might say *cockroach*.

My heart sped up. Had Brandon actually done it? Did she know? I waited.

Molly was silent for a while, then she said, "Your sister. The one who dumped Cole. She's doing well, yeah?"

I was confused by the change of subject, but I went along with it. "Val? She's doing great," I said. "She's engaged to my business partner, actually. And she has her own business now."

Molly nodded. "I knew that. Your grandfather told my dad. That's great. I haven't talked to Val since they split. Obviously Brandon took a side. But I secretly always thought Cole was a jerk." She laughed, the sound bitter. "Too bad I was dumb enough not to realize that like attracts like."

"What do you mean?"

She looked me straight in the eye. "I mean that Brandon is just like his buddy."

That was kind of a loaded statement. I knew Cole to be a liar and a cheater. I didn't know what else he might be on top of that, so I couldn't be a hundred percent sure what Molly was talking about here. But I wanted to keep her talking, regardless. "I see. So why would the cops be looking at him?"

"Because my dad told the police that he was unreachable and not where he was supposed to be last night."

"Your dad did? Is that what you were arguing about?"

She nodded and blew out a long trail of smoke, careful to direct it away from me and JJ. "It's my fault though. I told him I didn't know where Brandon was last night. We were supposed to all go out to dinner after the bazaar shut down. Brandon was actually supposed to come help out at the booth with me, but he didn't show. He didn't pick us up for dinner either."

"So wait. He really was MIA?"

"In a manner of speaking, yes. And I didn't want to get into it with my dad." She took a last drag from her cigarette and tossed the butt. "I don't know if you've been back long enough to recognize this, but it's really hard to keep people out of your business around here."

I had to laugh at that. She was a hundred percent right. "Oh yeah. That's why I left in the first place."

"So then why did you come back?" She seemed genuinely interested in my answer.

"Because I missed my family," I said honestly. "And I wanted to spend as much time with my grandfather as possible. It really became clear when my grandma died that people don't live forever."

"Yeah. I guess." She seemed a little sad. But then she shrugged it off. "It's probably easier when your family doesn't want to control everything you do."

Wow. That was kind of wild that Angelo would rat Brandon out to the cops like that. Grandpa had suggested there wasn't a lot of love lost there, but that sounded extreme.

But then why did he offer him up to Donna as her advisor?

I pretended not to know that her dad didn't like her husband. "Did Brandon and your dad normally get along? Did something cause him to . . . do that?"

Molly laughed. "You're kidding, right? My dad can't stand Brandon. And it's mutual."

"Was the newspaper sale making it worse?"

"Kind of. From what I could gather, the offer was good and would've given Donna and the investors more money than with the initial offer. Brandon thought it would be good for my dad to get a lump sum. He thought we should expand this place." She waved an arm at the co-op building. "And an expansion would benefit me and by extension, Brandon. This place is in my name too."

That explained a lot. Brandon's interest in the sale *was* self-serving, like I had guessed. "Your dad wasn't interested?" I asked.

She shook her head. "He likes things how they are. My dad is old school. Doesn't want to expand. He likes the quarterly dividends he gets from his investment because he can usually depend on them. He likes his place. Wants to leave it to me. Doesn't want to have too much to manage while he's still in it."

"And he and Brandon disagreed on this," I guessed.

"Often and loudly."

"So why did he want Brandon to advise Donna?" I asked. "That doesn't really make sense."

"My dad thought keeping the proceedings close would give him an advantage. He could see what was coming and try to manage it somehow. I guess he also thought he and I could convince Brandon otherwise. My dad was always kind of naive."

"But what if Donna sold and your dad refused to

expand?" I asked. "There was always that chance, so why would Brandon be so invested? He doesn't control that."

"He thought he'd get some of Dad's money either way. My dad gives me a share of the dividends," she explained. "Lump sum payment to Dad meant I'd get a chunk. Therefore he would too."

"How much are we talking?" I asked.

"I don't know exactly, but he was throwing around numbers in the low hundreds of thousands."

Well, that could be enough to cause someone to make a bad heat-of-the-moment decision. "Molly. Where was Brandon last night?" I asked carefully. "It sounds like you at least had an idea."

"Yeah. I knew." She didn't offer up the information.

Our eyes locked, Molly's defiant, mine—I hoped—calm.

"Look," I said, trying for a friend-to-friend tone. "My best friend might be on the chopping block for this Donna thing. I don't know Brandon well, but I do know he was involved and I'm wondering why. If there's someone who was maybe pressuring him." I didn't want to insinuate I thought he could've killed Donna because she'd probably punch me. "So if you have any context and you want to keep him out of trouble, please tell me what you know. Was he at Donna's Friday night after he left the high school in the afternoon?"

But now her posture had shifted—defensively, I thought.

"Brandon's not a killer, if that's what you're suggesting. He might be a weasel, but he's too much of a wuss to actually murder anybody," she said.

"I'm not. I promise." I crossed my fingers behind my back. "I'm just trying to figure out what was going on under the surface here."

Molly sighed. "He wasn't at Donna's."

"Then where was he?"

She leaned back against the wall of the building, the fight going out of her. "He was out with his new conquest," she said. "Pretty, this one. Kind of fancy, which fits his image of himself. I think he's tired of having a small-town wife, even if it's a prestigious small town." Molly pushed herself back up to a standing position. "He wants off the island. He's got some new girl who's probably going to be part of that new life when he pulls the trigger on it. I'm just here waiting for the shoe to drop, trying to set myself up so it doesn't matter when he leaves."

"You mean he was with someone else?"

"Yeah. He picked up some girl from the ferry. Took her to his office. Just shows how lazy he is that he can't even go off-island to have an affair," she said bitterly. "Gotta have her come to him and try to hide it."

"Did you confront him?" I asked.

"I couldn't be bothered," she said. "Let him go. I don't need him." She stood up a little straighter. "I have my own money and a lot of irons in the fire."

"I'm so sorry, Molly," I said. "But you're right. You don't need him."

"I don't," she agreed, jamming her hands in her pockets.

"Does your dad know what he was doing?"

"No. I just told him Brandon got tied up at work. Once I saw them go in the office, I came right back to the bazaar. Took Dad out for dinner myself." She smiled a little. "If he knew the truth, he'd kill him. My dad's Italian, after all. He's got a temper. As you saw at the tree farm."

Chapter 41

Molly slipped in the back door of the co-op to get back to work. I scooped up JJ and went back to my car, my brain churning through this new information. Of course I couldn't take her at her word that Brandon was at his office with some woman. Spouses were the worst alibis, even if they didn't actually like the spouse. Self-preservation was a thing, and no one wanted to be seen as a murderer's significant other.

I called Craig. He picked up on the first ring.

"I'm guessing you're talking to Brandon Tyson today?" I said by way of greeting.

"Good morning to you too. Mick and I just left his house, actually."

"Let me guess. Because his father-in-law suggested you should."

Craig paused. "How did you know that?"

"I just talked to his wife at the co-op. She and Angelo were having a bit of a disagreement about it, apparently. So what did he tell you?"

"He said he was in a business meeting last night. And gave me access to the security cameras to verify."

"Business meeting?" I laughed. "His wife told me he was with some woman."

"He was. Some lawyer from another firm."

"Do you believe him?"

"I believe the cameras that tell me he was in his office during the time that we believe Donna was killed. What kind of meeting it was, I don't really care."

I guessed I didn't either, except I felt bad for Molly. I remembered how devastating it was for my sister to be in a relationship like that. "You're sure they were there the whole time?"

"Except when they left to go have dinner. They went to a place in Duck Cove. I need to confirm with the restaurant when they open, but I have a receipt that looks pretty real."

I hissed out a breath. I wasn't sure what I wanted the outcome to be here—murderer or cheater—but I didn't like Brandon and I wanted him to be accountable for something. So it looked like Brandon was out as a suspect.

But that didn't mean Angelo was. I found it odd that he'd try to cast suspicion for something so serious on his son-in-law, no matter how he felt about him. Unless he was desperate and it was a matter of self-preservation. I said as much to Craig.

"Yeah, I'm curious about that too. We're going to talk to Angelo now," Craig said. "You said Molly is at the co-op too?"

"She is," I said.

"Good. She's on our list too. That whole crew is just way too involved."

"Molly's not. She just happens to be in the middle of the two of them. What about Todd?" I asked. "Did you talk to him yet?"

"Not yet. But I have it on good authority he was at the town green dealing with the Christmas tree, which wasn't lighting up during the latest round of tests."

Oh, dear Lord. "Seriously?"

"Yeah. And the town manager was there the whole time acting like his own personal drill sergeant, my source told me. Bernie eventually showed up to bail everyone out."

"Are you still going to look into him? And verify it?" I asked, although I could feel any hope for that lead slipping away. Our town manager was a stickler for certain things, and if he'd heard any inkling of electricity not working well, he'd be all over Todd like flies on a turd. There would be no avoiding that. So if he said Todd was there, he was likely there.

"Yes, Maddie. We are," Craig said, sounding amused.

"Keep me posted?"

He muttered something noncommittal and hung up.

I looked at JJ, who sat upright on the passenger seat. "Shoot. What now?"

He didn't respond, just flicked his tail.

"I still think something's up with Todd. Otherwise why was he fighting with Donna?"

JJ squeaked.

"He probably won't be such a priority to the police now," I mused. "Maybe we should go chat with him. What do you think?"

He squeaked again.

I took that as a yes and drove out of the parking lot, pointing my car in the direction of Turtle Point.

Selena Boyle and Todd Banks' house loomed large even on a street with some of the larger houses in Turtle Point. Val had told me it was massive, but I guess I hadn't realized the extent of it.

I knew Grandpa didn't love the newer-style homes that had been popping up on the island over the past decade, as people from other parts of the state migrated east looking for their own slice of paradise—but I did prefer the architectural look of them to some of the older homes. Not ours, of course—Grandpa and Grandma and other relatives before them had remodeled the house multiple times over the house's history so that now it had a newer, more unique look and feel to it than its similar-aged counterparts—the traditional boxy, brown Cape houses that dotted the island.

This house was another story altogether. It was more like a compound, stretching both sideways and backward, with a sunroom that seemed to elongate it even more. It even had a couple of turret-style rooms on each side of the home, bookending the sprawling, length-of-the-house second-floor balcony that, I was certain, offered a pretty impressive view of the sea. I was a sucker for turret rooms.

I parked out front, taking it all in. I knew they'd bought it over the summer, scooping up the last open lot in this development. They clearly did well for themselves, given the size and stature of the place. I'd heard some chatter about them, or rather Selena, around town. Selena had definitely thrown herself into island life in the few months they'd been here, getting involved in events like this one, hosting parties, being part of fundraisers. Seemed like they were planning to be here for a while.

Which would mean at the very least her husband would need to up his game as far as the work he did. And, you know, not be a murderer.

I wished I could ask for a tour, but I had a hunch I wasn't going to be invited in for tea. Todd Banks probably didn't want to see me at his door at all. But his van was here, along with another car, which likely meant he was home. So to the door I went, after telling JJ I'd be right back.

I rang the bell, listening to the elaborate chime inside the house. The door was yanked open a minute later and Todd stood there, looking extremely out of place against the backdrop of the all-marble foyer. At least he wasn't wearing that stupid coat. But I finally got a look at his face since it wasn't obscured by the hat he usually wore either. He had bulgy eyes—that was the feature that stood out. They were a nice blue, but they reminded me of an oversized bug. His brown hair was thinning a bit around the top, which was probably why he wore the hat religiously. He wore a pair of jeans that were smeared with dirt and a flannel shirt that was buttoned wrong, leaving one end hanging slightly lower than the other over his jeans.

He eyed me suspiciously. "Yeah?"

This guy really needed some social skills. "Hi. Maddie James. My house is—"

"I know who you are, and I tried to fix your house," he interrupted. "You said you had the other guy come and do it so it's really not my problem anymore." He started to shut the door in my face but I reached out and planted my palm against it.

"I'm not here about my house. I need to talk to you about Donna Carey."

At the mention of her name, Todd looked like he might throw up. "Look. I already talked to the police. I don't know anything."

"I'm here on my own, because my friend might be in trouble. Can I come in? Just for a minute?" I asked.

Todd looked like he wanted to say no, but he surprised me. With a quick flick of his wrist, he motioned me inside, leaving the door slightly ajar. I wondered briefly if it was a bad idea to be alone with him. This was a big house. If he murdered me, even his wife might not find me for days.

But I was here now, so may as well see what happened.

I stepped into a giant foyer, sleek with black-and-white accent furniture. Straight ahead of me, past a living room decorated in all white, was a full-window view of the ocean. Ahead and to my left was an open staircase that led to the second floor, which was visible from down here. The whole vibe was wide open and expansive.

"Beautiful home," I remarked.

Todd didn't acknowledge the comment. "Look. I don't know how I can help you. Like I said, the police asked me already and I told them. I wasn't there yesterday. I hadn't been back since Wednesday night when you came over. I have no idea what happened there."

"I heard it might've had something to do with her electrical system," I said, fudging a bit.

"Even if that's true, I'm still not sure what that has to do with me."

"You're the electrician," I said.

He crossed his arms in front of his chest defensively. "Not *her* electrician. She needed a whole system upgrade. Her system was old. That wasn't a job I wanted to do. And she didn't ask me to do it, anyway."

"What do you mean, not her electrician?" I asked, playing dumb. I'd already confirmed she wasn't using him for contest-related electrical work, but I wanted to see what he said.

He flushed a little. "I mean, not like that. I was . . . just helping with some small stuff to get her through this thing."

"What kind of small stuff?"

Todd rubbed his neck, which was now also turning red. "Stuff with the lights. Like I was doing for all the other contest people."

I shook my head. "I saw the spreadsheet. You weren't. Everything that was being done related to the contest was documented. She didn't have any requests in through the event channels."

"We should probably just tell her. Maybe she can help."

The voice came from behind Todd. He whirled around and I peered past him to find Eva Flores standing there, holding a mug, like she'd been over visiting. She did tell me she had known Todd and Selena for a while, but my guard was up now. What were these two up to? Had there been some sort of conspiracy between them? Donna and Eva were allegedly friends, but what if something had gone wrong?

"What are you doing here?" I asked Eva, trying to casually feel around in my pocket for my phone. Just in case.

She motioned for Todd to step aside. "After you came to see me, I knew I needed to connect with Todd. I guess we were both on the same page." She looked at Todd. "Todd was helping Donna and me with something. We needed to keep it quiet, so we used the guise of the Christmas lights contest. I was coming to tell him we should just tell the police about it. They may need the information to solve this."

"She thinks I killed Donna," Todd said flatly. "Now she probably thinks you helped me."

"What?" Eva stared at him, then me. "Oh my goodness, girl. Donna was my friend. The reason I was here at all." She looked like she was about to cry again. "This is all my fault. Because she helped me with something. And now I feel like I need to make it right. Maddie, why don't you come in. Todd, make more tea. And then we can tell Maddie what we were all working on."

Chapter 42

I still hesitated, glancing back over my shoulder at the car where JJ waited. "I have my cat with me."

"Well, go get him!" Eva said. "Go on," she added when I still didn't move. "I promise we're not going to kidnap you. I'm due at a meeting with your mother shortly. I wouldn't want to have to explain you going missing to her."

Maybe I was being naive, but I decided to talk to them. I needed information more than I needed to be overly cautious. Still, when I went out to the car to get JJ, I fired off a text to Lucas: *I'm at Todd Banks' house if you can't find me.*

He immediately texted back a whole string of question marks, which I ignored. I slipped the phone back in my pocket and carried JJ to the door. "Should I get Mick Ellory over here?" I asked.

"Lord no," Eva said, herding me farther into the house as Todd led us down to the fancy living room. "Not yet, anyway. Your grandpa needs a little more time."

I stopped in my tracks. "My grandpa?"

Eva nodded. "Yes. Sit." She waved at the couch. "Todd, the tea."

I sat, putting JJ on my lap. Todd slunk off to the kitchen. I was momentarily distracted by him. He was such an odd dude, getting yelled at and bossed around by all these people. Mostly women. I wondered what his wife was like, but I suspected it was the same story. Especially if they lived in a house like this. He didn't seem like he could get out of his own way to make the money this place would require.

Eva sat across from me. "While he's doing that, let me fill you in."

"Please," I said. "Because I'm really lost."

"Understandable. Let's catch you up." Eva took a breath, as if fortifying herself for what was next. "So, Donna and I go way back, as you know. We were in college together, and have stayed friends." Her eyes filled with tears again and she dabbed at the corners with her index fingers. "She referred me for this job."

I nodded. I knew all this.

"So I started coming out here to spend some time, meet people, get to know the vibe and what was going on. I wanted to make sure it was a good fit. I thought I could make a difference—still do—so I accepted, obviously. But one of the times I came out here, over the summer, a friend came with me. I wanted to stay for a while, so we got an Airbnb. My friend brought her cat."

I was about to interrupt and tell her to just get to the whole altercation with Todd already, but then I realized what she'd said—"her cat." Weird how so many things came back to cats lately—things that had nothing to do with my normal cat immersion.

Eva nodded. "My friend Margot—who was also Donna's friend—has show cats. At the time, she only had one. Jasmine."

Oh, boy. I was starting to get a sinking feeling about where this was all going. "Jasmine," I said, the newspaper article Katrina had shown me blinking like a red light in my head. "Some fancy breed, right? I'd never heard of it."

"Yes. You've seen the story, I take it?"

"Yes. Well, I really only looked into it recently." I glanced up as Todd returned with a tray of mugs. I couldn't stop thinking about how out of place he seemed with the tea tray and the mugs—and in the house in general. I took the mug with a murmured "thank you" and refocused on Eva. "There have been some attempts to sell some expensive cats around town. Christmas gift marketing and all that. But our animal control officer is looking into it. She found the article about the possibly stolen cat."

"There is no *possibly*," Eva said with an edge to her voice. "Jasmine was stolen. And Margot is traumatized. She put her whole life on hold to stay here and look for her. But she was never found. The theory for a while was that she was taken off-island and is being used to breed new hybrids. It seemed too cheeky—and dangerous—to keep her here."

"Wow. That sounds . . ." I tried to find the right words. Clearly there was a whole side to the cat world that I've never experienced and really had little to no idea about. Obviously I knew there were cat breeders, but I always thought about it as people breeding Siamese or Bengals or something we've all heard of. I didn't like it, but preferred to think of it as a small sampling. But this sounded . . . much bigger. Stolen cats? Hybrids? What on earth?

Was this what Donna had been involved in?

I glanced at the tea Todd had brought. I still wasn't sure if I wanted to drink it.

He watched me with a slightly amused look as if he knew what I was thinking. He took a seat across from me, angling his gaze toward the window instead of into the conversation.

Weird dude.

"It's horrible," Eva said. "Margot wasn't using Jasmine to make money. She loves her."

I nodded. "Okay. That's very sad, I agree." I resisted the urge to point out that cats in shelters could give just as much love as one that costs as much as three normal cars. "But what does it have to do with Donna, aside from her friendship with Margot?"

"Donna had been thinking of doing something different in her work for a while. She's also been into show cats and the whole cat fancier community for a long time. It started out as a hobby when Margot got into it, years ago. Donna went along with her to some shows and started doing some reporting, just for fun. This was not long after grad school. She was curious and even contributed to some major publications in the community. It really was a hobby for a long time, but it allowed her to stay involved with cats and keep up with something she was really interested in. She had her allergy problems, which kept her away from most of the big shows, but you know Donna."

I didn't, really. "Meaning?" I asked.

"Meaning that she always finds a way, especially if she sees a story. She started to get more involved when Margot told her about something that happened at a cat show about five years ago. A cat breeder was carjacked and her cats were stolen. It happened in Cleveland and not at the actual show, so the narrative was that she drove through a bad area. Thing is, there were enough rumblings that it was a setup that when Margot mentioned it to Donna, she got really interested in looking into it. She actually went out there and did some investigative reporting and, long story short, this whole story came out that someone had been paid to carjack this woman and take the cats. It really piqued Donna's interest. More research on her part and she started to see that a lot of shady stuff was going on in this world, and that's where she came up with the idea of a media company that focused on cat fancier stories. She thought it might keep the industry a bit more in check. So that's what she's been building."

"For five years?" That was commitment. And it also suggested that she might have been creating enemies along the way, if she was publishing stuff that outed bad—and in some cases probably illegal—behavior. "Did anyone know?"

"A few of us. She'd made a lot of contacts in the industry, and she'd been talking with a few people who were heavy hitters to see what people thought. And for the record"—at this she laughed a little—"I've been hanging around her too long. The people she talked to thought it was very much needed. There's a lot of interest in this space, but aside from a couple of magazines, no one is covering this for real. So it was very well received. But she hadn't gone live with anything yet. She wanted to have content in place, she was testing various formats and she was also trying to raise some money. Margot has money—she's been an investor since Donna brought it up, and she pledged even more when Jasmine went missing—but Donna wanted to attract other investors also. She was really close to making this work. Then"—she took a deep breath—"the Jasmine thing happened, right here on the island. And she decided that there was no way these people were going to infiltrate our island, right under her nose like that. She was solving this stolen cat case and this was going to launch her new platform. She expected to have a ton of investment interest once the story broke."

"Which was when?"

"Well, that's the thing. She was getting close."

I sat up straighter now. "She knew who had done it?"

"She had a very strong theory and she was trying to get enough evidence to nail down the story."

"So the threats. She thought they were about this and that's why she looped my grandpa in."

"Correct. Although she didn't tell him everything before she died."

That aligned with what Grandpa had told me: she'd been about to get him the information she'd gathered in her reporting.

And then she was killed.

Something Eva had said earlier had been nagging at me. "You said the theory for a while was that Jasmine was taken off-island. Has that theory been disproved?"

Eva nodded approvingly. "You are your grandfather's granddaughter. Good catch. Donna had a new theory after doing some deeper investigating right here at home. And she thought the thief might still be on the island."

That made my heart speed up a bit. Because that would be, if this person knew she might be onto them or at least suspicious, a motive to kill her.

I looked at Todd, who was still staring out at the ocean. "And Todd? What's his role?" That was the piece that still wasn't fitting together for me—what this mediocre-at-best electrician was doing to help them investigate.

Todd glanced at Eva. She nodded.

"Donna hired me to snoop around when she'd narrowed down the people she was looking at," he said.

I couldn't hide my surprise. "You?"

He flushed. "I'm a good landscaper. And I can do basic electrical. It was a way into the houses without being obvious. Eva suggested it. Look, I'm sorry about your grandfather."

"The people she was looking at are part of the Christmas light contest," Eva cut in smoothly. "We thought Todd was a good plant to gather some evidence for us. He wasn't obtrusive, he didn't have a big crew so things might take a bit longer, and he'd have opportunity to be at everyone's home who wanted help. And we knew these people would want help. That was something people have been asking for, apparently—help from the town if they needed it to get their lights hung and fix any issues."

That was true. Grandpa had mentioned it last year. I remembered he had scoffed at the idea. He was of the mind that people should be hanging their own lights. Hence why he was annoyed with Todd's "help" from the start.

"So Donna and I cooked up a plan to get Todd the town contract for the Christmas lights. Plus, we thought it was nice to help someone new get more acclimated and start to make a name for himself."

Neither of us mentioned the *kind* of name he'd made for himself.

"Okay, so who is it?" I asked impatiently.

It was Eva's turn to hesitate. She looked at Todd. He shrugged.

Finally she turned back to me. "You can't do anything with this information yet," she warned me. "We need to figure out a plan. We have to see if Jasmine is still here—and if they suspect we're onto them, they might do something with her."

"Fine," I agreed. "I won't. Who is it?"

"Camille and Ray Billings."

Chapter 43

Camille and Ray Billings. I sat back, stunned. "You think they stole Jasmine?" I asked. "But . . . how? Why them?" I knew Camille had cats—she'd mentioned it when she came by the cafe—but I didn't know she was into exotic ones.

What if she had stolen Frederick? She'd come by the house the other day to talk to me about the event when she could have just called. Maybe she *was* scoping the place, just not in the way Grandpa thought. Maybe Frederick had been hers and had gotten out—maybe he hadn't been dumped after all and she wanted him back.

"I think it presented itself as a moneymaking opportunity," Eva said simply. "Ray Billings works on yachts for a living. Margot was here on her yacht, docked in the marina."

I stifled a sigh. These people with their yachts. The last time a giant celebrity yacht had been docked here, it had been nothing but drama also.

"Did he have access to her boat, though? And how would he have known about the cat being so fancy?"

"He did have access," Eva said. "Margot hired his team to come in and clean the yacht every week while she was here. Even had him reupholster some seating for her. He may have picked up on the cat's worth while he was around. He has a bit of a reputation as a get-rich-quick guy. He's got a few failed businesses and a couple of bankruptcies to his name. Good googling," she added at my inquisitive look.

"But how would he get from there to stealing a cat and selling it?"

"It's not a stretch," Eva said. "That type of person sees animals as any other business opportunity. Dollar signs."

"Okay, so did she tell the police?"

"She did. They questioned him. He vehemently denied anything to do with it. Said he wasn't even on the island when the cat was stolen."

"Was that true?"

"Yeah, but doesn't mean anything," Eva said. "He had a whole crew. Who they also questioned, and who also denied it. But what was interesting was that a couple of them quit after that summer."

That didn't seem out of the ordinary for me. Those kinds of jobs were pretty seasonal, after all.

"So Donna had homed in on them. What did she find out?"

"She was still digging," Eva admitted. "If they did steal Jas, they covered their tracks pretty well. But there are breeders in town who have been actively pushing their product lately, and she was trying to see if there was any tie-in to Camille and Ray."

"Isn't Camille like a church lady?" I asked. "Seems out of character." Although Grandpa hadn't spoken really highly of her either. And clearly she had a competitive nature, just given the Christmas light contest. Which she hadn't won, or even been in the top three.

Eva gave me a skeptical look. "Most church people who talk about how church-y they are are full of crap."

She wasn't wrong.

"So you think she stole Jasmine. Did they know she might be onto them?"

"I don't think so. Donna was very discreet. And we didn't tell Todd why he was there. Just wanted him to get photos of any cats he saw."

"Was she doing anything else—setting up fake meets, doing fake inquiries?" I thought of my sister and Katrina's plan with a sinking feeling. Was Camille going to show up in that church community center? Then I realized with a jolt that it was her church. That was the vendor table I'd followed her to last night.

"She wasn't personally, but she had people poking around," Eva said evasively.

"Do you think she did something to Donna?" I asked bluntly.

Eva slumped back in her chair, dropping her head into her hands. "I don't know. If they found out she was sniffing around and it put their financial life in jeopardy, maybe so."

I turned to Todd. "And I'm guessing you really were working on the town tree yesterday and not at Donna's."

"Just like I told you," he said. "But I feel like someone was trying to set me up."

"Honestly? I feel like you're right," I said. "Someone who knew that you'd . . . had some complaints about your work."

The doorbell rang, startling all of us. Eva glanced at Todd. "Expecting someone?"

"No." He got up and went to the door. I sat up straight when I heard a familiar voice.

Mick.

Shoot. I jumped to my feet, startling JJ, who squeaked in protest. Too late. Mick, Craig, and Todd appeared in the living room. Craig shook his head when he saw me. Mick just looked amused.

"I thought that was your car out front," he said.

"Oh. Yeah, well, just finalizing the work on the house," I said with a smile. I didn't want Eva and Todd to suspect I'd been throwing Todd's name at them all along and that we were in this together.

"I see," Mick said. He turned to Eva. "Hi, Ms. Flores."

"Lieutenant." Eva stood. "I should be going too. Todd, speak later?"

He looked like he was about to protest as the two of us left the room, but he shut his mouth, seemingly resigned to what was to come.

Once we were outside, I turned to Eva. "Did Lt. Ellory already speak to you?"

She nodded. "Yesterday."

"And you didn't mention this to them." At her head shake, I asked, "So what happens now?"

"I'm hoping your grandfather can get a little more concrete information about them that could help us get the police to look into Jasmine again. Unfortunately cats aren't high on their priority list."

"But if they were threatening Donna, the cops will care about that." I glanced back at the house. "They really kicked Todd out for being bad at the job?"

Eva sighed. "He was supposed to be looking for evidence of Jasmine at their house. But he kept screwing up the job so they fired him before he could do it." She shook her head. "He's harmless, but he's really kind of useless. I'm not really sure what Selena is doing with him."

I got back in the car with JJ and pulled out my phone, noticing I had a missed call. Bones. The voicemail was simple: "Call me."

I called him back as I pulled away from the curb, heading back to Daybreak Harbor. "Were you able to get in?"

He laughed. "Seriously?"

"I know, sorry. Stupid question. Hit me. What'd you find?"

"Well. I found a ton of cat-related stuff. I didn't know there could be that much to say about cats," Bones said. "What is it with you cat people?"

"Just tell me what you found," I said through gritted teeth.

"A lot of info filed by year under the main folder, Cat's Meow Media."

I had to smile at that. Not a bad name.

"Standard stuff. Drafts of stories, notes, interview recordings. I didn't listen to everything, but none of it was password protected. I can send it. But I did find a bunch of files that were locked down. Notes, recordings, all in a folder labeled Project J."

Project Jasmine, likely. "Go on."

"Those aren't on the cloud. They're on her hard drive only. Everything else was on the cloud."

"You could get into the actual hard drive? Never mind," I said, catching myself. I had never wanted to know the nitty-gritty of Bones' other profession. The web design and management—the up-and-up part of the business—was all I needed to know about.

"But," he continued, ignoring me, "it was all still cryptic. No names, nothing identifying from what I scanned through. I'll send those unpacked files. Maybe some of it will mean something to you."

Bummer. It was probably a pipe dream that she'd laid out the whole story for us to bring to the police, clear Becky, and arrest the murderer. Still, maybe between

Becky and me—and Alice—we could figure something out.

"Thanks," I said. "I appreciate your help."

"Don't you want the rest of it?" Bones said.

"Oh. There's more?"

"Well, yeah. The goldmine isn't going to be on the computer. It's going to be on the dark web."

"The dark web? Why would Donna be using the dark web?" I was confused.

"Lots of reporters do. It's a way to connect with sources who want deep cover."

"You're kidding." I'd had no idea. I thought the dark web was all about stolen identities and sex trafficking.

Bones let out an impatient sigh. "I'm not. You wanna hear this or what, because I have other stuff to do."

"Yes. Sorry. Please." I turned onto my street. I needed to get this computer back to Alice now that Bones had gotten us some information from it.

"Your girl was having most of her conversations here. Emails with people who were running stolen-cat rings. Seemed like she was offering to turn her head on some stuff to get information on one case, or one supposed ring, in particular. Something she thought was happening out your way. Lots of references to the island. A lot of dead ends, but in the last few weeks she had homed in on this one email address who seemed to have information she needed on a stolen cat. The person had actually reached out to your girl for help. Someone had gotten busted out in Georgia with a cat they were breeding without a license. The cat was confiscated because authorities thought it was a hybrid, or something? That mean anything to you?"

"Like a hybrid of a wild cat?"

"Dude, no idea. This is your department. I'll stick

with computers. Anyway, the cat may be euthanized if no one comes forward for it with the right paperwork. Looks like it's due to happen on Monday and this person was making a last-ditch effort to save the cat. I don't know if that's helpful."

"Definitely. Can you send over all her correspondence over the last few months?" I pulled into the driveway.

"Sure. There's a lot. She was also looking into breeder scams where people were charging a lot of money for basically alley cats. And since a lot of this stuff wasn't completely legit, when people had issues with each other, they were taking them out in . . . let's just say, more violent ways."

Oh, boy. I thought the rescue world was cutthroat. "Like . . . murder?"

"Not sure, but there was one forum I found where some of these people hung out that were clearly using code words for things that didn't sound good."

"Yikes," I said.

"One more thing. Someone facilitated a transfer of 'cargo' off the island a few weeks ago. I'm trying to trace the email address to see if we can figure out who it is, because I'm guessing that might be the person you're looking for. But it's buried pretty deep and I need some more time."

"Bones, you're the best."

"Yeah," he said. "Anyway, I'll send you encrypted files for what I have so far. Password will come separately. So will the bill." Bones disconnected.

I had to laugh. He was a businessman, first and foremost.

I ran inside and took JJ out of his harness and leash, setting him free. He scampered off to the cafe doors, where Adele would let him in to play with his friends.

I ran upstairs to get the laptop, which I shoved in my bag, then back downstairs again, calling Becky as I went.

"I'm on my way over. We need Alice. And some time to huddle up and see what we can figure out."

Chapter 44

When I got back to the paper, Alice waited in the reception area for me. "Perfect timing!" she exclaimed. "I was just about to call those lovely detectives back and tell them I'd located Donna's computer in the spare office she used for some of her more private meetings." She winked at me. "I'll take you upstairs to Becky."

I followed her upstairs. We made a pit stop on the second floor and I handed over the computer, which she promptly went and locked in said spare office. Then we went up to the newsroom.

"I'll be in shortly," she promised.

I walked through the aisles of desks. There were more people than usual working for a Saturday, and the mood was somber. The usual bustle and excitement had been replaced with a funereal atmosphere, which was certainly fitting for the situation. I went to Becky's office. The door was closed, but she waved me in.

"Have you talked to Alice yet?" I asked.

She shook her head. "Haven't had a chance. I've been flat out since I got here."

I was surprised to realize it was nearly five. This day

felt like it had been five years long, and it wasn't over yet. "The cops released your car?"

"Yeah. Great. Until the next thing," she muttered, standing up. "Let's go to the conference room." She grabbed her laptop and led me through the newsroom and across the hall to the opposite side of the floor and into an empty conference room. Once we were inside with the door shut, she texted Alice to tell her where we were.

Alice joined us a few minutes later. "They just sent an officer over to get the computer. They were very grateful to have it," she said, sliding into a seat. "So, ladies. Let's talk. I know you have questions for me."

"So many," Becky said.

Alice nodded somberly. "I'm really devastated about this," she said, and it hit me that this was the second tragedy she'd dealt with in as many months. "I was so looking forward to a new start, a chance at a rejuvenated career. And Donna was so good to me." Her voice choked up and she took a minute to regain her composure. "I was grateful to be able to work on some reporting with her in the past months. But let me tell you—this cat stuff is intense."

She doesn't know the half, I thought.

"Donna wanted to show the good side of cat fanciers. That was one of the reasons Cat's Meow Media was born, but the deeper and deeper she got into that world, the darker she found it. And with her journalistic integrity and curious mind, she of course had to tell the truth about what she was seeing."

"She was looking into the stolen cat," I said. "Todd and Eva confirmed that."

"Todd? What does he have to do with this?" Becky asked.

"Apparently he was a plant. They wanted to use him for access into where they thought the cat was." I lifted my hands, palms up, at her disbelieving look. "I guess Eva knows him or something."

"So he didn't kill her," Becky said.

"Doesn't seem like it," I admitted. "And Brandon's off the hook too." I filled them in on that story.

"Not surprising," Becky said when I got to the cheating part.

"He's a weasel," Alice agreed.

"Yes. But listen. I got new information that sounds important. And could possibly send us down a whole new path. Alice—I need to know if you knew anything about this."

I told them about Camille and Ray Billings and Donna's suspicion that they were somehow involved with the stolen cat.

Alice's face was tight. "I knew she had someone she was looking at. She didn't tell me who. Wanted to protect me until she knew for sure, I guess."

"Well, if they did it and then somehow got tipped off that she was onto them . . ." I let my thoughts trail off.

"Then maybe one of them killed Donna," Becky finished. "Hang on a minute." She got up and almost ran out of the room.

While we waited, I pulled my phone out, found the password Bones had sent for the encrypted file in my texts, then opened the zip file that was in my email. By the time I did all that, Becky was back with a folder.

"Look at this." She threw it on the table in front of us.

I wasn't sure what I was looking at. It appeared to be something about ads for the paper. "What am I looking at?"

"Some of the ads that were running in the paper recently that got pulled. I remember this because it messed up the layout one day and I didn't find out until the paper already went to print. I was upset."

"So?"

"They were ads for exotic cats."

I looked at the paper again. "Who took them out?"

She jabbed at the page. At the very bottom, I could just make out a scribbled signature. Just a couple of letters, really. "I give up," I said. "Who is it?

"Ray Billings," she said grimly.

My eyes dropped to the letters again. I could just make out an R and a B now that she had pointed it out.

"When I asked why they'd been pulled, the ad department told me Donna had authorized it."

"Like she was punishing them. Oh wow. So they did know," I said slowly. "You know, I was curious why Camille seemed so annoyed that Donna was sponsoring the event and had supported the Todd contract. This is all starting to make sense now."

"They knew she was suspicious of something," Becky said. "But what, we don't know."

"Well, maybe this will help." I picked up my phone and pulled up the files. "Did you know that journalists use the dark web to communicate with sources?"

"Of course I did. I'm a journalist," she pointed out. "Besides, everyone knows that."

Everyone except me, apparently. "Do you?" I asked.

She made a frustrated noise. "Why are you asking?"

"Because Donna did." I showed them.

"How did you get this?" Becky demanded.

"Don't ask," I said.

"That's right. I forgot I don't want to know."

"Can you send them to me?" Alice asked. "I'll go through them tonight."

I didn't really want to send them out into cyberspace. Bones had me worried about the repercussions of that.

"I'll give you the log-in to my email and the password for the file," I told her. Alice had a reputation for keeping secrets extremely well. I wasn't worried about sharing it with her.

She nodded. "I'm on it. Going to head home and start looking right now."

"Thanks," I said. I turned to Becky. "Let's go get your car before they find another reason to search it. While we're there, I'll let Mick and Craig know they have another suspect or two to run down."

Chapter 45

The next morning, I was awakened by my phone nearly vibrating off my nightstand. I grabbed it before it could wake up Lucas.

It was a text from Alice: *Call me.*

I slipped into the hallway, blinking sleep out of my eyes, and did so.

"I think I know what she's up to."

"Who?"

"Camille. Well, if we can confirm it's her."

I inhaled sharply. "You found something." I'd fallen asleep last night going through the piles of information Bones had sent without getting anywhere. Now I felt bad. Alice had probably stayed up all night doing the same, but with better results.

"The source Donna was emailing with had evidence that there was an underground stolen cat ring. And that the main point of contact was possibly the same person she was asking about."

"Underground stolen cat ring?" I shook my head. You couldn't make this stuff up.

"I know, right? And with super-rare cats. Like, new breeds and breeds that are really close to their wild counterparts, at least according to the shorthand I was reading."

"And the cats were being sent here?"

"No. They were being shipped all over the country. Pretty fancy operation, with couriers involved and everything from the sounds of it. Anyway, the source was supposed to send Donna some correspondence with more concrete details. I can't find it, though. The emails kind of stopped."

"When was this?"

"Last Monday."

Yikes. I told Alice to keep me posted on anything else she found. I was heading back to my room, eager to pull out my own computer and dig back in, when my phone vibrated again. It was Grandpa calling from downstairs. Frowning, I answered.

"Can you come down?" he asked. "We've got company."

"At six a.m.? Yeah, I'll be right down."

"Everything alright?" Lucas asked, sitting up in bed.

I winced. "Sorry to wake you. Yes, go back to sleep. I need to go help Grandpa with something."

He didn't argue.

I brushed my teeth and hurried downstairs, stopping short in the kitchen to find it full with Grandpa, Mick, Craig, and Bernie Elliott. All eyes turned to me.

"What, no Scottie dogs?" Mick asked, deadpan. Craig hid a laugh behind a cough.

I looked at my jammies which, admittedly, were less cute than the ones I'd worn yesterday, mostly because there were no animals on them. They were just purple. "Sorry to disappoint. What's going on?" I poured myself some coffee and sat down.

"Your tip was helpful," Mick said to me. "We started looking into the Billingses and noticed a couple of things that are . . . interesting. Ray Billings was pretty broke when he met his new bride. But now he's driving a fancy car and throwing money around like he's got it. And he doesn't make a heck of a lot at the yacht club."

I looked at Grandpa. "Her first husband?"

Grandpa shook his head. "Jerry wasn't wealthy. They were comfortable, and maybe he left a life insurance policy, but it's more than that. I've been . . . doing some research into them based on a trail I was following for Donna."

I gaped at him. "Donna told you she suspected Camille?" I didn't think she'd told anyone. But it made sense. There was no one more discreet than Grandpa.

He nodded. "That last day. At my party. Made me swear not to tell anyone because she was worried about something happening to the cat if she was right and they caught on that she had a clue. And I know how you and Katrina are, so I didn't want to mention it until I had more to go on. So I started digging. And found out they've been busy with some remodeling, and they even built a new structure out back. One might call it a shed— they did, in fact, on their permit request—but it's a bit more than that. So I got to thinking about who might've done work out there." He glanced at Bernie, who wore that proud look again. He was reveling in this new police-consulting gig.

"You did work at her house," I said. I knew that, of course. Camille had told me. Obviously she trusted Bernie, because she's known him a long time. She didn't trust Todd, because she hadn't.

"Sure did," he said. "Her lights, and that structure back in the fall. And it's no shed."

"What is it?" I asked, wide-eyed.

"It's a cat house." Bernie looked proud of himself.

I got chills. "Cat house?"

"Yeah. For all their fancy cats. Guess they don't want 'em stinking up the house." He shook his head. "Cats should live with their people, I think. I know you do too," he said with a nod to me. "But they were different. And they also let them have lots of babies. Not cool."

He clearly hadn't caught on that she was running a cat breeding operation yet.

"She was definitely breeding cats, then," I said, eyes traveling to Mick.

He nodded. "Which is not my problem. It's Katrina's, if they don't have a license. Which I'm guessing they don't, if they're saying this is a shed. But if you're right about Donna being onto them, I think it's a viable avenue to pursue. They could have planned this attack on Donna and saw an opportunity to frame a subpar electrician for it. It's actually pretty brilliant, if that's what happened."

"They're also up to something else," Grandpa said. "There have been some regular deposits into their accounts. For big bucks. Starting last August."

Last August. When Jasmine was stolen.

Mick nodded slowly. "Which we can't pursue yet, because I'm waiting on my warrant to look into their financials officially, but it's good to know."

"I bet she stole Frederick too. Are you going to bring her in?" I asked.

"No."

I stared at him. "Why the heck not?"

"Because I'd much rather have something to bust her with." He grinned at me. "Katrina told me about the plan for Sam to meet this anonymous breeder tonight. I'd like to see if it's one of them. We can use that if we get any good info."

"Well," I said slowly, "I think I know a potential way to get some information. Or at least gauge the reaction."

I told them what Alice had just told me, leaving out her name and how we'd gotten the information. "So we were already planning to have Sam ask for a really unique cat. We can up the ante, maybe have her offer a lot more money for, like, some near-illegal hybrid."

Craig was staring at me in fascination. "I never knew the business of cats could get this shady."

"Neither did I," I admitted.

I could see the wheels turning in Mick's head as he strategized. "It's not a bad idea. If they bite, we have a way in."

"Are you going to wire her up?" I asked.

Mick snorted. "We're not on *CSI*. And I don't have a warrant. But I'm going with my gut that your friend didn't kill Donna. If that's true, we need a nudge in the right direction to get to the bottom of who did."

"Is that too dangerous?" I asked, looking at Grandpa.

"They know what they're doing," he assured me. "And Samantha is a smart girl, Maddie."

"We'll be right outside," Mick said.

There was one issue I could see, though. "We're assuming this is Camille. And maybe it is, ultimately. But what if she sends someone else? And by the way, Camille knows our family. She'll know Sam and figure out that we're onto her. And Sam won't know—"

"We're working with Sam," Craig interrupted. "And I don't think there's any danger of her being recognized. I've seen her outfit." At this, he grinned. "Our guess is they'll send someone else. She doesn't seem to be the face of anything, from what we've looked into so far. But that's why we need your help with something."

I frowned. "What?"

"Can you get your hacker friend to see if he can trace her on the dark web? If I can find something that shows she paid for a fake license or fake papers for any of these cats, or any records of moving stolen product, that would be perfect."

My mouth fell open. How on earth did he know about Bones? "What do you mean?" I managed finally.

"Come on, you think we don't know you were at the paper yesterday? It was pretty convenient for Alice to find that laptop later on," Craig said, his mouth tipped up in a smile.

"Don't worry, we're not going to bust you. Or your friends," Mick said. "You may actually have helped us. But that leaves this room and we'll arrest all three of you, got it?" He looked from me to Grandpa to Bernie. We all nodded, even though I could tell Grandpa wasn't happy to be lumped in with the civilians.

"Ask him to get me what he can by three today, at the latest. We'll get your sister all set up at the church later." Mick rose to go and Craig followed suit.

"I'm coming too," I said, also standing up.

"The public is welcome at the tree lighting, of course," Mick said, patting me on the shoulder. "Which jammies will you be wearing?"

Chapter 46

"You really think she's a killer?" I asked, pulling my JJ's House of Purrs knitted hat down farther over my forehead. "I mean, trafficking stolen cats is one thing. Killing someone, though . . ."

Katrina and I were sitting in her personal car—not the ACO van for once—around the corner from the United Methodist Church, where Mick had warned us to stay out of the way while they organized Sam's meet with whoever from this organization was about to show up.

"I don't know," Katrina said, eyes glued to every car or pedestrian that passed by us—which was a lot given the level of activity as people got ready for the tree lighting. It wasn't quite like preparing for New Year's Eve in Times Square, but for Daybreak Harbor, it was close. Non-residents new to our island were lining up to get the best spots on the town green, where the giant tree waited to be lit up in all its glory.

They hoped. As long as someone had checked Todd's work.

"You think Sam will be okay?" I asked. I worried about my little sister. She wasn't used to doing things like this. It occurred to me that I shouldn't be either, but that was a problem for another day.

"She'll be fine. Mick's all over it." I could tell she was nervous too, despite her efforts to not come off as such.

Especially since Bones, who was charging me a fortune for this little exercise, had come through. He had at least two emails arranging courier service for "delicate cargo" that he could track back to an email from Ray Billings' office. Which was still a little iffy for deniability purposes because the argument could easily be that someone else in the office had sent them, but it fit the narrative we'd been cobbling together.

Camille and Ray were definitely doing something they shouldn't be. Whether that included murder, well, we had no way of knowing.

But I had my strong suspicions.

"I hope they know what they're doing with the script they gave her," I said.

Katrina finally looked at me, exasperated. "Would you chill. You're making me nervous."

"At least you're finally admitting it," I said.

"I just can't believe all this was going on under my nose," she said. "I'm really disappointed in myself."

"Katrina. You can't be. How would you have any clue?"

"Come on. The flyers, for one."

"Those just started going up. They were getting greedy, I suspect," I said. "Using Christmas as a way to try and make an extra influx of cash. Especially with tourists in and out of here. Less chance of someone local getting caught up in their scams."

"Still. I should've been more aware. And I should've pursued the Jasmine thing more."

"How? You're not an investigator," I argued. "I'm sure your chief would've taken issue with you spending your time doing that anyway."

"It's no excuse, Maddie."

"Stop being so hard on yourself. It's annoying. We all want to save the world but at some point we have to come to terms with the fact that we can't." I glanced at my phone as Mick texted me.

All in place and Sam's ready to go.

"They're ready," I said, sitting up straighter. Sam was due to meet her contact at four thirty. The plan was for her to go in a few minutes early. At four twenty, we saw her walking down the street.

Or at least we assumed it was her. The bright red wig and giant glasses she wore were definitely a contrast to her usual look. She glanced around when she reached the church steps, then hurried inside.

"I don't see anyone else, though," Katrina said.

I shrugged. "Maybe they'll be here right on time."

My phone vibrated with another text. Figuring it was Mick, I picked it up.

And realized it was Bones. I scanned the message, then sat up straight. "Oh, crap," I said softly.

Chapter 47

Leaving Katrina in the car, I got out and raced to the church steps, taking them two at a time, intent on getting to my sister before she got too far into whatever she was walking into. But once I burst through the main doors, I realized I had no idea where the community room was. It had to be downstairs somewhere, I reasoned. But there were no visible stairways where I had come in.

I ran through the pews to the back of the church, catching sight of a door to the side of the altar area, or podium, or whatever one called it—I had no idea. I found bathrooms. And thankfully, a stairwell. I ran down the stairs, almost tripping in my haste to reach the bottom, when I heard voices.

Pulling up short, I flattened myself against the wall and listened. The voices were coming from the big room at the end of the hall. I'd found the community room.

"I don't understand." My sister's voice. "I just wanted a cat. I don't want to get involved in whatever this is."

"You're a terrible actress." The other female voice, cool as the cucumbers she sold on a daily basis, hit me like a punch to the stomach. Bones had been right. So had Mick.

Camille Billings wasn't the face of all this. She was the puppeteer. And she had more than her husband doing her dirty work.

Hoping Katrina had alerted Mick that something was up, I inched forward and risked a glance into the room. I saw three cat carriers on the table, and I could hear distraught meows emanating. I had to do a double take when I realized that Frederick was in the first one. And he was mad, holding the door with his claws and crying.

Beyond them, my sister, sitting against the wall, hands and feet bound with some sort of rope, her wig on the floor next to her. But what startled me most was the still figure on the floor. A man. I couldn't see his face, but I could certainly see the blood pooling around his head.

And Molly Longo with a role of duct tape, about to slap a piece over Sam's mouth.

I took a breath and stepped into the room. "Molly. Stop," I said.

Both Molly's and Sam's heads snapped in my direction, Molly startled and Sam relieved. "What are you doing here?" Molly snarled, grabbing a knife off the table. A big one. Like a hunting knife.

I took a step back, hands up. "Look. Just let my sister go. She didn't do anything."

"Except try to bust the operation." Molly shook her head. "What is it with your family? Everyone wants to play cops and robbers. Can't even back off when I leave a warning note in your house. Get in here." She waved the big knife at me.

I couldn't move as I processed what I'd just heard. She had broken into our house, into Grandpa's room, and stolen Frederick. What on earth?

She advanced on me with the knife. "I said move!"

"I'm coming." I stepped in.

"Over here." She motioned to the wall next to Sam.

I hesitated.

She went over and jammed the knife against Sam's throat. I heard my sister make a strangled sound, her eyes wide with fear.

"Okay!" I moved slowly toward her, pausing in front of the cats as Frederick rattled the cage, clearly distressed. "It's okay, honey," I said softly, reaching through the wire to try to give him some comfort. And maybe open the door so he could bolt and distract her, giving us a chance to take her down.

"I said over here!" She reached for me, yanking me away from the cats and shoving me against the wall. She threw a piece of rope at me. "Tie your ankles."

Reluctantly, I did what she said, gauging my options. She was taller and faster than me—darn swimmer's stamina—but also a smoker, so maybe I could get the upper hand. If I fake tied the knot . . .

"A real knot," she snapped, obviously onto what I was doing.

Crap. I complied. "How did you get involved in this?" I asked her. "You know this is nuts, right? Why did you steal our foster cat?"

"Nuts. Sure." She laughed, but there was no mirth. She placed the knife just out of my reach, grabbed my hands and tied those together too. "More nuts than being stuck here on this craphole island with my clingy father and a cheating husband, you think?"

I didn't think she actually wanted me to answer, so I stayed quiet.

"As for your foster cat, he was one of Camille's. I saw him when we came to your grandfather's party. I wasn't sure how he'd gotten to you, but he's a big-bucks cat. I couldn't let him get adopted for fifty bucks or whatever you do-gooders charge. That was the point of this whole operation. It was supposed to give me enough money to get out. Until Camille and her loser husband had to get greedy." She gave the still man's form a vicious kick with her combat boot.

Ray. I winced, wondering if he was still alive.

"And Super Newswoman had to try and save the day. Seriously, everyone has to be so *righteous* all the damn time." She stood, picking up her weapon again. The cats in their carriers were getting more stressed with the tension in the room. The screeches were louder and the cage rattling was getting more intense.

"You killed Donna," I said.

"Yeah, I did. She was screwing everything up. All the upcoming shipments of cats were canceled because she was sniffing around. Which meant I wasn't getting paid. Because whatever Camille got up front she sure wasn't sharing."

"But electrocuting her? Why?"

Molly smiled a little. "Clever, right? I knew this electrician was a real dope. My dad had trouble with him, your grandpa did, and I knew Donna did too." She shrugged. "Doesn't take a genius to figure out how to fray a wire and make a puddle. I hoped everyone would think he finally lost it from all the criticism. You actually did," she said. "I was hoping people would listen to you about that. You almost did me a favor."

"Where is Camille? Did you kill her too?"

She ripped off some tape and slapped it on Sam's mouth. "No. She's not worth it. But I did find out where this little meet was supposed to take place so I could give at least one of them what they deserved."

"Wait," I said, before she could do the same to me. "You know it was all for nothing, right? That Donna had already shared what she'd found out? There's nowhere to go from here, Molly."

For the first time, uncertainty flashed across her face,

but it was once again replaced by defiance. "If she did, I wouldn't be here right now," she said. "And I'm about to be out of here for good, so Camille can take the actual fall, like she deserves. She's been screwing me over since we agreed to work together. I hope they bust her hard."

She ripped off another piece of tape and slapped it over my mouth. "Adios," she said. "And PS? A lot of her cats aren't really pedigreed. It's mostly a scam." She slipped her knife into a belt on her waist and started for the door.

I tried to loosen the ropes on my wrists. Where was Mick? He was supposed to be right outside. Hadn't Katrina alerted him? Molly was going to take off. She clearly wasn't stupid and probably had some transportation set up to get her off the island, and then she'd be gone.

But the ropes weren't coming off, and she was almost out the door.

The banging from the carriers had reached epic proportions. Then, mercifully, it stopped. And Frederick succeeded in slamming the door open. With a screech that sounded like a mountain lion, he barreled for the door, startling Molly. She tripped over him, stepping on his tail in the process, which elicited another scream from Frederick, who launched himself at Molly. They both went down in a blur of fur.

And then, finally, Mick, Craig, and two other cops burst in.

Chapter 48

"Took you long enough." I rubbed my wrists where the rope had bit into my flesh. I had a red slash across my face where I'd ripped the tape off. Sam had a matching one, along with a bandage on her neck where Molly had dug in a little too hard with the blade when she was mad at me. One of the cops was speaking to her in the hallway. The others had put Molly in the back of the patrol car and brought her to the station. I wondered what Angelo would do now.

"Sorry. But when Katrina called, we were busy with the FBI," Mick said.

"FBI? How were they involved in this?"

Mick grinned. "Your buddy Todd is not all he appeared to be. Probably a good thing he had another profession all along."

I stared at him, sure I'd heard incorrectly. "Todd Banks is FBI?"

"Technically, his name is Todd MacKenzie. But yes, he's a special agent. So is his wife. Who isn't really his wife."

"She's an agent too?" This was getting wild.

"They were here on an undercover assignment related

to RICO charges. Specifically, interstate transportation of stolen property, which in this case were high-end cats," Mick said.

I was stunned into silence. The FBI had been watching what was going on with the cats on our island. It was a lot to take in. "Did . . . Donna know he was FBI?"

"No," Mick said. "But her buddy Eva did. Eva and Todd really were friends from way back, and she helped him make a case for why they should be here. They tapped her to put the plan in place because she was in charge of the event. Eva just 'suggested' that they plant him to gather information as the electrician. You know, one of those jobs that makes you kind of invisible. She fed Donna the whole plan about Todd being the on-call guy for all the houses involved in the contest once they found out Camille was entering."

I had to admire a well-organized plan. "When did they realize the bigger crimes were happening, though?"

"Apparently it all started with that stolen cat last summer," Mick said. "Since then, at least a hundred cats had been traced back to this operation. And Donna's reporting was a huge help in bringing more of the story to light."

"The FBI knew what Donna was doing?"

Mick nodded. "Donna gave Eva copies of all the evidence she'd accumulated when she started getting threats. Eva shared it with the FBI."

Donna had been smarter than the average bear after all. I shook my head. "Thank goodness Todd has another job, because he would've been out of business fast as an electrician."

Sirens blared as the ambulance with Ray Billings in it pulled away, heading for the hospital. He was alive, but with a serious head injury from where Molly had hit him over the head with a porcelain cat food bowl when he'd entered the church community room. I refocused on Mick.

"But Molly as the killer. That's still blowing my mind. Did you have any idea?"

"No," Mick admitted. "That was definitely thanks to your guy. We'd had Camille pegged for the murder. Or Ray."

I felt a surge of pride for knowing such a competent hacker.

"How did Molly get involved anyway?" Mick asked.

I told him what I'd been able to glean from what she'd said to me in the church. "Sounds like she was boots on the ground, organizing shipments and stuff. But really it sounded like she was backed into a corner with life in general. Kind of like a trapped wildcat looking for a way out."

"Well, her husband was a real piece of work." He filled me in on how Brandon *was* two-timing his wife—but she wasn't the only one he was two-timing. His rendezvous with Mystery Woman had been only one piece. She was also the attorney representing the firm that wanted to buy the paper, which his firm was actually handling on the back end and had appointed him liaison. So he was getting paid by his employer, and would get a cut from the other firm if he could get Donna to sell. And sleeping with the other attorney to boot—a puzzle piece Grandpa had been responsible for putting together, according to Mick.

"No wonder she lost her mind," I said, grateful Val's experience had turned out much better. "And her father on top of it. He seemed like he was kind of stifling her. She said he was clingy, but that's probably putting it mildly."

"I'd say. Worked with her, lived on the same street, knew her every move." Mick shook his head. "I'd have lost it too."

"Did you ever find out why he was trying to pin this on Brandon?" I asked.

Mick nodded grimly. "My guess? He knew Molly was involved somehow—maybe not the actual murder—and was trying to protect her."

"You're kidding."

"Still piecing it together, but she was MIA the afternoon of Donna's death. We think he tracked her but got to her too late, so tried to figure out the best way to try and save her. Landed on getting rid of the crappy husband."

"Wow." Talk about dysfunctional. "I knew Angelo was weirdly attached to her," I said. "But I had no idea it was like that. Are you guys charging him with anything?"

"Possibly obstruction of justice. We have to figure it out."

"What about Camille?"

"She was about to make a run for it. Agent Boyle got her at the ferry dock." Selena, Todd's fake wife. "She and hubby will probably see federal prison time."

Ouch. "And what about the cats at her house?"

"They're rounding them up and assessing them. If they're not actually stolen—or wild—I'm sure you and Katrina will inherit that problem." He grinned. "Speaking of wildcats. How did you know the cat would attack her?"

"I didn't," I admitted. "I wanted him to scare her. I actually think they scared each other and when she stepped on his tail, he got mad."

Mick barked out a laugh. "Leave it to a cat."

Then I remembered the last puzzle piece. "What about Jasmine?" I asked, panicked. "Is she really about to be euthanized in Georgia?"

"Got it covered," Mick said. "The FBI contacted the shelter, said the cat was evidence in a crime. Her owner is flying there as we speak to get her."

"Thank goodness." That would've been horrible. But at least that part had a happy ending.

"Come on." Mick slung an arm around my shoulder. "You should go check out the tree lighting. Enjoy a little of this crazy holiday."

We found Sam and went outside. Grandpa, Lucas, Val, Ethan, and Katrina were waiting in front of the church. Lucas pulled me into a bear hug. Grandpa was out of his chair with his cane as he hobbled over to see Sam.

And there was Becky, racing over to us. I should've known she'd be here to get the story in real time. But as she reached me, I could see she was crying.

"Oh, don't cry, we're fine," I assured her, giving her a hug.

"I'm not crying about you." She swiped at her eyes. "I mean, I'm glad you're fine, of course," she rushed to add. "But we just heard that Donna's niece wants to take over the paper. She's young, but she's always been interested in journalism even though her dad tried to talk her out of it. And she doesn't want to sell!"

"That's amazing!" I hugged her again. That had to have lifted a huge weight off her chest. Well, that and not being a suspect in a murder.

We all turned as the crowd let out a cheer. The Daybreak Harbor Christmas tree lights blazed on in all their multicolored glory. Todd "Banks" MacKenzie, who stood on the steps of the church, turned to me and grinned. "I brought in a real electrician to save the day," he said.